HARDCASTLE'S AIRMEN

HARDCASTLE'S AIRMEN

Graham Ison

This first world edition published in Great Britain 2006 by
SEVERN HOUSE PUBLISHERS LTD of
9–15 High Street, Sutton, Surrey SM1 1DF.
This first world edition published in the USA 2006 by
SEVERN HOUSE PUBLISHERS INC of
595 Madison Avenue, New York, N.Y. 10022.

British Library Cataloguing in Publication Data

Ison, Graham
    Hardcastle's airmen
    1. Hardcastle, Detective Inspector (Fictitious character) - Fiction
    2. Police - England - London - Fiction
    3. Detective and mystery stories
    I. Title
    823.9'14 [F]

    ISBN-13: 978-0-7278-6368-3
    ISBN-10: 0-7278-6368-1

This title, as with all others from Severn House, is printed on acid-free paper.

Typeset by Palimpsest Book Production Ltd.,
Polmont, Stirlingshire, Scotland.
Printed and bound in Great Britain by
MPG Books Ltd., Bodmin, Cornwall.

Glossary

ALL MY EYE AND BETTY MARTIN: nonsense.
BAILEY, the: see 'Old Bailey'.
BEAK: a magistrate.
BOB: a shilling (now 5p).
BUCK HOUSE: Buckingham Palace.

CART, IN THE: in trouble.
CID: Criminal Investigation Department.
CLINK: prison. Clink Street, London, was the site of an old prison.
COLDSTREAMER: a soldier of the Coldstream Guards.
COMMISSIONER'S OFFICE: official title of New Scotland Yard, headquarters of the Metropolitan Police.
CONK OUT, to: to suffer engine failure.
COPPER: a policeman.
CULLY: alternative to calling a man 'mate', ie friend.

DDI: Divisional Detective Inspector.
DICKIE BIRD: a word (rhyming slang).
'DILLY, the: short for Piccadilly and its environs; a haunt of prostitutes.
DOGBERRY: a policeman or watchman (*ex* Shakespeare).
DOG'S DINNER, a: a mess.
DOXY: a woman of loose character.

EARWIGGING: listening.
EIGHT O'CLOCK WALK, to take the: to be hanged.
EYEWASH: nonsense.

FEEL THE COLLAR, to: to make an arrest.
FRONT, the: theatre of WW1 operations in France and Flanders.

GLIM: a look (a shortening of 'glimpse').

GREAT SCOTLAND YARD: location of an army recruiting office, not to be confused with New Scotland Yard.

GROWLER: a taxi.

GUM TREE, UP A: stuck, in difficulties.

GUV *or* **GUV'NOR:** informal alternative to 'sir'.

JILDI: quickly (*ex* Hindi).

JUG-AND-BOTTLE: the bar of a public house where one could obtain beer in either a bottle or in one's own jug to be consumed off the premises.

KNOCKED OFF: arrested.

NEWGATE COLLAR: a hangman's noose.

NICK: a police station or prison; alternatively, to steal.

NICKED: arrested.

NINETEEN TO THE DOZEN, to talk: to talk very fast.

NOSE: an informant.

OLD BAILEY: Central Criminal Court, London.

OLD HARRY: the devil (hence 'play old Harry', cause trouble).

PEA-SOUPER: a thick smog.

PLONK: the mud of no-man's-land.

PROVOST, the: military police.

QUEER IN THE ATTIC: of unsound mind.

QUID: one pound sterling.

RAGTIME GIRL: a sweetheart; a girl with whom one has a joyous time; a harlot.

RECEIVER, The: senior Scotland Yard official responsible for the finances of the Metropolitan Police.

RECORD: record of previous convictions.

RFC: Royal Flying Corps.

ROZZER: a policeman.

SAM BROWNE: a military officer's belt with shoulder strap.

SCRIMSHANKER: one who evades duty or work.

SHILLING: now 5p.

SKINT: broke.

SKIP *or* **SKIPPER:** an informal police alternative to station-sergeant, clerk-sergeant and sergeant.

SMOKE, The: London.

STRETCH, a: one year's imprisonment.

SWADDY: a soldier. (*ex* Hindi).

SWAN: go around in a carefree or casual way.

TOBY: a police area.

TOPPED: murdered or hanged.

TOPPING: a murder or hanging.

TUMBLE, a: sexual intercourse.

TUPPENNY-HA'PENNY: a contraction of twopence-half-penny, indicating something or someone of little worth.

TURN UP ONE'S TOES, to: to die or be killed.

TURPS: short for turpentine, a cleaning spirit.

UNDERGROUND, The: London Underground railway system.

UNDER THE DAISIES: dead.

VAD: Voluntary Aid Detachment: wartime nursing auxiliaries.

WAR OFFICE: Department of State overseeing the army. (Now a part of the Ministry of Defence.)

WHISTLE: a suit (rhyming slang: whistle and flute).

WON'T WASH: can't be got away with.

One

The snow had been falling for more than an hour, and even the chill wind sweeping the length of Kennington Road in Lambeth had failed to deter it from settling. Now some two inches deep, the white blanket deadened all sound save that of the popping gas lamps and the occasional passing tram, its dim yellow lights and mournful bell marking its ghostly journey. It was nearing seven o'clock on the evening of Thursday the eleventh of February 1915. It would be another two months before London suffered its first air raid, and lighting restrictions had yet to be imposed.

A constable from the local police station hammered loudly on the door of number 27. But it was some time before the door was opened.

Divisional Detective Inspector Ernest Hardcastle, head of the CID for the A or Whitehall Division of the Metropolitan Police, appeared in his shirtsleeves and an unbuttoned waistcoat.

'Bloody hell, boy, I'm in the middle of my supper. It'd better be important.'

'It is, sir,' said the PC. 'A copper's been shot on Rochester Row's ground.'

'Is he badly injured?'

'He's dead, sir,' said the PC.

'Whereabouts on Rochester Row's ground?' asked Hardcastle as he turned from the door. 'You'd best come in, lad, while I get my coat. And wipe your feet or you'll have Mrs Hardcastle after you.'

The PC glanced at the sodden message form in his hand. 'Cowley Street, sir.' Taking off his cape and shaking the snow from it before entering, he followed Hardcastle into the tiny hall.

'Best get me a cab, then.' Hardcastle donned his jacket, and took his chesterfield overcoat, bowler hat and umbrella from the hooks that hung next to a mirror.

'Outside, sir, ready and waiting. I was lucky to find one. There's not many about in this weather.'

'I've got to go out, Alice,' called Hardcastle to his wife, who was in the kitchen.

'Shall I put your supper in the oven then, Ernie?' But even as she said it, Alice Hardcastle knew that it was a futile question; she had been married to a policeman long enough to know that when so high-ranking an officer as her husband was called out, it was unlikely that he would be home before breakfast, if then.

'No, don't bother, love,' said Hardcastle. 'I could be some time.' The DDI was not a man given to exaggeration, and he knew that the murder of a police officer would be a time-consuming enquiry. But even he did not realize how extended this particular investigation would become.

Charles Marriott, the first-class detective sergeant from Cannon Row police station, had been called out too, and was already in Cowley Street, a bare ten minutes walk from where he lived in police quarters at Regency Street.

As Hardcastle alighted from his cab, Marriott stepped across and raised his hat.

'Good evening, sir. Bad business.'

'It's this damned war, Marriott,' grumbled Hardcastle. 'The whole bloody world's gone mad.' He glanced at the body, a groundsheet-covered mound upon which the snow was lightly falling. The constable's helmet lay nearby, a poignant reminder of what had occurred. 'Who is he?'

'Robert Crispin, sir, PC 550A, attached to Rochester Row.'

Hardcastle grunted. 'Commissioner been informed?'

'Yes, sir,' said Marriott. 'Mr Hudson telephoned him the minute word came in.'

Sir Edward Henry – himself the victim of a shooting in 1912 by one Albert Bowes who had been refused a tram-driver's licence – had ordered a telephone line to be run from Paddington Green police station to his home in Kensington in order that he could be contacted at any time of the day or night. And any failure immediately to inform him of the murder

2

of a police officer would undoubtedly result in a very uncomfortable interview for several people. Starting with the superintendent of the man's division.

'What's known about this, Marriott?' Holding his umbrella aloft, Hardcastle put his other hand in his pocket and stared around at the murder scene. There was a taxi, behind the wheel of which its driver occasionally blew on his mitten-clad hands, and several policemen hunched beneath their capes. Beside them stood Detective Sergeant Wood and Detective Constables Henry Catto and Fred Wilmot, umbrellas raised, coat collars turned up.

One or two lights were on in the surrounding houses, and from one a man was leaning out of a window trying to see why there was such a commotion in the usually quiet Westminster backwater.

'It was witnessed by the cabbie, sir' – Marriott nodded towards the waiting taxi – 'and a Mrs Isabel Plowman.' He pointed at the nearest house. 'She lives there.'

'We'd better have a chat with her then. In the meantime, get someone to arrange the removal of Crispin's body to Horseferry Road mortuary. And tell them to advise Dr Spilsbury that I'll be wanting him for the post-mortem.' Hardcastle glanced across at Wilmot and Catto. 'Well, don't just stand there. Get knocking on doors and find out if anyone heard or saw anything. And start with him up there.' He pointed at the man in the window. 'Shouldn't have needed telling,' he muttered. 'Don't know what the Job's coming to.'

A maid showed the two detectives into the sitting room. Isabel Plowman was seated by the fire, warming her hands. She was an attractive young woman, probably no more than twenty-five, and Hardcastle judged by her elegant appearance and the richness of the furnishings that she had substantial means.

Her black evening robe, a combination of soft satin and ninon, was just short enough to reveal a trim ankle and a glacé kid court shoe with an embroidered heel. A black evening cloak with a fur collar had been thrown carelessly over a nearby chair; a pair of long gloves, a feathered hat and a handbag lay beside it.

'I'm Divisional Detective Inspector Hardcastle of the

3

Whitehall Division, ma'am, and this is Detective Sergeant Marriott.'

Mrs Plowman cast a coquettishly appraising glance at Charles Marriott before returning her gaze to Hardcastle. 'What a dreadful business, Inspector. I don't know what the world's coming to,' she said, more or less echoing Hardcastle's own thoughts when he had arrived at the scene of PC Crispin's murder. She rose to her feet and gave the bell-pull a brief tug. Moments later the maid reappeared. 'Mary, get these officers some whisky. I'm sure they need something to keep the cold out on a night like this. You look absolutely frozen, gentlemen,' she added, returning her gaze to the two detectives.

'Very kind of you, ma'am,' murmured Hardcastle.

'Do sit down, gentlemen.' Isabel Plowman indicated a settee with a wave of her hand, before resuming her own seat beside the fire. The maid turned to a side table and began to pour the drinks.

'Perhaps you would tell me exactly what you saw, Mrs Plowman.' Hardcastle glanced at Marriott to make sure that he had his pocket book out, ready to take notes.

The woman waited until the maid had handed the two detectives their whisky and left the room, closing the door behind her.

'I'd sent out for a taxi just before six to take me to Rules for supper with Charles Napier . . .' Mrs Plowman began.

'And who is this Mr Napier, ma'am?' interrupted Hardcastle.

'A gentleman friend, Inspector.' Isabel Plowman raised her eyebrows slightly, as though Hardcastle's question was an irrelevant and unnecessary intrusion into her private life. But then she felt impelled to explain. 'My husband Edward was shot down and killed over Lille last year, in the opening stages of the war. He was a major in the Royal Flying Corps, you see.'

'I'm sorry to hear that, ma'am,' murmured Hardcastle, and left a suitable pause after those brief words of condolence. 'However, you say you were going to supper with this here Mr Napier . . .'

'Yes, and then we were going on to the Gaiety to see *Tonight's The Night* at eight o'clock. It has George Grossmith and Leslie Henson in it, you know. I'm told it's very good.' Mrs Plowman gave a gay little laugh.

Hardcastle was not greatly interested in the play Mrs Plowman was going to see, or for that matter who was in it. 'Perhaps you'd get to the point of this business, ma'am, if you'd be so kind.'

'Yes, I'm so sorry, Inspector.' The woman became serious again. 'Here am I prattling on when one of your colleagues is lying dead outside. Well, the cab arrived, but as we were leaving, the driver told me that he'd seen a man on the portico of the house next door to this one. So I told him to stop the moment we saw a policeman, which we did in Barton Street, I think it was. I told the policeman what my driver had seen, and he got into the cab and we drove him back here.'

'What happened next, Mrs Plowman?' prompted Marriott, looking up from his notes.

'The man was still there and the policeman called on him to come down. But whoever he was, he had a gun, because the next thing that happened was that I heard what sounded like two shots and the policeman fell to the ground.'

'Did you catch sight of the man on the portico, Mrs Plowman? Can you describe him?' asked Marriott.

'Just a dark figure, that's all.' Mrs Plowman looked apologetic. 'It was the cab driver who saw more of him.'

'Did you see the going of this man?' asked Hardcastle.

'No, I'm afraid not, Inspector. I was too concerned about the policeman. I tried to do what I could for him, but to no avail. He was already dead.'

'Have you had medical training then, ma'am?' asked Hardcastle sharply, unhappy at the thought that an amateur had made such a decision. 'I mean, didn't you think of calling a doctor?'

'There was no point. As I said, the policeman was already dead, Inspector. I'm a part-time VAD at Charing Cross Hospital, and I'm afraid I know death when I see it.' Isabel Plowman stared sadly at the flickering flames of the fire before looking at Hardcastle again. 'And I've seen it all too often of late. Anyway, I sent the cab driver to get help and he came back a few minutes later with another policeman.'

Hardcastle and Marriott stood up. 'Thank you, ma'am. And thank you for the whisky. Most welcome. I'll have an officer take a statement from you shortly.' Hardcastle pulled out his

5

watch, glanced at it and dropped it back into his waistcoat pocket. 'I reckon you'll have missed the theatre,' he said.

Isabel Plowman gave Hardcastle a wan smile. 'I've already sent a message to Charles saying that I shan't be there, Inspector,' she said.

As the two detectives returned to the street, PC Crispin's body was being loaded into a police van.

'Wood,' said Hardcastle, beckoning to the other sergeant. 'Get in there and take a statement from Mrs Plowman, and while you're about it, get an address for this Charles Napier. I'll need to talk to him.'

'Napier, sir?' queried Wood.

'He's the chap Mrs Plowman was supposed to be going to the theatre with.'

'What can Napier tell us, sir?' asked Marriott as Wood departed. He could not see that Mrs Plowman's supper companion would have anything to contribute.

'Shan't know till we ask him, shall we?' said Hardcastle curtly. 'In the meantime, we'll have a chat with this cabbie.'

The cab driver was reading a copy of the *Star* that he had spread across his steering wheel. He glanced up as Hardcastle approached.

'It's too cold to hang about out here, so we'll use the back of your cab for a chat,' said Hardcastle, and waited until the driver had joined him and Marriott in the passenger compartment. 'Now then, tell me what happened. And we'll start with your name.'

'Grimes, guv'nor. Albert Grimes.'

'Right then, Mr Grimes. Go on.'

'I come here to pick up the lady, guv'nor.'

'How did you know she wanted picking up, eh?' Hardcastle, a stickler for detail, always made sure he got all the relevant information.

'Her maid come out and give me a shout.'

'Where was this?'

'Great Peter Street. Poor little bitch must've been waiting a while. Fair frozen to the marrow, she was. Anyhow, she 'ops in the back of me cab and I come round 'ere. Well the lady comes out almost straight off. "Rules, cabbie," she says, and then asks me if I knows it, all hoity-toity. I told 'er I'd been

6

a licensed 'ackney carriage driver nigh on twenty year, horse and motor, and knows the Smoke like the back of me 'and. And I certainly knows 'ow to get to the oldest restaurant in London. It's in Maiden Lane, see, guv'nor, off of the Strand.'

'I'm sure you're very good at your job, Mr Grimes, but can we get on with it?'

'Oh, yeah, right.' Grimes took out a voluminous red handkerchief and blew his nose noisily. 'Well, just as we was pulling away, I caught a glimpse of this geezer standing up there.'

'Where exactly?' asked Hardcastle.

The cabbie extended a forefinger and pointed at the portico of the house next door to Mrs Plowman's. ''Ere, lady, I says, there's some bloke up there. Is that your 'ouse? No, she says, but stop when you sees a policeman. So I rounded the corner into Barton Street and saw this copper straight off. The upshot was we took him back to Cowley Street and I pointed out where I'd seen this geezer. An' he was still there an' all. So this copper what I'd picked up gives 'im a shout, like, to come down. The next thing that 'appens is that the shooting starts, and the copper goes down.'

'Where did this man go after that?' asked Hardcastle.

'Don't ask me, guv'nor. Soon as the bullets started flying, I was down on the ground next to me cab. Bert Grimes knows when to take care of 'isself, I can tell yer.'

'What did he look like?'

'Well, like I said, I only caught a glim of 'im, but he was all in dark clobber, see. I was lucky to 'ave seen 'im at all, I s'pose.'

'And did you see him when you first drove into Cowley Street?'

'Nah! I was looking for the 'ouse number, see. I never looked up, but when I was turning, after I'd picked up the lady, I spots 'im.'

'Then what happened?' asked Marriott, looking up from his pocket book. 'After the shooting.'

The cabbie switched his gaze to Hardcastle's sergeant. 'When I got up, the lady was kneeling down by the copper, trying to do something for 'im, I s'pose. She said she was a nurse.' Grimes emitted a coarse cackle. 'Wouldn't mind 'aving 'er nurse me, I can tell yer. Anyhow, she said as how to get in me cab and go and find another copper and bring him back here quick.'

'Say anything else, did she?' asked Hardcastle.

'Yeah, she said the copper had snuffed it. I had to go as far as Victoria Street before I found another rozzer an' all.' Grimes sniffed and wiped the back of his woollen mitten across his nose. 'Is that it, then, guv'nor?' he asked, pulling out his watch. 'I must've lost a few bob 'anging about 'ere waiting for you.'

'You'd've been here forever if this man had shot you instead of my policeman,' said Hardcastle without any show of sympathy. 'And the answer's no. One of my sergeants will be here shortly to take a statement from you.'

And with that Hardcastle and Marriott left Albert Grimes muttering to himself about the unfairness of the world.

'Looks like Crispin disturbed a burglar, sir,' said Marriott.

'That's what I was thinking,' said Hardcastle, 'but I'm not in the habit of counting my chickens before they're hatched. There might be more to this than meets the eye.'

'What now, then, sir?' asked Marriott.

'Back to the house. From what our Mr Grimes said, it's possible that the maid saw something when she went out to find a cab for Mrs Plowman.'

At the front door of Isabel Plowman's house they met DS Wood.

'All done, Wood?'

'Yes, sir.'

'All right. Take a statement from Grimes the cabbie, and don't forget to get his badge number and plate number. He reckoned he saw this man, but he hasn't got any idea what he looked like.' Hardcastle pointed his umbrella at the figures of Henry Catto and Fred Wilmot, who were sheltering in the porch of a nearby house and stamping their feet in a vain attempt to keep them warm. 'Have they finished knocking on doors, Wood?'

'Yes, sir. No one saw or heard a thing,' said Wood, 'except for the man leaning out of the window. He said he was in his sitting room, reading, when he heard the shots, but by the time he got to the window it was all over. He didn't see anyone running away, just the PC lying there with Mrs Plowman leaning over him.'

'Well, it's no good them standing there. Tell them to get up on that portico where this cove was spotted, Wood. See if they can find anything. Cartridge cases in particular.' And with that Hardcastle knocked on Mrs Plowman's front door once again.

'The mistress is still in the drawing room, sir,' said the maid.

'As a matter of fact, it's you I want to speak to, lass, but I'd better have a word with the lady of the house first.'

Isabel Plowman was still warming herself in front of the fire, but now she had a glass of champagne in her hand. 'Oh, Inspector, you're back again.'

'Sorry to bother you, ma'am, but I'd like a word with your maid if that's all right.'

'Certainly, Inspector. Do you want to talk to her in here?'

'No, ma'am, the kitchen'll do fine, thank you all the same.' Hardcastle had interviewed servants before and knew that they were likely to speak more openly in the absence of their employer.

'Well if you're sure,' said Mrs Plowman, 'but tell her to make you a cup of tea, or give you another glass of whisky, whichever you fancy.'

Two

Hardcastle and Marriott descended the back stairs from the entrance hall and into the huge, stone-flagged kitchen. Set into one wall was a cast-iron range, and adjacent to it a large wooden dresser; beside it a tall stand held a selection of iron saucepans and cooking pots. Beneath a window giving on to the basement area was a sink flanked by wooden draining boards. Through an open door on the far side of the room, Hardcastle glimpsed a clothes wringer.

'Well, now, lass, you're Mary, is that right?' said the DDI. Taking off his overcoat, he settled himself on a wooden chair near the kitchen range. He held his hands towards the heat and then rubbed them together vigorously.

'Yes, sir.' The girl was a pretty little thing, no more than eighteen. Her blonde hair, piled high on her head, was surmounted by a frilly lace cap. 'Would you like a cup of tea, sir?' she asked Hardcastle, at the same time shooting a glance and a shy smile at the handsome Sergeant Marriott.

'That would be very welcome, lass.' Hardcastle waited while the girl filled the heavy wrought-iron kettle and placed it on the range. 'What's your surname, Mary?'

'Hutchings, sir.' Mary busied herself setting out bone china cups and saucers.

'Don't bother with all that, Mary, the kitchen stuff'll do for us policemen.'

'The mistress wouldn't like that, sir,' said Mary, and continued to place the best china on the scrubbed table.

'And where d'you live, Mary?'

The girl looked at him in surprise. 'Well, here, sir,' she said. 'I live in.'

'Yes, but where do your people live?'

'Oh, I see. Dorset, sir, but I come up here to get work. Three years ago now.'

'And who else is on the staff, Mary?'

'It's only me now, sir. There used to be a butler working here – Mr Timms he was called – and Gerald the footman, but they went off to the war. Poor Mr Timms got hisself killed at . . . I think it was at some place called Ee-press.' Clearly having trouble pronouncing Ypres, Mary stumbled over the word. 'But the mistress never got no one else in, not after the master was killed last year. Not that she'd've got no one, not with the war an' all.'

'Mrs Plowman said she sent you out just before six o'clock to find a taxi, Mary. Is that right? And for goodness' sake sit down, girl.'

Mary smiled as she sat down opposite Hardcastle. 'Yes, sir. The mistress was going out to dinner with Mr Napier and then on to the theatre. I had to go all the way to Great Peter Street and I was blue with the cold by the time I found one, what with the snow an' all.'

'Now then, when you left the house or when you returned in the cab, did you see anything, or hear anything unusual? Did you, for example, see anyone on the portico of the house next door?'

'No, sir.' The girl stood up and spooned tea leaves into a large brown pot before pouring water on to them. 'It's terrible, ain't it, sir, that poor policeman getting killed?'

'Yes, it is, Mary. Tell me, what d'you know about this Mr Napier?'

'He's a gentleman friend of the mistress, sir.'

'And has he called at the house ever?'

The maid paused, as if unsure whether to answer.

'This is just between you, me and Sergeant Marriott here, Mary,' coaxed Hardcastle.

'Two or three times, sir,' said the girl hesitantly. 'He sometimes calls to take the mistress to supper or the theatre.'

'I wonder why he didn't call this evening,' mused Hardcastle. 'Any other gentlemen callers, were there?'

'Not that I can recall, sir,' said the maid and turned away to pour the tea.

But Hardcastle did not believe her, and wondered whether she was being overly loyal to her employer.

*   *   *

11

It was nigh on half past nine by the time that Hardcastle and Marriott arrived at Cannon Row police station which, like New Scotland Yard opposite, had been designed by Sir Norman Shaw and built, on the site of a half-finished opera house, with Dartmoor granite hewn by convicts.

Hardcastle pushed open the door of his office on the first floor and was surprised to see the uniformed figure of Superintendent Hudson sitting at his desk. Arthur Hudson was the officer who commanded A Division and had been called out at the news that one of his constables had been murdered. Sitting nearby was Sub-Divisional Inspector Harry Marsh who had charge of Rochester Row, the police station to which the ill-fated PC Crispin had been attached.

'Good evening, sir.' Hardcastle took off his hat and coat and hung them on the stand in the corner before sitting down. He nodded in Marsh's direction. 'Harry.'

'A bad business, Ernie,' said Hudson. 'I didn't go to Cowley Street. You don't want people getting in the way.' He was one of those rare officers who avoided interfering with detectives going about their business. 'So what can you tell me?'

Hardcastle outlined what he had learned so far. 'And I've got Catto and Wilmot searching the area, sir, just in case anything was dropped. But my first thoughts are that it was a burglar who was surprised trying to break in.'

'Anything pointing to a particular individual?'

'Not at the moment, sir, but at a guess I'd say he was someone with a lengthy record behind him.'

'What makes you say that?'

'Probably thought that if he was caught, he'd go down for fourteen years penal servitude this time, and decided to take a chance on shooting his way out.'

Hudson nodded. 'You may have a point there, Ernie.' He stood up. 'Well, I'll get out of your way, but keep me informed.'

'Of course, sir.'

'By the way,' said Hudson as he slipped on his greatcoat, 'I've broken the news to Crispin's wife. She's understandably distraught, but we're doing what we can for her. They had three children, you know. All under the age of ten.'

No sooner had Hudson and Marsh departed than DC Henry Catto appeared in the doorway of Hardcastle's office.

'Well, Catto, find anything?'

'I had a good look round the area and on the portico in particular,' said Catto. 'It was obvious that someone had been up there from the disturbed snow, but nothing that we could identify.'

'What the blue blazes d'you mean by that, Catto?' demanded Hardcastle. 'You know I don't stand for sloppy reporting.'

'Well, there wasn't any footprints,' said Catto nervously. 'Nothing clear like. I mean nothing that we could look at and compare with a boot or shoe. If we ever found one, sir. But there was these, sir.' The DC opened his gloved hand to reveal two brass cartridge cases.

'Were they on the portico?'

'Yes, sir.'

'Touched them with your bare hands, have you?'

'No, sir,' said Catto indignantly. 'Certainly not, sir.'

Hardcastle peered closely at Catto's find and then glanced up at Marriott. 'Get those across to the Fingerprint Bureau at the Yard and then to that firearms chap, Marriott. See what he's got to say about them.' And, turning to Catto, said, 'All right, lad.' He waved a hand of dismissal, but then paused. 'Nip downstairs and bring me a copper's helmet, Catto, and don't waste any time.'

Utterly confused by the DDI's latest order, Catto fled to do Hardcastle's bidding.

'What d'you think, sir?' asked Marriott.

'It's what I thought when I was talking to Mr Hudson, Marriott. I reckon we're looking for a professional burglar, and he knew that if he was nicked, he'd go down for at least a fourteen stretch. But he made a mistake in shooting a copper, and he'll take the eight o'clock walk for that, you mark my words, Marriott.' Hardcastle paused to fill his pipe with his favourite St Bruno tobacco.

Catto entered the office carrying a helmet. 'You asked for this, sir,' he said, still failing to understand why Hardcastle should want an item of constable's uniform.

But the DDI did not explain. 'We got a full house over there, Marriott?' he asked, nodding towards the main CID office.

'Yes, sir,' said Marriott. 'Mr Rhodes called them all in the minute the news came through.' Detective Inspector Rhodes was the officer in charge of the Cannon Row sub-division's detectives.

'Good.' Emitting a plume of smoke into the air, Hardcastle crossed the corridor and opened the door of the CID office. 'Right, lads,' he said as the detectives rose to their feet. 'You all know what's happened. I'm of the opinion that we're looking for a burglar who was disturbed by PC Crispin. Well I'm going to disturb him a bit more when I find him. Disturb him with a Newgate collar at eight o'clock one morning down Pentonville. But I ain't doing it on me own. I want you lot out on the streets now. Talk to your noses and tell 'em that Ernie Hardcastle don't take kindly to having one of his own murdered, and that he's coming after them unless they give up this killer. Got that have you?'

The assembled detectives murmured assent. When Hardcastle was roused everyone suffered, and they almost felt sympathy for London's criminal community.

Hardcastle handed the helmet to Marriott and took out his wallet. Extracting a pound note, he dropped it into the helmet. 'But before you go, pass that round,' he said. 'Crispin had three small children. And I don't want to hear the chink of coins neither. Just folding stuff. Got that?'

'Yes, sir,' chorused the detectives, hurrying to find at least a ten-shilling note.

'Come, Marriott. There's one or two undesirables we shall give a personal talking to right now,' he announced.

It was a small, smoky pub on the edge of A Division and the conversation stopped the moment the two detectives strode in. The habitués knew Hardcastle and knew what he was. And Hardcastle knew it was a good place to start.

The landlord was there in a trice, wiping the top of the bar. 'Evening, guv'nor. The usual?'

'Yes, please, Josh.' Hardcastle turned so that he was leaning with his back against the bar, and surveyed the clientèle. The customers stared back. They knew that so senior a detective as Hardcastle did not just call in for a drink at this pub when there were more salubrious alehouses on his division. But they knew that Hardcastle knew that this particular tavern was a regular thieves' kitchen.

Josh Arkwright put two glass tankards of best bitter on the counter. He made no attempt to ask for money and Hardcastle made no attempt to pay.

The DDI took a lengthy draught of beer, set his tankard down on the bar and wiped his moustache with the back of his hand. 'Now listen to me,' he said loudly, turning to face the customers once again. 'At about a quarter past six this evening, a robber shot dead one of my policeman in Cowley Street.'

There was an immediate buzz of conversation. The murder of a policeman was extremely unsettling. Unsettling because the police would not leave the criminal fraternity alone until his killer had been found. And that meant that thieves and robbers would have a very distressing few days, if not weeks, until the murderer was arrested. And the assembled petty thieves, robbers and cracksmen knew it.

'So, gentlemen,' continued Hardcastle once the hubbub had died down, 'I want to know who did for my copper. Every man jack in the Metropolitan Police Force – and there's nigh on twenty thousand of them – is going to come looking for him, and there's no telling what else they might find while they're looking.' He took another pull on his beer. 'Unless, of course, someone who knows him gives him up. You know where my office is, but any copper or any nick will do. But I want to know and I want to know soon.' He and Marriott finished their beer and strode out with a final nod to the landlord.

A silence followed the departure of the detectives. The drinkers knew very well that when the police started a search for the killer of one of their own, houses, workshops, outhouses and lock-ups would be searched, felons would be arrested, and the criminal register at courts throughout the Metropolis would be much fuller than usual.

Hardcastle had arrived at his office early on the Friday morning. After toying with the first reports and statements concerning the death of PC Crispin, he rose and crossed the narrow roadway between Cannon Row police station and New Scotland Yard. It was drizzling with rain and yesterday's snow had turned to a dirty slush.

His first call was on Detective Inspector Charles Stockley

Collins, head of the Fingerprint Bureau, but he had disappointing news. No identifiable fingerprints had been found on the cartridge cases recovered by DC Catto.

Next, Hardcastle made his way to a pokey little office tucked away in the basement of the Yard. There, Hardcastle found Detective Inspector Percy Franklin. Franklin had, of his own volition, developed an interest in firearms and was eventually given somewhat grudging authority to set up a testing room.

'Well, Mr Franklin,' began Hardcastle, 'what can you tell me?'

'Interesting, sir,' said Franklin, crossing to a side bench littered with pistols, revolvers, rifles and various pieces of disassembled weaponry. 'I think you might have had a bit of luck with this one.'

'I think I'll be needing it, too,' muttered Hardcastle.

'I'm fairly certain these cartridge cases that your man found are point seven-six-three millimetre.'

'What's lucky about that?' asked Hardcastle, himself no expert in firearms.

'It means that there are not many makes of weapon that could have fired them.' Franklin took up a magnifying glass and examined the cases afresh. 'They were undoubtedly used in a self-loading pistol, and in my opinion most probably a Bergmann or a Luger.'

'Can't you tell which?'

'Not straight off, no, but I'd put money on the Luger.'

'Why d'you say that, Mr Franklin?'

'There's a war on, Mr Hardcastle,' said Franklin with a wry laugh. 'Chances are some swaddy picked it up in the trenches and brought it home as a trophy of war, so to speak.'

'Or I'm looking for a German,' said Hardcastle gloomily. He was never a man to jump to unwarranted conclusions. 'Dr Spilsbury's doing the post-mortem this afternoon and I daresay he'll find a couple of bullets in Crispin's body. Will that help any further?'

Franklin shook his head. 'I doubt it, sir,' he said, 'but when you find the weapon, I should be able to tell you if it's the pistol that fired them.'

Hardcastle grunted an acknowledgement. 'That's easier said than done, Mr Franklin.'

*   *   *

16

From Scotland Yard, Hardcastle went straight to St Mary's Hospital in Paddington where Dr Spilsbury, the pathologist, was wont to conduct his post-mortem examinations.

As Hardcastle had forecast during his conversation with Percy Franklin, Dr Spilsbury did indeed extract two bullets from the body of the late PC Crispin.

'I think those are what you're looking for, Inspector,' said the pathologist as he dropped the small pieces of metal, one after the other, into a kidney-shaped enamel bowl. 'I hope they help you to find whoever killed your policeman.'

'Oh, I'll find him, Doctor,' said Hardcastle vehemently. 'Have no fear of that.'

'They were also the cause of the constable's death,' Spilsbury added drily, pointing at the bullets with a pair of forceps.

'I suppose now's as good a time as ever to catch this bugger Napier at home, Marriott,' said Hardcastle, glancing at his watch. 'Where is it he lives?'

'Albert Hall Mansions, sir, just behind the Albert Hall.'

'Would be, I suppose,' said Hardcastle drily, but then surprised his sergeant by revealing a little knowledge of the area. 'They was designed by Norman Shaw, Marriott,' he continued. 'Same architect as designed the Yard. And what's more, they've got special rooms with baths in 'em. Bathrooms, they call 'em.'

'How d'you know all that, sir?' asked the bemused Marriott.

'You should know,' responded Hardcastle. 'When you're walking a beat on night duty with nothing else to do but read plaques and look at monuments, it's surprising what you pick up.'

'But I thought you did your foot duty at Old Street, sir.'

'Got nothing to do with it, Marriott,' said Hardcastle mysteriously, but then explained. 'When I was on G Division as a PC I got sent up here as aid to B Division for some damned concert. Spent all night wandering round the back streets.'

Charles Napier appeared to be in his mid-thirties. He had pomaded hair and a neatly trimmed moustache. And he looked a picture of health. Hardcastle wondered briefly why he wasn't in the armed forces.

17

'Mr Napier, I'm Divisional Detective Inspector Hardcastle of the Whitehall Division, and this here's Detective Sergeant Marriott.'

'Really? And what can I do for you, gentlemen?' Napier opened the door wide. 'Do come in,' he said.

It was a splendid sitting room, richly carpeted. The wall adjacent to the fireplace was almost completely covered with framed photographic prints, most of which seemed to take ships as their subject. Another wall was taken up with an oak bookcase, the length and height of the room, that was crammed to overflowing with expensively-bound volumes. In one corner, on an easel, stood a somewhat risqué painting of a nude mulatto girl.

'Are you a painter, sir?' asked Hardcastle.

'Heavens no,' said Napier. 'It's as much as I can do to write my name. No, Inspector, that was a gift from a grateful client.'

'A client, sir?'

'Yes, I deal in antiquarian books.' Napier waved a hand at the bookcase. 'Some of which are still with me, I regret to say. Unfortunately, Inspector, the war has not done a great deal to help my trade. Strangely enough, much of it was with the Continent, but now that France and Belgium are theatres of war, and the Trading with the Enemy Act forbids selling books to Germany—' He broke off with an embarrassed laugh. 'Not that I'd wish to do business with the Hun in any event, Inspector, not now I've heard about the atrocities they've committed in Belgium,' he added hurriedly. 'However, what was it you wished to speak to me about?' He waved a hand at a chesterfield settee. 'Do take a seat, gentlemen.'

'I understand that you were supposed to be meeting Mrs Plowman last night, sir,' began Hardcastle.

'Quite correct, Inspector.'

'And you and she were to dine at Rules, I believe.'

'Indeed we were, but she sent me a message saying that a policeman had been murdered right outside her house and that she was engaged with the police. But then you'd know that, of course.' Napier carefully fitted a cigarette into an amber holder. 'I'm afraid I don't quite see the point of your coming here, Inspector. As I'm sure you know, I was nowhere near Cowley Street when this awful crime occurred.'

18

'I wondered why you had not called at the house for her, Mr Napier, given that you'd done so previously.'

Napier frowned. 'How did you know that?' he asked.

'I have my sources, sir.' Hardcastle had no intention of identifying Mary Hutchings as his informant.

'Well, as it happened, I had to meet a client in the West End at a half past five, and there just wasn't time for me to go down to Westminster and pick up Isabel. She agreed to meet me at the restaurant.' Napier paused. 'It is to my chagrin that I wasn't there. In view of what happened, I'm sure she could have done with some moral support.'

'Quite so, sir,' said Hardcastle rising to his feet. 'I just like to make sure of the facts, sir, so perhaps you'd be so good as to give me the name of the client you met.'

Napier did so without hesitation.

And with that Hardcastle departed, leaving behind a somewhat bemused Napier and taking with him an equally bemused Marriott.

'What was the point of that, sir?' asked Marriott as they searched for a cab in Kensington Gore. 'I mean it was pretty obvious that he couldn't have had anything to do with it.'

'Like I told Napier, Marriott, I like to make sure of my facts, and we've only got Mrs Plowman's word for it that he wasn't there.'

'But he might have been, sir. Right now, they're corroborating each other.'

'You're catching on fast, Marriott,' said Hardcastle as he waved his umbrella at a taxi. 'And what's more, I've got a bit of a suspicion that Master Napier back there isn't Mrs Plowman's only beau.'

'She's certainly a good-looking woman, sir,' said Marriott. 'Very easy on the eye.'

'Yes,' said Hardcastle, 'I noticed. But get someone to check with this here client Napier was supposed to have met.'

It was on Saturday evening, however, that the investigation into the murder of PC Robert Crispin took a new twist.

Superintendent Hudson had ordered Sub-Divisional Inspector Marsh, within whose area Cowley Street lay, that he should keep all beats full in the vicinity and post extra patrols. Somewhat naïvely, Hudson believed that the killer might return to the area to complete whatever felonious enterprise had been interrupted by the arrival of PC Crispin. It was not a view shared by Hardcastle, who was certain that anyone who murdered a policeman would put as much distance as possible between himself and the scene of his crime.

In the event, it was the superintendent who was right, and the DDI who was wrong.

Hardcastle had finished his supper and had settled in front of the fire with that day's copy of the *Daily Mail*. He was about to fill his pipe when there was a knock at the door.

'I'll go, Ernie.' Alice Hardcastle wiped her hands on her apron and walked to the front door.

'Evening, ma'am.' The constable saluted.

'Oh, not again,' said Alice. 'I suppose you want the inspector.'

'I've a message for him, ma'am.'

'Wait there then and I'll get him.' Alice took a step back. 'Ernie, there's a PC at the door.'

Muttering an oath, Hardcastle threw down the newspaper and stepped into the hall. 'What is it, lad?'

The constable proffered a message form. 'Murder in Cowley Street, sir.'

'*What?*' Hardcastle snatched the form from the officer's hand and stared at it in disbelief. 'Well I'll go to the foot of our stairs,' he exclaimed. He nodded to the constable. 'All right, lad, get back to the nick and telegraph Cannon Row. Tell 'em I'll be there as soon as possible.'

'Very good, sir.' The constable saluted once again, crossed the road outside and hastened towards Kennington Road police station.

Three

Hardcastle was in a towering rage by the time he reached Cowley Street. Despite Superintendent Hudson's precautions, someone had somehow gained entry to Isabel Plowman's house and murdered her.

Two or three uniformed constables stood around, 'idling and gossiping', to quote the regulations; they were the first recipients of the DDI's wrath as he alighted from his cab. 'Get round your bloody beats,' he said angrily, gesturing at the group of greatcoated policemen. 'You're wasting your time standing round here like dying ducks in a thunderstorm.' Turning to DCs Catto and Wilmot, who were in conversation near the front door of Mrs Plowman's house, he demanded to know the whereabouts of Detective Sergeant Marriott.

'He's there, sir.' Catto hastily raised his hat and pointed.

Indeed, as Hardcastle approached the Plowman house, he was confronted by his sergeant standing at the open front door of the house. 'When did this happen, Marriott?' he demanded.

'The maid discovered Mrs Plowman's body at about a quarter to eight, sir.'

'You mean the maid was in the house?' demanded Hardcastle incredulously.

'Yes, sir, but apparently she was in the kitchen. Never heard a thing. I've had all the neighbours spoken to and they didn't hear or see anything either.'

'The area been searched?'

'Yes, sir, the minute the uniformed police arrived, but no sign of anybody, and nothing lying about that would point to the killer.'

'Pity those beat-duty men weren't here when they should've been,' muttered Hardcastle. 'Where's the body?'

'In the drawing room, sir.'

'What did the divisional surgeon have to say?' continued Hardcastle as Marriott led the way into the sitting room.

'Certified death, the result of gunshot wounds, and left, sir. I suggested he waited for you, but he said he'd another case to go to.'

'Where?' Hardcastle hoped that there was not yet another murder on his patch.

'Chelsea, he said, sir.'

'Thank God for that,' muttered the DDI, and walked into the house.

Mrs Plowman's body was sprawled across the very settee upon which Hardcastle and Marriott had been seated only forty-eight hours previously. A satin slipper lay on the floor next to an embroidered silk cushion, a blackened hole in its centre clearly visible. As for the victim, it appeared that the bullet had entered the woman's head just below her left eye.

'Looks like whoever done for her put that cushion over her face to deaden the sound, Marriott,' commented Hardcastle. 'Which means that whoever it was likely knew the maid would be in the house somewhere. Or guessed there was someone. He must have been a strong bugger, too.'

'Seems to put paid to the idea that it might have been a disturbed burglar, sir,' said Marriott.

'Yes, I think you're right, Marriott,' said Hardcastle. 'And that might just make our job a lot easier.' But in that regard, Hardcastle could not have been more wrong.

'D'you reckon whoever murdered PC Crispin was actually after Mrs Plowman, sir?' asked Marriott.

'A strong possibility,' said Hardcastle. Returning to the front door, he beckoned to Catto and Wilmot.

'Yes, sir?' said Catto.

'You and Wilmot go all over the house and see if you can find any evidence of a break-in. And don't forget the upstairs windows. But don't touch anything, don't disturb anything and don't go down the basement. I'll have a look round there after I've talked to the maid.' Hardcastle glanced at his sergeant. 'We'll do that now, Marriott,' he said.

'I took the liberty of sending for Dr Spilsbury, sir,' said Marriott as the pair descended the stairs to the kitchen. 'Said he'd get here as soon as possible.'

'Good,' said Hardcastle. 'Now we'll see what young Mary's got to say for herself.'

When the two detectives reached the kitchen they found a tearful Mary Hutchings being comforted by Detective Sergeant Wood.

'All right, Wood,' said Hardcastle, 'get upstairs and wait for Dr Spilsbury. When he arrives, let me know.'

'I made the girl a cup of tea, sir,' said Wood. 'There's some left in the pot if you're interested.'

'God Almighty, Wood,' thundered Hardcastle crossly, 'I've got other things to do but sit here drinking tea.' He turned to the maid, still sobbing into a piece of wet muslin. 'Well, Mary, what can you tell me?' he asked, the tone of his voice becoming immediately conciliatory.

'Nothing really, sir. I was down here trying to get some supper started for the mistress and I went upstairs and there she was, the poor thing. It was horrible, sir.' And once again Mary dissolved into tears. 'I've never seen a dead body before,' she added between sobs.

'What time was this that you went upstairs, Mary?' asked Hardcastle gently.

The maid glanced at the wall clock. 'About a quarter to eight, sir. I went up to see what the mistress wanted for supper. She only ever has a very light meal at this time of night, you see, and I didn't want to get her nothing she didn't want.' She paused. 'Sometimes she'll have had something to eat at the hospital, sir, before she comes home. She nurses there, see.'

'Yes, we know that,' said Marriott. 'And had she been at the hospital today?'

'Yes, she had, sir. She's up there most days.'

'And which hospital is that?' Marriott knew the answer because Mrs Plowman had mentioned it, but, like his chief, always sought corroboration whenever possible.

'Charing Cross, sir,' said Mary, the intonation in her voice implying that Marriott should have known that too.

'And what time did she arrive home this evening?' Hardcastle asked.

Once again Mary glanced at the clock. 'I think it was about half past six, sir. Maybe a little earlier.'

'And did you let her in?'

'Oh no, sir. The mistress has her own key, but she rang down for me and I know she'd only just come in because she'd still got her outdoor coat on. She was standing in the sitting room, and she asked if I'd make her a cup of tea. Fair parched, she reckoned she was.'

'And what time did you take the tea up to her?'

'I didn't, sir. She came down to the kitchen a few minutes later and sat right where you're sitting. She often did that. She liked to have a chat, did the mistress, and she'd tell me all about the poor soldiers what she'd been nursing. It was terrible, what she had to put up with. She once said that hardly a day passed but that someone on her ward had died of his wounds.'

'And after your little chat, Mrs Plowman went back upstairs again, did she?'

'Yes, sir.'

'At what time?'

'Just before seven, it must have been.'

'And that was the last time you saw Mrs Plowman alive was it, Mary?' asked Hardcastle, taking back the questioning.

The maid let out a convulsive sob. 'Yes, sir,' she said, and burst into tears again.

'So she was murdered between seven o'clock and a quarter to eight,' mused Hardcastle. 'Now, Mary, I want you to think very carefully about how you answer my next question. Did you see or hear anything at all after your mistress went back upstairs?'

'No, sir, nothing at all.'

'You didn't hear the sound of anyone breaking into the house? Or perhaps someone letting himself in with a key?'

'No, sir. Like I said to the other policeman, I never heard nothing at all. You don't never hear nothing down here with the door shut and the range blazing away.' Mary paused guiltily. 'And I was singing. I like singing when I'm working, and I shut the door because I didn't want to disturb the mistress.'

'Did Mrs Plowman have any callers this evening?'

'No, sir, no one. Leastways, none that I know of. But like I said, I mightn't have heard even if there had been.'

For a moment or two Hardcastle sat in silence before posing his next question. 'When did Major Plowman die, Mary?'

Mary looked up in surprise at the change in questioning. 'It was last year, sir. If I remember aright it was November. Yes, now I come to think of it, it was definitely November.'

'And did Mrs Plowman take it badly?'

'Well, I don't know, sir. The mistress was a very reserved lady. Most of the time you never knew what she was thinking, except when she was talking about them poor soldiers in Charing Cross. But on the day she heard about the major, I went up to the sitting room to collect the afternoon tea-things and the mistress was standing there with a telegram in her hand. "Mary," she said, "the master's been killed". Just like that. Sort of matter-of-fact.'

'Did she tell you what had happened?'

'Yes, sir. She said that his aeroplane had been shot down at somewhere called . . .' The girl paused, searching her mind for the name. 'Lille, sir,' she said eventually. 'It's in France, I believe.'

'How soon after this did Mrs Plowman start going out with Mr Napier, Mary?'

The girl looked embarrassed by the question and remained silent.

'Mary, my job is to try to find out who killed your mistress, so you've got to tell me everything you know.' Hardcastle spoke in kindly tones to the young girl, coaxing her into answering what she must have thought to be an invasive question.

Mary dabbed at her eyes with the corner of her apron. 'It was almost straight away, sir,' she said, but sounded guilty at revealing what she believed to be a confidence. 'She said that she was only a young woman and couldn't spend the rest of her life as a widow.'

'And how old *was* Mrs Plowman, Mary?'

'Twenty-five, sir. I remember that because she gave me a glass of sherry on her birthday and it made me feel all woozy.' The maid gave a shy smile. 'She told me she was twenty-five, and said she was getting old. But she wasn't. I mean, twenty-five ain't old, is it, sir?'

Hardcastle turned to Marriott. 'You getting all this down, Marriott?' he asked.

'Yes, sir,' said Hardcastle's sergeant, and glanced up from

his pocket book. 'Did Mrs Plowman show you this telegram, Mary?'

'No, sir. She just had it in her hand.'

'What'll happen to you now, Mary?' asked Hardcastle.

'I don't really know, sir. I don't know if I could find another position. I was very happy here with the mistress, and with the major when he was home, but I wouldn't want to go into no factory. I know some girls what's gone to work down Woolwich Arsenal, but that's terrible.' Mary stared at Hardcastle. 'They've all got yellow faces, sir, from the stuff they have to work with.'

'Will you go home then?'

'I was thinking about it, sir.'

'I know you said you came from Dorset, Mary, but where exactly?'

'Clapgate, sir. It's a village about two or three miles from Wimborne Minster. My father's the blacksmith there. Not that there's much work for him now they've taken the horses away.'

'Taken the horses?' Hardcastle turned to Marriott. 'What's she talking about?'

'The army has requisitioned a lot of horses, sir, for duty at the Front.'

'How d'you know that, Marriott?'

'My brother's in the Middlesex Regiment. He told me.'

'Bit of a mine of information, you are, Marriott, and no mistake,' said Hardcastle, and faced the maid again. 'Did Mrs Plowman have any other gentlemen callers, Mary, apart from Mr Napier?'

There was a long pause.

'Mary?'

The girl hesitated, but then said, 'Yes, sir, quite a few.' It was evident that she was reluctant to admit it.

'I see. And this was after the major was killed, was it?'

Mary looked away, staring at the kitchen range.

'I need you to help me find out who murdered your mistress, lass,' Hardcastle reminded the girl.

'There was some before, sir,' mumbled the maid. 'But only after the major had gone off to France.'

'D'you remember the names of any of them?'

'Some, sir. There was a Captain Lawton and a Mr Staples.

26

They're the only ones I can remember, but there was others.'

'And you let them into the house each time they called, did you?'

'Not always, sir. Sometimes the mistress would call down and say something like, "It's all right, Mary, I'll go," and she'd let 'em in herself.' Mary paused again, clearly wondering whether to reveal more of her late mistress's social activities. 'I think one or two of 'em had a key, sir.'

Hardcastle glanced meaningfully at Marriott. 'And did Mr Napier have a key, Mary?'

'I think so, sir. The mistress said it was so I wouldn't have to be bothered answering the door.'

Which, to Hardcastle, seemed a very odd statement from a woman who employed a maid. Unless she had an ulterior motive for keeping the frequency, and perhaps the identity, of her callers from the sole remaining member of her staff.

'Did you ever have days off, Mary?' asked Marriott.

'Oh yes, sir. One day a week. Usually a Thursday, but very often the mistress would tell me she wouldn't be needing me on other evenings, and I could go out. She'd say something like she was going out to supper or the theatre, and there'd be no need for me to wait around. And she'd often give me a couple of bob. She was very generous like that, was the mistress.'

'And *did* she go out on those occasions?'

'I don't know, sir. I s'pose she did, but most times I went out too, having the opportunity like. I've got a friend who's a maid a few doors down, and if she was off as well we'd sometimes go to the Bioscope in Vauxhall Bridge Road. Specially if it was a Charlie Chaplin film. We'd have a good laugh at that.'

'Did Mrs Plowman mention that she was going out tonight at all, Mary? I mean, being a Saturday evening, I'd've thought she might have been out on the town.'

'No, sir,' said Mary, 'she never said nothing. It is a bit unusual though. She hardly ever stayed in of a Saturday night. P'raps she was tired after her hospital work.'

'Well then, did she happen to mention that she was expecting a caller?'

'No, sir, she never said.'

27

'Excuse me, sir.' Detective Sergeant Wood stood in the doorway of the kitchen. 'Dr Spilsbury's here.'

'Right. You take a statement from Mary here, Wood, and Marriott and me'll go and have a chat with the doctor.'

The tall, slender figure of Dr Bernard Spilsbury was attired in full evening dress, a black cape slung carelessly back from his shoulders. Catto, standing nearby, was holding the doctor's silk hat, unsure what to do with it. Spilsbury, even at thirty-eight years of age, was a distinguished pathologist. His damning evidence had secured the conviction of the wife-murderer Hawley Harvey Crippen in 1910 after Crippen and his paramour Ethel Le Neve had been arrested by Chief Inspector Dew following a chase across the Atlantic.

'Ah, Doctor, I'm sorry to have called you out,' said Hardcastle. 'You look as though you were at a slap-up dinner somewhere.'

Spilsbury smiled. 'As a matter of fact, Hardcastle, I was at the theatre, and a damned boring play it was too. I was glad to have been called out. To tell you the truth, I'd fallen asleep at the start of the second act. Now then, what is it you have for me?'

Hardcastle led the pathologist into the sitting room where Isabel Plowman's body was still lying exactly as Mary had found it. 'I think I may have wasted your time, Doctor,' he said.

'Time's never wasted examining a cadaver *in situ*, my dear Hardcastle.' Spilsbury knelt on one knee, so that his head was level with that of the dead woman, and peered closely at the wound. 'I presume that you're about to tell me when this young woman died,' he added without looking up.

Hardcastle was not sure how Spilsbury had guessed that. 'Having spoken to the housemaid after you were called, Doctor, I established that the murder took place between seven o'clock and a quarter to eight.'

Spilsbury stood up. 'Excellent,' he said. 'Well, Hardcastle, all I have to do is to conduct the post-mortem examination and see if I can find some more bullets for you. As a tentative suggestion, I would say from my initial examination that you're looking for a right-handed gunman. I'll be able to tell you more later on, but the entry wound being below the left eye would seem to indicate that your murderer held the cushion in place with his left hand while discharging the firearm with the right. But as I say, it's only a tentative suggestion. D'you think this has any connection with the murder of your policeman on Thursday?'

'I don't know, Doctor,' said Hardcastle, thinking that looking for a right-handed gunman would not reduce the field of search by very much, 'but if you find a bullet that our firearms man can match to those that killed PC Crispin, then I reckon the answer will be yes.'

'That would be a help, I suppose,' said Spilsbury. 'Well now, perhaps you'd have the cadaver taken to St Mary's in Paddington. I prefer working there and that's where all my instruments are.'

'Of course, Doctor, and once again, I'm sorry to have called you.'

'Not at all, my dear Hardcastle, not at all.' And with that, Spilsbury took his silk hat from Catto and made for the front door where his chauffeur-driven car was waiting.

'Well, Catto, find anything, did you?'

'Find anything, sir?' Catto frowned.

'God dammit, man, I sent you and Wilmot to look for signs of a break-in.'

'Oh that, sir, no. We went all round and the windows were all locked.'

'That's as may be, Catto, but had they been tampered with? These wooden sash windows might have a lock on 'em but they can be slipped as easy as pie. All you have to do is slide a penknife up between the lower and upper windows and the job's done. Then our murderer could have locked it again and let himself out of the front door after he'd topped Mrs Plowman. On the other hand, he might have forgotten to lock it again. Did you find any windows where the catch *wasn't* on?'

Catto, on the receiving end of yet another little homily on crime investigation, dithered. 'I don't think so, sir.' He now doubted his initial assertion that all the windows had been locked.

'Oh, you don't *think* so, eh, Catto?' said Hardcastle acidly. 'Well, you're paid to think, lad, and you're paid to investigate.

29

Either they're locked or they ain't, so go round and check again. *All* the windows, mind, but don't touch any of them. And then go down and ask the maid if the windows are kept locked, or if they ain't, which ones are and which ones aren't. Got that, have you?'

'Yes, sir,' said Catto.

Hardcastle turned to Marriott. 'Remind me to get Mr Collins from the Fingerprint Bureau over here, Marriott, to see if he can find something on them window frames that might help us.'

'Er, there was one thing, sir,' said Catto.

'What?'

'There was a leather belt in the dining room, sir.'

'Well, where is it, man?'

'It's still there, sir. You told me not to touch anything.'

Hardcastle let out an exasperated sigh. 'Show me, then.'

Catto led the way into the dining room. On the floor, just inside the door, lay a leather belt. Hardcastle picked it up and examined it. 'Looks like an army belt, Marriott,' he said, turning it over in his hands. 'Ah, and there's a number on the inside: 14315. What's that mean, I wonder?'

'That could be the man's regimental number, sir.'

'Should make it easy to find the owner then, Marriott.'

'Not necessarily, sir. Each regiment numbers its men from one, and there are a lot of regiments.'

Hardcastle frowned. 'A right bloody Job's comforter you are, Marriott.'

'There's another thing, too, sir. If some of Mrs Plowman's gentlemen friends had keys to the house, mightn't one of them have let himself in, murdered her, and left again? All by the front door.'

'You might be right, Marriott,' said Hardcastle gloomily. 'And although we only know of Napier and the two whose names young Mary gave us, I've a nasty suspicion there could've been more. It's beginning to look as though our Mrs Plowman was a bit of a flighty piece. Which reminds me. Did Napier's alibi check out?'

'Yes, sir,' said Marriott. 'Bert Wood interviewed the client Napier met on Thursday and he said he met Napier in the Nerone Lounge off Trafalgar Square to discuss some business.'

'I wonder what he was doing this evening,' muttered Hardcastle as he and Marriott returned to the sitting room and waited while two constables removed Mrs Plowman's body.

'Want me to have it checked, sir?'

'Not for the moment, Marriott. But in the meantime, I think we'll have a look round.' Hardcastle crossed to the far side of the room and opened the fall flap of a mahogany bureau. 'Never know what the inside of a lady's desk will tell you,' he said.

For a few minutes the DDI rummaged around among the contents, occasionally muttering to himself about its untidiness.

'There's a few letters here, Marriott, and one or two telegrams. We might just get a few more names of Mrs Plowman's gentlemen admirers if we're lucky.' He plucked one telegram out of the pile of correspondence. 'Now this is interesting.' Without revealing the contents, he turned to Marriott. 'Nip down to the kitchen and see if young Mary can remember the exact date that Mrs Plowman received the telegram about Major Plowman's death.'

Only minutes later, Marriott returned. 'It was the tenth of November last year, sir,' he said.

'Can she be sure of that?' asked Hardcastle.

'Yes, sir. She apparently remembered it because it's her father's birthday.'

'Interesting,' mused Hardcastle. 'This here telegram's dated the tenth of November 1914, but it's nothing to do with the bold major getting shot down. It's from someone called Cecil asking Mrs P to meet him at the Savoy Hotel at eight o'clock. It says here there'd been a change of plan, whatever that meant.'

'Is that relevant, sir, apart from giving us another name of one of Mrs Plowman's fancy men?'

'Possibly, Marriott, possibly,' said Hardcastle mysteriously. 'You see, there's no telegram here about the major getting his come-uppance at the hands of old Fritz. Now I'd've thought that a bereaved widow would have hung on to a missive like that, wouldn't you?'

'What are you getting at, sir?' asked the mystified Marriott. 'Are you suggesting that she might not have been a widow? Was playing fast and loose?'

31

'You might be right, Marriott. Remember what Mary said about her mistress not showing any emotion at the news. It's just possible that this was the telegram that Mrs Plowman was holding when she told Mary that the major had been shot down over Lille. Why should she have done that, I wonder? I reckon she was up to something.' Hardcastle let out a sigh. 'Well I think that's all we can do here, Marriott. Bring those letters with you and we'll have a good go through them. Might throw up a few names. And get a PC stationed on the door for the time being.'

'Right, sir,' said Marriott, mildly irritated that Hardcastle had sent the uniformed officers away when he had arrived. He gathered up the letters and telegrams, and secured them with an elastic band he found in Mrs Plowman's bureau.

'Ah, Catto, just the man,' said Hardcastle, as he returned to the hall.

'Yes, sir?'

'Tenth of November last year.'

'Sir?' Catto looked suitably perplexed.

'There was someone called Cecil who'd arranged to meet Mrs Plowman at the Savoy Hotel at eight o'clock that evening. Get up there and see if you can find out his surname.'

'Isn't it a bit late, sir?' asked Catto.

'It's a funny thing about hotels, Catto,' said Hardcastle, 'but they're open twenty-four hours a day.'

'Yes, sir.'

'And before you run away, Catto, what about the windows?'

'Mary said that they're always locked, sir. She goes round the house every night before she turns in. She reckoned that Mrs Plowman was very particular about it.'

Four

Whenever possible, Hardcastle's Sundays always followed the same pattern. Today he found himself unable to settle to his normal routine. He would have preferred to be in his office at the police station, but he knew that there would have been little for him to do. He just had to wait.

But that was not all. The usual tranquillity of the household had been disrupted when the nineteen-year-old Kitty announced that she had obtained a job as a conductress with the London General Omnibus Company.

Hardcastle flew into a rage at his daughter's brazenness, but his real concern was the danger in which she might be placing herself, and he did not hesitate to say as much.

'London's not full of men of dubious morals, whatever you may think, Pa,' Kitty said spiritedly. 'Anyway, it means that if I'm working on the buses, it'll release another man to join up.'

'Well, I'm not having it,' thundered Hardcastle. 'And less of your cheek, young woman.'

'It's too late now, Pa, it's done. I can't go back on my word and you can't stop me.' Kitty was a strong-minded girl, and strong though her father was, he knew that there was no shaking the girl once her mind was made up.

Hardcastle lit his pipe, puffed furiously at it and lapsed into a moody silence.

After the Hardcastles' usual lunch of roast beef and Yorkshire pudding, followed by steamed syrup pudding – conducted in a painful silence – Kitty had flounced out of the house, declaring that she was going for a walk with her current boyfriend. Intent on avoiding their angry father, the seventeen-year-old Maud mooned about the house, and Walter, the youngest at fifteen, disappeared to his bedroom where he spent the afternoon poring over a map upon which he daily charted the progress – or lack of it – of the conflict that was currently consuming the nation's interest.

Hardcastle himself, however, was unable to put his mind to anything, and it was not only the argument with Kitty that had disgruntled him. He glanced at the *News of the World*, but cast it aside before he had even turned the first page.

Alice Hardcastle, having done the washing-up, with the unwilling help of Maud, sat opposite her husband beside the blazing fire and continued with her self-imposed task of knitting socks and mufflers for soldiers. In common with most policemen's wives, she made a point of never discussing her husband's cases with him, but the murder of a police officer touched every police family, the thinking being 'there but for the grace of God . . .'

'Are you going to find him, Ernie?'

'I will, Alice, if it's the last thing I do,' said Hardcastle. 'Just because there's a war on is no excuse for going about killing coppers. Don't you worry, I'll see him hanged. Even if I have to stay on after my pension falls due.'

'What about the PC's family?' asked Alice.

'Three bairns, all under ten,' said Hardcastle. 'God knows how she'll manage, but Arthur Hudson's doing what he can. Of course there's a collection round the division, and for that matter, the whole of the Force.'

'Well if there's anything I can do, let me know,' said Alice.

'Aye, I will,' said Hardcastle, gazing into the fire. He leaned across to the small side table and put his pipe in the ashtray. 'D'you fancy a cup of tea, love?'

'Yes,' said Alice, and went to stand up.

'I'll make it,' said Hardcastle, rising from his chair.

The scene in the Marriott household in the police quarters at Regency Street was very similar to that in the Hardcastle ménage. But the tragedy was brought more sharply home to the Marriotts, because the Crispins lived in a flat in the same block.

Marriott's wife Lorna watched her husband with growing concern. 'You might as well settle down and read the paper or something, Charlie,' she said. 'There's nothing you can do on a Sunday afternoon.'

'Perhaps not, love,' said Marriott, 'but I feel I ought to be at work. He was good copper, was Bob Crispin.' He stared moodily into the fireplace. 'And now, on top of that, the poor woman who saw it all's been murdered.'

'I'll make a cup of tea,' said Lorna, and then glanced at their two children, playing happily on the rug in front of the fire. 'Mind you don't disturb your father,' she cautioned.

On Monday morning Hardcastle was able to get back to the investigation of the double murder that had been occupying most of his thoughts on Sunday.

When he arrived at his office, as usual at half past eight, Catto was hovering.

'Well?' barked the DDI.

'I went to the Savoy Hotel, sir . . .' Catto began.

'I should hope so. What did you find out?' Hardcastle entered his office and hung up his coat and hat, and dropped his umbrella into the stand, its ferrule hitting the metal tray with a clatter.

Catto thumbed open his pocket book and coughed deferentially. 'There were two men called Cecil who stayed at the Savoy Hotel on the tenth of November last, sir,' he said. 'One was called Cecil Yates, the other was called Cecil Underwood.'

'So what did you find out about them?' demanded Hardcastle testily. 'For God's sake, man, get on with it. You're not giving evidence up at the Bailey now.'

'Yes, sir. Er, no, sir. Cecil Yates stayed there for one night only with a Mrs Yates. Cecil Underwood was an American gentleman who was over here on business. He was on his own and he stayed for a week.'

'I hope you got their addresses,' snapped Hardcastle.

'Er, yes, sir.' Catto started to read them out. 'Cecil Yates lives at Eaton Place—'

'Don't tell me, lad. Tell Sergeant Marriott. Did you by any chance get a description of the woman who was with Yates?'

'No, sir. I asked the hall porter but he couldn't remember on account of it being a long time ago.'

Hardcastle nodded. 'Thought that might be the case, Catto. Never mind, I've a good idea it was Mrs Plowman pretending to be Mrs Yates. Ask Sergeant Marriott to come in.'

'We're meeting Mr Collins at the Plowman place, Marriott,' said Hardcastle when, a few minutes later, the sergeant appeared in the doorway. 'He's having a look round the house for fingerprints.'

'Of course, Ernie,' said Detective Inspector Charles Stockley Collins as he moved around the Cowley Street house with a magnifying glass, 'ever since the Stratton brothers were hanged, dyed-in-the-wool villains have been more careful where they put their fingers.'

'I suppose so, Charlie.' Hardcastle, in common with all detectives, knew of the 1905 Deptford oil-shop murders, the first case in which the police had secured a conviction on fingerprint evidence. 'But I'm beginning to think that I'm dealing with a gentleman murderer, so to speak, and he might not have been so well informed.'

'Well, there's quite a few prints here, Ernie,' said Collins when he had completed his examination. 'The problem is that most of them will belong to people who've had legitimate access to the premises. I'll get one of my lads to nip round to the mortuary and take a set of Mrs Plowman's prints so we can eliminate them. And while I'm here I'll take a set of the maid's as well.' He sighed. 'I reckon you've got a job on your hands, Ernie, and that's a fact.'

'I'd already come to that conclusion,' said Hardcastle and turned to his sergeant. 'Take Mr Collins down to the kitchen, Marriott, and see if you can find Mary Hutchings.'

Following a hurried lunch of a meat pie and a pint of beer at the Red Lion pub immediately outside New Scotland Yard, Hardcastle and Marriott made their way to Wellington Barracks in Birdcage Walk. Hardcastle had decided that his questions about the strange find of the army belt at Cowley Street could best be answered by a soldier familiar with such accoutrements.

''Alt, who goes there?' Recognizing immediately that the two policemen were clearly not soldiers, the khaki-clad Coldstream Guards sentry raised his rifle, the fixed bayonet pointing threateningly at Hardcastle.

'Police,' said Hardcastle, by now accustomed to such military wartime precautions.

'Report to the guardroom, sir,' said the sentry, and main-tained his rifle at the port until the DDI and Marriott had entered the small building inside the gate.

'Good afternoon, gents,' said the sergeant of the guard. 'And what can I do for the law?' he asked, remaining seated behind his desk.

Hardcastle regarded the red-sashed guard commander suspi-ciously. 'How did you know that?' he demanded.

'It's the training, sir,' said the sergeant with a grin, choosing not to reveal that he had overheard Hardcastle's response to the sentry.

'I'm Divisional Detective Inspector Hardcastle, Sergeant, and I've got an important query about a piece of military equipment found at the scene of a murder.'

The sergeant fingered his moustache. 'I reckon the best bloke you can see is the major quartermaster, sir. What he don't know about stores and kit ain't worth knowing.' He half turned in his chair. 'Williams,' he bellowed, 'get your fat little body out here sharpish.'

Within seconds an immaculate soldier appeared and crashed to attention beside the sergeant. 'Sarn't,' he screamed.

'Take these police officers across to the regimental quar-termaster's office, and don't get lost.'

'Where's that, Sarn't?' asked the young soldier.

'Oh my sainted aunt!' exclaimed the sergeant. 'In the head-quarters block. Where d'you think it bloody is, lad, across the road at Buck House?' And, oblivious to the guardsman's pres-ence or feelings, he said to Hardcastle, ''Alf the time these Kitchener's volunteers don't know their arse from their elbow, sir. Frankly, I don't know why the Brigade takes 'em, mixing 'em with proper soldiers.'

Setting off with jerky, marionette-like movements, Private Williams crossed the parade ground at a fast pace, and Hardcastle and Marriott had some difficulty in keeping up with him.

Eventually, however, they were shown into an office, a sign on the door of which proclaimed its occupant to be Major (QM) Thomas Duggan, Coldstream Guards.

'And what can I do for you, Inspector?' asked Duggan once introductions had been effected.

Hardcastle produced the belt that had been found in Isabel Plowman's dining room and handed it to Duggan. 'I was wondering if you could help me to identify the owner of this, Major.'

The quartermaster examined the belt carefully, turning it over in his hands. Eventually he placed it in the centre of his desk, rubbed his hands together and uttered a scornful laugh. 'I can tell you this much, Inspector. The owner of this is an idle, scurvy knave. It's not been polished in years.'

'I daresay, Major.' As far as Hardcastle was concerned, the soldierly inefficiency of the belt's owner contributed nothing to his enquiry. 'But it's the number inside that I thought you might be able to assist me with.'

'Doubt it. There are about eighty regiments in the army, give or take, and that's not counting the gunners, the engineers, the artisans, the Indians or the other assorted odds and sods. And each regiment starts its numbers from one.'

Which was exactly what Marriott had said. 'So that's not likely to help me find out who it belongs to, is it, Major?'

'No help at all, Mr Hardcastle, because it's a German Army belt.' Major Duggan stood up. 'I suppose you could drop a line to the Kaiser,' he added with a chuckle.

Hardcastle was not at all pleased to learn that the belt which had mysteriously found its way into Mrs Plowman's dining room was German Army issue. Coupled with Inspector Franklin's opinion that the weapon used to murder PC Crispin was probably a German pistol, it seemed to point to the murderer being German.

'It don't make sense, Marriott,' said Hardcastle. 'How, in time of war, could a German soldier murder one of my policemen, then come back, gain entry to Mrs Plowman's house and murder her too?' He took off his shoes and began massaging his feet.

'If it's the same killer, sir,' said Marriott.

'What d'you mean by that, Marriott?' asked Hardcastle, glaring at his sergeant.

'Well, I know what Mr Franklin said, sir, and I know we found a German Army belt, but we're not sure it was the same man who killed them both. Or even if it was a German who was responsible. After all, that Charles Napier reckoned he used to do business with the Germans before the war, and he must've gone over there to do that. He could've laid hands on a pistol and a German Army belt *before* the war started.'

Hardcastle replaced his shoes and his spats, and began slowly to fill his pipe. 'You're a right Job's comforter and no mistake, Marriott,' he said.

'He was at pains to tell us that he wasn't doing business with the Germans any more. Well, he couldn't be, so why bother to tell us unless he was trying to shift suspicion away from himself?'

Hardcastle considered that. 'You might be right, Marriott. I never mentioned that we knew it was a German pistol that killed them and I never said anything about the belt.'

'Exactly, sir. A bit suspicious, that, I'd've thought. Mind you, like I said, Bert Wood checked his alibi for the Thursday, so if it's the same—'

'Yes, all right,' said Hardcastle. 'I'd worked that out for myself.'

As if to confirm what Marriott had been saying, the DDI's sketchy prognosis that one killer was to blame for both deaths was confirmed later that afternoon by a report from the Yard's firearms expert. The bullet that Dr Spilsbury extracted from Mrs Plowman's cranium had been passed to Inspector Franklin, and he was in no doubt that it had been fired by the same weapon that had killed PC Crispin.

'Of course, sir,' said Marriott, once Hardcastle had imparted this latest piece of information. 'On the other hand, the belt that Catto found may have been lost, or might even be a trophy of war that the late Major Plowman brought back before he was killed. And the pistol might have been brought back by a British soldier, as Mr Franklin suggested.'

'You're probably right, Marriott,' said Hardcastle, regarding his sergeant with a sour expression, 'but be that as it may' – he glanced at the clock – 'I think now would be a good time to visit this Mr Cecil Yates.'

It was about half past six when Hardcastle and Marriott arrived at the house in Eaton Place.

'I'm here to see Mr Cecil Yates,' said Hardcastle to the manservant who answered the door.

The butler peered haughtily down his nose at the two detectives on the doorstep. 'Is the master expecting you?' he asked, an imperious tone in his voice.

'I doubt it,' said Hardcastle, who was quite accustomed to dealing with those members of the servant class who thought they were as good as their employers. He produced his warrant card. 'Just tell him that Divisional Detective Inspector Hardcastle wishes to see him. And I don't want any obstruction from you either, cully.'

'I see. You'd better come in, I suppose.' Somewhat affronted by Hardcastle's brash approach, the butler left the two policemen in the large entrance hall, turned on his heel and made for a door on the far side.

'I can see he's one of them what thinks the bell tolls for him, Marriott,' muttered Hardcastle, displaying a surprising insight to the poetry of John Donne.

The butler returned. 'The master will see you in the drawing room,' he said, clearly disappointed that his employer had agreed to see someone who had called without an appointment. 'This way.'

Cecil Yates looked up from a copy of *The Times* as the two detectives were shown in. He stood up, carefully folded the newspaper and placed it on a side table, neatly aligning it with other journals and magazines, all of which were in a tidy, regimented array. Hardcastle got the impression that Yates was a man who appreciated order in his life.

'Well, gentlemen, I'm intrigued. And what, pray, brings the police force to my door?' Yates – Hardcastle guessed he was fast approaching forty years of age – dropped his pince-nez into the top pocket of his plum-coloured velvet smoking jacket and brushed at his neatly-trimmed moustache. A glass of whisky stood on a small table close to the chair in which he had been sitting.

'Mrs Isabel Plowman, sir,' said Hardcastle, unwilling to waste too much time on the social niceties with a man whom he had already decided was a philanderer.

'Mrs Plowman?' Yates furrowed his brow as though giving the name some thought. 'I'm not sure that I—'

'Lives in Cowley Street, Westminster. Or *did* live there, I should say. I'm investigating her murder.'

Suddenly Yates's veneer of superiority vanished. 'Her murder?' he gasped, and half fell into his chair. 'My God! When did this happen?'

'On Saturday evening last, sir,' said Hardcastle as he and Marriott sat down, unbidden, on a leather settee. 'I understand that you and she stayed at the Savoy Hotel on the night of Tuesday the tenth of November last year.'

'What ever makes you think that she and I—?'

'The hotel management was quite sure it was you, sir,' said Hardcastle, although he was by no means certain himself. The fact that DC Catto had come back with this Cecil Yates's address did not necessarily mean that he had got the facts right. However, that Yates acknowledged knowing Isabel Plowman, albeit in a roundabout way, seemed to confirm to Hardcastle that the information was correct.

Yates leaned forward, putting his head in his hands. 'Murdered! I can't believe it.' He looked up. 'How did it happen, Inspector?'

'She was shot, sir.'

'God Almighty, who would have wanted to harm her?'

'Can we get back to the night of November the tenth last, sir,' said Hardcastle, convinced that Yates's behaviour was in part contrived histrionics. 'You did stay at the Savoy that night.'

'I think I possibly did, Inspector, but there's nothing wrong with that, surely?' said Yates, becoming defensive.

'I take it, then, that you were seeing the lady quite regularly.' It was an assumption on Hardcastle's part. There was no evidence that Yates's partner had been Mrs Plowman, but he thought that it was not far from the truth.

'Well, yes. We went out to dinner and to the theatre quite often.'

'I'd like to be certain about the particular date I mentioned, Mr Yates,' persisted Hardcastle.

By way of a reply, Yates crossed to the table upon which his newspapers and magazines rested, opened a drawer and withdrew a small leather-bound book. 'My diary,' he explained, holding it aloft, and spent a few seconds thumbing through it. 'Yes, you're quite right, Inspector. Isabel and I did spend the night at the Savoy on November the tenth.' He returned the diary to the drawer and sat down again. 'But why is that so important, given that you told me she was murdered last Saturday?'

'Did Mrs Plowman seem at all upset that evening, sir?'

'No, not at all. In fact she was her usual gay, carefree self. What makes you ask?'

'According to her maid, that was the date she received notification of the death of her husband.'

'But that's ridiculous,' said Yates. 'She was widowed well before that.'

'It was on that date that she summoned her maid to the drawing room,' continued Hardcastle. 'Mrs Plowman was holding a telegram and told the maid that Major Plowman had been shot down over Lille, and that he was dead.'

'Good God!' Yates reached across for his whisky glass and took a sip. 'But I was sure that Edward had been killed almost at the outset of the war.'

'Did she actually tell you that, sir?'

'Well, not exactly. She sort of implied that she'd lost her husband at the beginning of the Battle of Mons.'

'When did you last see Mrs Plowman, sir?'

'Just before Christmas.' Yates spoke with hesitation.

'Why as long ago as that, Mr Yates? I mean why haven't you seen her since?'

'We, er, had a disagreement.'

'What was that about?' persisted Hardcastle.

'I asked her to marry me, but she refused. She said that she wasn't ready to marry again, so soon after Edward's death.'

Hardcastle remained silent, fixing Yates with a penetrating gaze.

'Well, that's not entirely true. She said there was a very good reason why she couldn't marry me, although she wouldn't say what it was. But I worked it out a matter of days later.'

'How was that?' asked Hardcastle.

'I saw her at the Garrick Theatre in Charing Cross Road. She was with another man.'

'Oh I see,' said Hardcastle, a half smile playing around his lips. 'And did Mrs Plowman see you?'

'Er, yes, Inspector, she did.'

'Did she speak?'

'No. As a matter of fact, she cut me dead.'

'Were you there on your own?' asked Hardcastle.

There was a long pause before Yates replied. 'No, I was with a lady of my acquaintance,' he said, somewhat ruefully.

'Did you know this man Mrs Plowman was with?'

'No, I'd never set eyes on him before.'

Hardcastle stood up. 'Well, thank you for your assistance, Mr Yates.'

Once in the street, Hardcastle hailed a taxi. 'Scotland Yard, cabbie,' he said, and turning to Marriott, added, 'Tell 'em Cannon Row and half the time you finish up at Cannon Street in the City.'

'Yes, sir, I know,' said Marriott, wearily. He had received Hardcastle's little homily on almost every occasion they had taken a taxi back to the police station.

'It seems to me, Marriott,' said Hardcastle, settling himself against the cushions of the cab and pushing his legs out straight, 'that Mr Yates and Mrs Plowman thoroughly deserved each other.'

'If what Mary Hutchings said is true, sir,' said Marriott, 'I reckon that Mrs Plowman had a string of admirers and wasn't too bothered about which of them she shared her bed with.' He paused for a moment or two. 'D'you reckon Major Edward Plowman is dead, sir?'

'You took the words right out of my mouth, Marriott,' said Hardcastle. 'And tomorrow morning, we'll do some checking up.'

Five

The funeral of Police Constable Robert Crispin took place at St Matthew's Church in Great Peter Street on the Tuesday morning following his murder. It was an impressive affair. The roads from the funeral parlour in Regency Street, near where the unfortunate officer had lived with his wife and three small children in police quarters close to the Marriotts, were lined with policemen. Most were from Crispin's own division, but there were also officers from the neighbouring B and C Divisions. Despite a near freezing wind that would normally have demanded greatcoats, all wore ceremonial uniform with snake-clasp belts, white gloves and, those who had them, medals.

In an eerie silence, save only for the sound of hooves and marching men, the hearse, its horses with sable plumes, was followed by a contingent from Crispin's own station, and led by the tall figure of the Commissioner, Sir Edward Henry – the wind occasionally ruffling the feathers of his cocked hat – Superintendent Arthur Hudson, Sub-Divisional Inspector Harry Marsh, and Hardcastle.

At the church the coffin was borne in by six constables drawn from Crispin's relief, commanded by an inspector and a sergeant.

In sonorous prose, the presiding clergyman spoke of Crispin's devotion to duty, his unfailing service to the public and his willingness, in common with all policemen, to lay down his life to preserve the King's Peace. The only interruption came from Mrs Crispin, whose quiet sobs could be heard throughout the service.

That afternoon, Hardcastle and Marriott visited the War Office in Whitehall. To his surprise, he found it to be an oasis of

44

tranquillity. The only occupant of the vast entrance hall was an ageing messenger with Boer War medal ribbons on his blue uniform jacket.

'And what can I do for you, gents?' he asked.

'Police,' said Hardcastle, 'and I need to see someone about an officer who's been killed.'

'Ah!' said the messenger thoughtfully. 'What regiment?'

'Royal Flying Corps,' said Hardcastle.

'Mmm!' The messenger scratched at his ragged moustache. 'Bit of a problem that, guv'nor, so to speak. A lot of them flyers is attached from all sorts of different regiments, see. Hold on and I'll see what I can do.' Disappearing into a small glass-panelled cubicle on the far side of the entrance hall, the messenger conferred with one of his colleagues.

'You wouldn't think there was a war on, would you, Marriott?' muttered Hardcastle while they waited. 'Seem to be taking it a bit too easy for my liking. Never asked to see our warrant cards. We could be German spies for all he knows.'

But before Marriott could respond, the messenger returned. 'I'll take you up to see Colonel Armstrong, gents. My mate reckons he'll be able to help.'

The messenger led them up a staircase, and along several echoing corridors, until Hardcastle and Marriott were eventually shown into an office overlooking Horse Guards Avenue.

'George Armstrong, gentlemen,' said the colonel as introductions were effected. 'How may I help you?'

Armstrong was close to sixty and, Hardcastle correctly surmised, had been recalled at the outbreak of war to replace one of his fitter fellows who was now doing duty at the Front.

The DDI briefly explained about the murder of Isabel Plowman and that he was seeking information concerning the death of her husband, Major Edward Plowman of the Royal Flying Corps. 'I've had two different dates given me, Colonel,' he continued. 'One suggests that he was killed at the start of the Battle of Mons; the other is that he was shot down over Lille shortly before the tenth of November last year.'

'I see. If you'll bear with me, Inspector, I'll see what I can find out for you.' Armstrong struck a brass bell on the corner of his desk and seconds later an Army Service Corps warrant officer appeared through a communicating door from an adjacent office.

'Yes, sir?'

'Mr Warrender, these gentlemen are police officers. Be so good as to see what you can dig up about this Major Plowman, will you?' said Armstrong, handing the warrant officer the notes he had made.

'Shan't keep you a moment, sir,' said Warrender, and returned to his own office.

Armstrong stared gloomily out of the window. 'Good chap is Warrender, Inspector,' he said, 'but I fear it may take even him a bit longer than that. We're losing men hand over fist. Officers too. The life of a second-lieutenant on the Western Front is reckoned to be six months now, at best. In the RFC they calculate it in days. Can't keep up with it, you see.' He gave a cynical laugh. 'And to think that last August they were talking about it being over by Christmas. It wouldn't surprise me if it lasted another ten years, the way things are going.'

But a continuation of Armstrong's gloomy prognosis was curtailed by the return of Warrender holding a manila file.

'There's no record of this Major Plowman being killed, sir,' he said to Colonel Armstrong. 'In fact, there's only one Plowman in the list of killed in action, and he was James Plowman, a captain in the Essex Regiment attached to the Royal Naval Division. Anyway, sir, I've sent a runner to see if we can find anything about Major Plowman, like when he was commissioned and so on.'

'What on earth was a soldier doing at sea?' exclaimed Hardcastle, yet again baffled by the army.

'The Royal Naval Division are sailors fighting as infantry, sir,' said Warrender with a smile. 'It was Mr Churchill's idea – he's First Lord of the Admiralty – but of course they need a few soldiers to show 'em how it's done.'

'Is there any tea on the go, Mr Warrender?' asked Armstrong. 'I'm sure these gentlemen could use a cup.'

'I'll arrange it, sir,' said the warrant officer, and disappeared once more to his own office.

'There's a problem with RFC chaps,' said Armstrong. 'If they're shot down in enemy territory and taken prisoner, it may be some time before the Huns notify us. On the other hand, if they crash in thick woodland, or something like that, their bodies may not be found for days. Weeks even.'

'But Mrs Plowman was quite adamant that she'd received notification of her husband having been killed on the tenth of November last, Colonel,' said Hardcastle.

'I thought you said she'd been murdered.' Armstrong raised his eyebrows, clearly wondering how a dead woman could be adamant about anything. 'Ah, the tea,' he said as a soldier appeared with a tray, upon which were cups and saucers and a large brown teapot.

'We spoke to her maid, Colonel,' said Hardcastle, as the soldier began to pour the tea, 'and she told us about Mrs Plowman receiving a telegram to that effect. There was no mention of him having been taken prisoner. But a friend of hers told us a different story. According to him, she'd said Major Plowman was killed at Mons at the outbreak of the war.'

'I see,' said Armstrong, but it was fairly clear that he did not see. 'Well, I daresay that Warrender will get to the bottom of it.'

But Warrender did not get to the bottom of it, at least, not in a way that was satisfactory to Hardcastle. Some twenty minutes later he returned. 'According to the latest information, sir,' he said to Armstrong, 'Major Edward Plowman, a regular Royal Flying Corps officer, is attached to Number Four Squadron. In fact he's the squadron commander, and is currently based at St Brouille, but we've had no reports of his death or capture.'

Armstrong glanced at the warrant officer. 'Is he a pilot or an observer, Mr Warrender?'

'A pilot, sir.'

'I'm much obliged, Mr Warrender,' said Armstrong, by way of dismissal.

'Very good, sir,' said the warrant officer and retreated to his own office.

'Well, it seems that your chap wasn't killed when you thought he was, Inspector, although he could've died recently, I suppose. Is there anything else I can do for you?'

'If he is still alive, Colonel,' said Hardcastle, 'he'll need to be told about his wife's murder.'

'Mmm! Yes. Want the army to do that for you, eh?'

Hardcastle was tempted to say that he had no intention of crossing to France personally to inform Major Plowman of his wife's death, but confined himself merely to thanking Armstrong for his offer. 'I would be grateful if you will, Colonel,' he said.

'Certainly, Inspector,' said Armstrong, 'and I'll inform you when that's been done. I daresay he'll be granted compassionate leave to make the funeral arrangements. If he *is* still alive.'

For the next ten minutes they drank their tea while Colonel Armstrong gave forth of further desultory comments about the progress of the war.

'Well, I don't know, Marriott,' said Hardcastle as the pair walked back to Cannon Row police station. 'It's a bloody dog's dinner.'

'Sounds to me as though our Mrs Plowman was a lady who enjoyed male company, sir.'

A brief smile played around Hardcastle's lips. 'Cuckolding her husband while the poor bastard's risking his life at the Front, you mean?' he said.

'If he's still alive, sir,' said Marriott, repeating what Colonel Armstrong had said. 'But one thing's pretty certain: it looks as though he wasn't killed when Mary the maid said he was. Or when Cecil Yates reckoned he was. I suppose it's possible she made up this yarn so that the maid wouldn't think she was cheating on her old man.'

'Well, if she's offering her favours to anyone who takes her fancy, it could make for a long list of suspects,' said Hardcastle gloomily.

The following morning, a soldier appeared in Hardcastle's office and crashed to attention on the bare boards before saluting. He was immaculate: boots shining, puttees correctly wound, and cap – with a burnished badge – squarely placed on his shaven head.

'Corporal Green, sir, from the War Office. I'm Colonel Armstrong's runner.'

'And have you run all the way from the War Office?' asked

Hardcastle mischievously as he shook his head in amazement at this display of military theatre.

'Er, well, no, sir.' Green spoke hesitantly. In common with members of Hardcastle's staff, who were never sure when Hardcastle was being serious, the corporal was a little flummoxed by a question he imagined should be considered with some gravity.

'Is it about Major Plowman, lad?'

'Yes, sir.' Corporal Green unbuttoned a breast pocket and extracted a piece of paper that he handed to the DDI.

Hardcastle skimmed the unfamiliar army message form and nodded. 'All right, lad,' he said. 'Perhaps you'd thank Colonel Armstrong for his prompt assistance.'

'Yes, sir. Thank you, sir.' Green saluted once again, executed a smart about-turn and left the office.

Hardcastle crossed the corridor and opened the door of the detectives' office. 'Marriott, a moment of your time.'

Returning to his office, Hardcastle read the note again. 'This is a rum do and no mistake, Marriott,' he said as his sergeant entered. 'According to Colonel Armstrong, Major Plowman is still alive. He's been told about his wife's murder and is coming home to sort out the funeral.' Reaching for his pipe, he scraped out the bowl and filled it with tobacco. Once the aroma of St Bruno filled the office, he leaned back in his chair. 'Sit down, m'boy,' he said.

'D'you mind if I smoke, guv'nor?' Marriott, recognizing that Hardcastle was in one of his more informal moods, lapsed into a familiar mode of address.

Hardcastle waved a hand of assent. 'This is turning out to be a right bugger's muddle, m'boy,' he said, using one of his favourite expressions. 'Now why should Mrs Plowman have told her maid that the major was under the daisies, I wonder?'

'Like I said before, guv'nor, perhaps she didn't want young Mary wondering why she was entertaining other men while the major was still alive and kicking,' said Marriott.

'You could be right, m'boy,' agreed Hardcastle. 'More convenient to tell her that he'd turned up his toes. Wouldn't want the servants thinking she was playing fast and loose while her poor husband was risking life and limb every day up in one them new-fangled aeroplanes. I tell you this much,

49

m'boy, you'd never get me up in one of those things. All wood and string from what I've heard.' He put his pipe in the ashtray. 'Have we still got a PC posted on the Plowman house?'

'Yes, sir.'

'Good. Get a message passed to him, and the reliefs, saying I'm to be informed when Major Plowman turns up. The sooner we get round there and have a few words with him the better.'

But rather than wait for Hardcastle to call on him, which is what the constable had been told to tell the major would happen, Plowman came to the police station.

At ten o'clock the following morning, the station officer tapped deferentially on Hardcastle's office door.

'There's a Major Plowman to see you, sir,' he said.

'Send him up, Skipper,' said Hardcastle, 'and ask Sergeant Marriott to come in.'

Wearing a well-cut 'maternity jacket' – the curious wrap-over tunic that distinguished RFC officers and men – breeches, polished Sam Browne belt and riding boots, Edward Plowman looked as though he had just stepped out of a Savile Row tailor's rather than having only recently returned from the Front.

'I understand from the constable outside my house that you wish to see me, Inspector.'

'Yes, I do, but I left word that I'd call on you.'

'It was no problem for me to come here,' said Plowman, glancing around Hardcastle's austere office.

'Take a seat,' said Hardcastle. 'This is Detective Sergeant Marriott,' he added as Marriott entered the office.

Placing his cap on the corner of Hardcastle's desk, Plowman sat down and took a silver cigarette case from his breast pocket. 'D'you mind?' he asked.

'Carry on, Major.' Hardcastle began to fill his pipe. 'My condolences on the death of your wife,' he mumbled; he was not much good at utterances of sympathy.

'Thank you,' said Plowman, as the distinctive aroma of his Turkish tobacco filled the office. 'Perhaps you would tell me what happened, Inspector.'

Briefly, Hardcastle outlined the sequence of events, starting with the murder of PC Crispin the previous week. 'All I can tell you, Major, is that my constable and your wife were killed with the same automatic pistol, but whether the same finger pulled the trigger in each case, so to speak, is something we haven't discovered. Yet.'

From time to time Plowman nodded gravely as Hardcastle described what had happened. 'And you have no idea who was responsible, Inspector?'

'Not at the moment, sir, but rest assured whoever was guilty will take the eight o'clock walk. You have my word on it.'

From the expression of doubt on his face, Plowman did not seem unduly hopeful that this stolid policeman opposite him had the necessary qualities needed to solve a complicated murder. But the major was not the first to make that mistake. 'Do you have any clues at all?' he asked, in a somewhat disdainful manner.

'The police firearms expert is convinced that the weapon used was German, probably a Bergmann or a Luger.' Hardcastle paused. 'And even more curious was that we found a German Army belt in the dining room of your house.'

Plowman did not seem at all surprised at this somewhat bizarre discovery, and shrugged. 'A lot of soldiers collect souvenirs, Inspector.' It seemed that he had already made up his mind that a soldier was responsible for the murders. 'We try to discourage it, of course, but it's very difficult. More to the point, have you reached any conclusions about the reason for my wife's murder?' He seemed very matter-of-fact about Isabel Plowman's violent death, and Hardcastle assumed that his experiences on the Western Front had hardened him to the extent that he had become inured even to his wife's demise.

But rather than answer Plowman's question, Hardcastle countered it with one of his own. 'D'you happen to know a Mr Charles Napier, Major?'

Plowman raised his eyebrows. 'No. Who is he?'

'Or Cecil Yates? Or perhaps Captain Hugo Lawton?'

'Certainly I know Hugo Lawton. He's a flyer.'

'What about James Staples?'

'I don't know him personally, but I know of him. He's a friend of Lawton. But why are you asking me about these people?'

'I'm told that they were all friends of your late wife, Major.'

51

Plowman's chin dropped, and for a moment or two he remained in brooding contemplation. Leaning forward, he stubbed out his half-smoked cigarette in Hardcastle's ashtray. 'Friends, you say?' he said, glancing up. 'May I ask how you came by this information, Inspector?'

'In the course of my enquiries, Major,' said Hardcastle somewhat smugly. He had no intention of revealing the source of that information, and was particularly keen to safeguard the identity of Mary Hutchings, the Plowmans' maid. He had a feeling that she may yet have more to tell him, and he could do without her being browbeaten into silence by Major Plowman. 'I take it that those names mean nothing to you, apart from Lawton and Staples.'

'No, they don't.'

'I understand that Mr Yates escorted your wife to the theatre on occasions,' continued Hardcastle, 'and sometimes to restaurants.'

'Don't see any harm in that,' said Plowman gruffly. 'She was a young woman and there's no reason why she should have been starved of a social life just because I was at the Front.' The comment was perhaps a token of loyalty to his dead wife's reputation, but he sounded unconvinced.

'You're a pilot, I'm told, Major.' Hardcastle was already confirming his earlier view that the late Isabel Plowman was a woman who did not practise sexual abstinence while her husband was away, and decided to let the matter drop. Neither did he mention to Plowman the lie of his own 'death'; something that both he and Marriott presumed Isabel had created to guard against suggestions that she was an adulteress. It was becoming rapidly clear that, apart from Captain Hugo Lawton, none of the names he had mentioned could be described as *family* friends.

'Who told you I was a pilot?' demanded Plowman.

'The colonel at the War Office who arranged to have you informed of your wife's death.'

'Yes, well, such matters are supposed to be military secrets,' mumbled Plowman.

'Sounds a bit risky.'

Plowman afforded Hardcastle a bleak smile. 'That's one way of putting it, Inspector,' he said. 'We've lost a few good men in recent months. The Hun is pretty damned good at shooting us down. I've lost seven of my pilots and observers since the war started.'

'But surely as a squadron commander you don't go up in these aeroplanes, do you?'

'Of course I do, Inspector. One cannot command a squadron by sitting on one's arse in an office. However, more to the point, when will my wife's body be released for burial?'

'Almost immediately, I imagine, Major. I'll have a word with the coroner's officer and let you know.'

'Thank you,' said Plowman, rising from his chair. 'A bad business, Inspector. One has grown to expect this sort of thing in Flanders, but to hear of it happening here, close to the seat of government, beggars belief.'

If Plowman's statement was an implied criticism of the police, Hardcastle chose to ignore it.

Six

Captain Hugo Lawton did not prove difficult to find. Within an hour of Hardcastle's enquiry, Colonel Armstrong at the War Office was able to tell Hardcastle that the young airman was based at Number One Reserve Squadron at Gosport.

'Would you like me to tell the commanding officer that you're going down there, Inspector?'

'Thank you, Colonel, that would be helpful,' said Hardcastle, resigned to a long train journey that may well turn out to have been a waste of time.

'And how the devil do we get to Gosport, Marriott?' Hardcastle demanded as the pair strode back up Whitehall to the police station.

'Train from Waterloo to Portsmouth Harbour and across on the Gosport ferry, sir,' replied Marriott promptly. 'About a couple of hours in all, I should think. We could be there and back in a day if we start tomorrow morning, sir.'

'And I doubt we'll find out anything,' grunted Hardcastle.

After being subjected to the usual military routine that was a prerequisite of entering any army unit in time of war, Hardcastle and Marriott were eventually admitted to the Royal Flying Corps establishment on the Hampshire coast.

'Yes, Inspector,' said the man who met them. 'George Armstrong telegraphed from the War House to say you were coming. Something to do with a murder, I understand. I'm Perry Tyler, by the bye.'

'Good of you to see us, Major.' Hardcastle had recognized the crowns indicating his rank that Tyler wore on the shoulder straps of his tunic. 'You must be busy at the moment.'

'Enough to keep us going, what?' said Tyler with a laugh. 'All the chaps here are experienced flyers and they're learning

54

to be instructors. Frankly, the drain on our pilots and observers at the moment makes it difficult for us to keep up with demand. We're sending young men out to France with only a few hours solo flying time. They'll probably take this lot for active service soon, and that'll leave us in the cart and no mistake.' The major gave an expressive shrug with his shoulders, and waved at two vacant chairs in his tiny office. 'Do sit down, gentlemen, and tell me how I can help you.'

Hardcastle began to explain about the murders of PC Crispin and Isabel Plowman, but got no further than mentioning the woman's name.

'Good God! D'you mean Edward Plowman's wife?' Tyler was clearly shocked by the news. 'I know him well. He's out with Four Squadron at St Brouille.'

'He's back home for the funeral, Major,' said Hardcastle, and continued with his account of what had occurred in Cowley Street last week. 'And so it would help if I could see Captain Lawton.'

'Heavens, d'you think he might have had something to do with this awful business then?'

'Not at all.' Hardcastle rebutted the suggestion smoothly, but in his book everyone was a suspect until proved otherwise. 'But I understand that Captain Lawton knew both Major Plowman and his wife. He may have some information that might assist me in my enquiries,' he added, somewhat woodenly.

'Really?' Tyler seemed to sense a whiff of adultery in what Hardcastle had said, but if he did he made no comment. He stood up and crossed to the window. 'You'll have to wait a while, Inspector,' he said, pointing towards the sky. 'He's up there at the moment.' He glanced at the clock on the wall. 'Should be down quite soon though. I hope.' He laughed callously. 'These Farmans are the very deuce to get down on terra firma.' He rubbed his hands briskly together. 'I daresay you could sink a glass of ale after your journey from London, eh? Come along to the mess and we'll see what we can do.'

Major Tyler led them across the edge of the runway to a wooden hut that had a sign over the door proclaiming it to be the 'Officers' Mess', mounted the steps and pushed open the door.

The inside of the mess was Spartan, but an attempt had been made at homeliness. A worn carpet covered the bare wooden boards, and at one end there was a bar over which presided a corporal in a white jacket. Behind him, on the wall, was a chipped wooden airscrew. In one corner stood a piano, its top beer-stained and scarred with cigarette burns.

'What'll it be, Inspector?'

'A pint of bitter would be acceptable,' said Hardcastle.

'And you, Sergeant?' asked Tyler.

'The same, please, sir,' said Marriott.

The three men sat down at a table in the corner and waited for the mess corporal to bring their drinks.

They had been talking for some fifteen minutes, mainly about the war, when the door opened with a crash.

'Ah, here's Lawton now, the noisy bugger,' said Tyler. 'Get a beer and come over here, Hugo. The police want a word with you, my lad.'

Captain Hugo Lawton was a fair-haired, good-looking young man in his early twenties. But beneath the 'wings' insignia on his tunic there was already the white and mauve ribbon of the Military Cross, the first awards of which had been made only seven weeks previously.

'A beer for one of the workers, Corporal,' bellowed Lawton in the direction of the bar, and then sat down with Tyler and the two detectives. 'What's this all about then, Skipper?' he asked of his squadron commander.

But before Tyler could answer, the DDI introduced himself. 'I'm Divisional Detective Inspector Hardcastle of the Metropolitan Police,' he began, 'and this is Detective Sergeant Marriott.'

'Bloody hell!' said Lawton. 'Sounds serious.'

'It is,' said the DDI. 'I'm investigating the murder of a policeman in London—'

'I don't see what that has to do with me,' interjected Lawton.

'And Mrs Isabel Plowman.'

'Oh no! Not Isabel?' Young Lawton's face went ashen. 'I don't believe it. When did this happen?'

'Last Saturday,' said Hardcastle.

'But there was nothing in the papers about it.'

'The name was withheld from the press until Major

56

Plowman could be informed in France,' said Hardcastle, although the London newspapers had contained reports of 'two shocking murders in Westminster'.

'My God!' Lawton took a sip of his beer. 'This is terrible. Who would want to kill Isabel?'

'I understand that you knew Mrs Plowman quite well, Captain Lawton,' Hardcastle continued, wondering whether Lawton's show of shock was genuine surprise at the news of the woman's death, or that the police had, in some way, associated him with her so quickly.

'I knew them both, Inspector,' said Lawton, appearing to recover quite rapidly. 'Edward and Isabel.'

Apparently sensing that his presence might in some way be inhibiting Hardcastle's questioning, Major Tyler rose from his seat. 'If you'll excuse me, Inspector, I must grab a sandwich. I have a lecture to give very soon. I'm sure that Hugo will entertain you to lunch when you've finished.'

'Thank you, Major,' said Hardcastle, and waited until Tyler had walked through to an adjoining hut that housed the dining area of the mess. 'When you say you knew both Major Plowman and his wife, Captain Lawton, just how well did you know Isabel?'

'Ted Plowman and I were at Sutton's Farm aerodrome together for a while. It's down near Hornchurch. He'd often invite me back to his place in London whenever we had a day or two off. That's when I met Isabel.'

'But you carried on seeing Isabel after Major Plowman was posted to France, didn't you?' suggested Marriott.

Surprised by the intervention, Lawton switched his gaze to Hardcastle's assistant. 'Whatever makes you think that, Sergeant?' he asked, resentment clear in his voice that the question had come from someone he perceived to be a non-commissioned officer.

'Because we have been told so by a reliable witness, Captain Lawton.' Hardcastle had little doubt about the reliability of Mary Hutchings. 'And you also had a key to the house in Cowley Street, Westminster.' It was a guess, but he was fairly sure, particularly in view of what the maid had told him, that Lawton *did* possess a key.

'Now look here,' protested Lawton, the youthful bonhomie

57

he had possessed on his arrival in the mess now all but vanished. 'I don't know what you're implying, Inspector, but I can assure you that—'

'How often did you bed her, Lawton?'

Hugo Lawton was now in the difficult position of not knowing the identity of Hardcastle's informant, or precisely what had been said. 'Look, I don't see that what Isabel and I did is any of your damned business.'

'It is when she's murdered, young man,' said Hardcastle. 'You might well be engaged in duty of national importance, but it don't stop me arresting you if I think you're obstructing me in the execution of *my* duty. So we'll have the truth and then we can all get about our business.'

Lawton lit a cigarette without offering one to either of the two detectives. 'I hope this won't go any further, Inspector,' he said, 'but Isabel and I did have a fling.'

'By which you mean you slept with her, I suppose,' said Hardcastle, brutally crushing what the young man had doubtless regarded as a romantic interlude.

'Yes,' whispered the red-faced Lawton, looking down at the table.

'Shouldn't think the army goes too much on you having a tumble with another officer's wife,' commented Hardcastle, further adding to Lawton's discomfort, 'particularly when her husband's risking life and limb over the trenches.'

'It was only the once,' said the miserable Lawton.

'I see, and that makes it all right, does it?' Hardcastle took out his pipe and began filling it with tobacco. 'When was the last time you saw Mrs Plowman, Captain?'

Lawton considered the question for some time before answering. 'It must have been about three weeks ago, I suppose,' he said.

'And where was that?'

'At Cowley Street. I took her out to supper.'

'And then you went home with her and shared her bed, did you?'

'Yes.'

'So you bedded her more than the once.'

'Yes.'

'How many times before that had you taken advantage of

her favours?' Hardcastle took out his matches and spent time getting his pipe going. He gazed through the smoke. 'And at what stage of your relationship with Mrs Plowman did she give you a key to her house?'

'Round about Christmas, I think.'

'And do you still have it?'

'Yes.'

'Then I'd be obliged if you gave it to me, Captain.'

Lawton withdrew a key ring from his pocket, slowly removed a latchkey from it and placed it on the table.

Hardcastle pushed the key in Marriott's direction and then looked at Lawton. 'Where were you last Saturday evening, Captain?' he asked.

'Here,' said Lawton. 'Well, here and down at the local pub, the King's Arms. A whole crowd of us went down there in Max Vilsack's car.'

'Who is Max Vilsack, sir?' asked Marriott, looking up from his pocket book.

'He's a captain here. He's an American.'

'What the hell's an American doing in the Royal Flying Corps?' asked Hardcastle, yet again bemused by the military.

Lawton grinned. 'He heard there was a scrap going on over here and decided to join in, Inspector. He's a very good flyer. Did some barnstorming with a flying circus in the States apparently.'

'And where can I find this Captain Vilsack?'

Lawton frowned. 'Why d'you want to see him?'

'Because if you're telling me the truth about your movements last Saturday, he'll be able to verify it, won't he?'

Lawton glanced at his watch. 'The skipper said I was to take you into lunch,' he said in a vain attempt at thwarting Hardcastle's desire to check his story.

'Don't bother about that, Captain Lawton,' said Hardcastle. 'We're not hungry and we've got work to do. Now, if you just tell me where I can find Captain Vilsack, I'll leave you to enjoy your meal.' Not that Hardcastle thought he *would* enjoy it after the bruising interview he had just undergone.

Lawton stood up and walked to the door. 'That hut is where the instructors are to be found, Inspector,' he said, pointing to another wooden building. 'I'll take you over there. The skipper would play old Harry if he knew I was letting you wander about the aerodrome on your own.'

Three or four young men were lounging about in armchairs in the hut, chatting and reading newspapers and magazines.

Lawton walked over to a rakish captain, his tunic unbuttoned, feet on a small table, who was reading a copy of *John Bull*. 'Max, these gentlemen are police officers. They'd like a word with you.'

Vilsack stood up, an ingenuous grin on his face, and pushed out a hand. 'Pleased to meet you,' he said in a strong American accent.

'Perhaps we could speak somewhere privately,' said Hardcastle.

'Yeah, sure. I guess outside is the most private you'll get in this place.'

Hardcastle turned to Lawton. 'Thank you, Captain. I won't keep you from your lunch.'

For a moment or two, Lawton dithered, not wanting to leave these two policemen, principally because he guessed what Vilsack was going to say to them. But in the face of Hardcastle's stony stare, he eventually capitulated. Sketching a salute he strode back towards the mess.

The two detectives and Vilsack stood outside the instructors' hut on the lee side, away from a chilling crosswind that had recently got up.

The American hunched his shoulders. 'I guess that if that breeze stiffens it'll put paid to flying this afternoon,' he said. He lit a cigarette after tapping it on his thumbnail for a few seconds. 'So, Officers, how can I help you?' he asked.

'I'm Divisional Detective Inspector Hardcastle,' said the DDI. He took out his pipe and attempted to light it, but gave up. Even where they were standing, a capricious wind blew out his match. 'Captain Lawton tells me that you and he, and a number of other officers, went out last Saturday evening, Captain Vilsack. Is that correct?'

'Hell, Detective, what's young Hugo been up to that the police are taking an interest in him?'

'I'm investigating the murders of a police officer in Cowley Street, Westminster, last Thursday, and of Mrs Isabel Plowman forty-eight hours later.'

'Hell!' exclaimed Vilsack again. 'Isabel's been murdered?'

'You knew her?' asked Hardcastle, his gaze narrowing.

'Sure I knew her. So did half the guys on this base, I reckon.'

'What exactly d'you mean by that, Captain Vilsack?'

Vilsack laughed. 'I guess you're a man of the world, Detective. Isabel Plowman was a very entertaining girl. Quite a few of the guys here found their way to Cowley Street. I certainly spent one or two very pleasant nights with her.'

'How did you meet her?' Hardcastle was unhappy that his previous assessment of Isabel Plowman having a string of lovers was being confirmed. Finding her murderer would be even more difficult than he had first thought.

'Hugo Lawton introduced us. We'd gone up to Town one evening to take in a show, and she was there with some other guy. A foppish-looking feller. Struck me as being a sort of arty type, if you know what I mean.'

'What was his name?'

Vilsack ran a hand through his hair. 'Give me a minute, Inspector. Yeah, got it. Same as the car.'

'Same as the car?' echoed Hardcastle, furrowing his brow in bewilderment.

'Yeah, Napier. That's what the guy was called. Charles Napier. Anyway, Hugo knew Isabel and he made the introductions. His brother was there, too. We'd arranged to meet up with him.'

'Who, Napier's brother?'

'No, Hugo's. Sebastian Lawton. He was there with some filly. I think he said she was a chorus girl. Quite a looker, she was.' Vilsack thought about that for a moment. 'Mind you, Detective, she could've been a hooker.'

'A hooker?' asked Marriott, unfamiliar with the term.

'Yeah, sure. A prostitute.'

'Last Saturday, Captain Vilsack.' Hardcastle steered the conversation back to confirming Captain Lawton's story.

'What about it?'

'Were you and Captain Lawton out together?'

'Yeah, sure. We went to the King's Arms. It's a local bar.'

'And how long were you there?'

'Hell, I don't know. We were late getting down there. Ten o'clock maybe.'

'And was that the first time you'd seen Captain Lawton that evening?'

Vilsack considered the question. 'I guess it was,' he said. 'I'd been across to Portsmouth town to buy a leather coat. The kit they give you here is no damned good for keeping out the cold, and I can tell you it gets pretty damned chilly when you're up in one of those things.' He gestured towards an aeroplane standing on the edge of the airfield, where a group of fitters were struggling to tie it down in the face of the increasing wind.

Hardcastle thought that if ten o'clock was the first that Vilsack had seen of Hugo Lawton, the young man would have had ample time to return from London before going to the local pub. Clearly further enquiries were going to be necessary.

'And where were you during the early part of the evening, Captain Vilsack?' Hardcastle asked.

But Vilsack saw through the question immediately. 'Now just you hang on, Detective,' he said angrily. 'I had nothing to do with Isabel's death. Why would I want to kill the girl? Hell, why would anyone?'

'That's what I'm attempting to find out, Captain Vilsack,' said Hardcastle mildly. 'So where were you?'

'After I got back from Portsmouth, I had a few drinks in the mess. Ask anyone. And when Hugo turned up, we pushed off to the King's Arms. That'd be about a quarter to ten, maybe ten o'clock,' said Vilsack, confirming the time.

'And where had Captain Lawton been during the earlier part of the evening?'

'No idea, Detective. I guess you'll have to ask him that.'

The two detectives walked away from the American and made their way to Major Tyler's office, but he was not there, and Hardcastle recalled that the CO had said something about giving a lecture.

'I suppose we'll have to leave it, Marriott. Can't very well tramp about the place without Tyler's say-so.'

'What d'you make of it all, sir?' asked Marriott. 'It's beginning to look as though Mrs Plowman kept open house for these flyers.'

'It's a bloody dog's dinner, Marriott,' muttered Hardcastle.

'Sounds to me as though Isabel Plowman would jump into bed with anyone who asked her, and that's going to make our task a bloody sight more difficult than it is already.'

'Everything all right, Inspector?'

Hardcastle turned to see Perry Tyler hurrying towards them. 'We're up a bit of a gum tree, as a matter of fact, Major,' he said, and went on to explain about Lawton's alibi. Or lack of it.

'You'd better come inside, Inspector,' said Tyler, leading the way back to his office. Striding through the outer office, he demanded tea from the sergeant-clerk on duty there.

'D'you think Lawton had anything to do with this dreadful business, Inspector?' Tyler sat down behind his desk and waved the detectives to chairs.

'Strictly between you, me, Sergeant Marriott and the gatepost, Major, it seems that Mrs Plowman was fairly free with her favours. We already know of four or five men with whom she seems to have been intimate.'

'Good God!' Tyler gave the impression of being shocked by this revelation. 'And Edward's away fighting for King and Country,' he said in apparent despair. 'Damned poor business, eh what?'

'And then there's Captain Vilsack, Major.'

'The Yank? What about him?'

'He also admits to having had an affair with her.'

'Christ!' It evidently seemed to Tyler that there was no end to the sexual activities of the officers under his command. 'So what d'you want me to do, Inspector?'

'I don't want to involve the military police if I can help it,' Hardcastle began, having no intention of involving them anyway if it could possibly be avoided.

'Neither do I,' said Tyler quickly.

'But I'm interested to know where Lawton and Vilsack were last Saturday night,' said Hardcastle, idly wondering what dark secrets Tyler wanted to prevent the military police from learning.

'Is that when Isabel was murdered?'

'Yes, it was. So far, all I have is Captain Vilsack's word that Lawton was with him at some time after ten o'clock. As for Vilsack himself, he claims he was in Portsmouth buying an overcoat.'

Tyler pondered the problem for a moment or two. 'I'll see what I can do, Inspector,' he said eventually, 'but it's rather difficult keeping track of what these young chaps do in their off-duty time. When death's just around the corner, they tend to live for the moment, eh what?'

But Hardcastle was not going to leave it too long. If necessary, he would return to Gosport and make formal enquiries among each and every officer there. 'Thank you for your assistance, Major,' he said, rising from his chair.

'Won't you stay for a cup of tea?' asked Tyler.

'No thanks. We have to get back to London.'

It was on the Gosport ferry that Marriott reminded Hardcastle that Major Perry Tyler had also known Isabel Plowman and it was possible that their acquaintanceship may well have extended to her bedroom.

'Yes, I'd thought of that, Marriott,' said Hardcastle glumly. 'We'll deal with him in due course.'

The train to London was packed with sailors going on leave, and some of their shore-based fellows snatching a weekend in the capital.

Fortunately for Hardcastle, his status allowed him to travel second class, and he and Marriott were not bothered too much by the rowdy matelots further down the train. But he was in a gloomy mood and hardly spoke another word until they reached Waterloo.

Seven

The following morning, Hardcastle arrived at his office at eight o'clock. He was still in the same mood of deep depression that he had been on his return from Gosport the day before, a mood not improved by the pea-souper of a fog that came off the river and swirled in the streets around Cannon Row police station and New Scotland Yard opposite. From time to time, the foghorns of tugs, leading strings of barges on their ponderous way to and from the Pool of London, penetrated the office.

'Well, Marriott, it's a right dog's dinner,' said Hardcastle for about the tenth time since leaving the Royal Flying Corps airfield. 'It strikes me that our Mrs Plowman was game for anyone as how took her fancy.'

'D'you reckon one of the airmen for the topping, sir?' asked Marriott. 'It seems she had quite a few gentlemen friends from among that lot.'

Hardcastle snorted. 'You got a better idea, Marriott?' he demanded crossly.

'Not really, sir, no.' The sergeant recognized that his chief was in a bad mood and, deciding that no good would come of exacerbating that ill temper, lapsed into silence.

'Well, to hell with Mrs Plowman,' continued Hardcastle. 'I'm more concerned with catching whoever killed our copper.'

'Catch one and we've caught the other, I reckon, sir,' ventured Marriott, safe in the assumption that he was reflecting Hardcastle's own view of the double murder.

'That's certainly the case according to Mr Franklin, the firearms inspector. He says the same gun killed 'em both, and I don't see the weapon getting handed round.'

'I wonder if any of Mrs Plowman's fancy men have served in France, sir,' said Marriott thoughtfully.

'What if they have?'

'I was thinking about the pistol and the German Army belt, sir. If one of those airmen brought them back from the Front, they might just have used the weapon and deliberately left the belt to lay a false trail, so to speak.'

'It had crossed my mind, Marriott,' said Hardcastle. 'I think it's time we enlisted the help of Colonel Armstrong. Or, more to the point, that sergeant-major of his. What's his name?'

'Warrender, sir, and he's not a sergeant-major, he's a staff quartermaster-sergeant.'

'Oh, for God's sake don't split hairs, Marriott.'

'No, sir.'

'I don't think we can rely too much on that Major Tyler down at Gosport, either,' continued Hardcastle. 'I've a shrewd suspicion he might have been dipping his wick with the fair Isabel an' all.' He stood up. 'No time like the present. Come, Marriott.'

'Er, it's Saturday, sir.'

'What's that got to do with the price of fish?' demanded the DDI.

'I don't somehow see Colonel Armstrong being at the War Office on a Saturday, sir.'

'God Almighty!' exclaimed Hardcastle, 'there's supposed to be a bloody war on. Are you telling me that the British Army don't fight on a weekend?'

'Shall I telephone him, sir? Make sure he's there,' suggested Marriott in an attempt at placating his querulous inspector. 'Might save us a walk up Whitehall.'

'Yes, all right,' said Hardcastle testily. He always took the view that if he was at work, so should everyone else be.

But Marriott returned a few minutes later with the news that Armstrong was not at his office and would not be there until Monday morning.

'Well, it'll have to keep, I suppose,' grumbled Hardcastle. 'One thing's certain, Crispin's killer ain't going to escape me, however long I have to wait to see him topped.'

'Unless the Hun does it for us,' said Marriott, risking a grin.

'What's that supposed to mean?' If anything, Hardcastle's temper had shortened even further by the news that he was unable to pursue his enquiry with the War Office until Monday.

'If it was one of the airmen, sir, he might get shot down in the meantime.'

Hardcastle grunted. 'I'm not having the bloody Germans doing my job for me, Marriott, and that's a fact.'

'Ah!' said Colonel Armstrong, 'that shouldn't be too difficult.' He struck the bell on his desk and summoned SQMS Warrender. 'Mr Warrender, Inspector Hardcastle here wants our help with regard to the RFC officers at Number One Reserve Squadron at Gosport.'

'Very good, sir.' Warrender glanced at Hardcastle. 'What exactly was it you wanted, sir?'

'Is it possible to find out if any of them have served in France, Mr Warrender?'

'May take a little while, sir,' said the warrant officer. 'I shouldn't say this, but it's not always easy to get hold of officers' records at the moment.'

'How long is a little while, Mr Warrender?' asked Marriott.

'A couple of days at the most, Sarge.'

And with that the police had to be satisfied.

It was, however, the following day that Corporal Green, Colonel Armstrong's runner, appeared once more in Hardcastle's office. Again executing a textbook salute, he presented the DDI with a list of names.

'With Colonel Armstrong's compliments, sir,' said Green, handing over a sheet of paper.

'Thank you, Corporal,' said Hardcastle, acknowledging the NCO's second salute with a wave of his pipe. He shouted for Marriott and settled back in his chair to study the information that SQMS Warrender had obtained.

'There's seven names on here, Marriott,' said Hardcastle when the sergeant had joined him. 'There's Major Tyler, and Captains Lawton and Vilsack, plus four others, all lieutenants: Baxter, Hartley, Morrison and Rowe-Smith. All of them have served in France at some time since the outbreak of the war.'

'Does that mean we'll have to interview them all, sir?'

'Yes,' said Hardcastle, a monosyllabic reply that, for him, was remarkably restrained. He did not relish a return to the windswept airfield at Gosport. 'That Warrender fellow's quite good,' he continued. 'He's made a note on here that one of the lieutenants, Hartley, is a transfer from the Royal Fusiliers and was at Mons.'

But on reflection, Hardcastle realized that little would be gained by talking to any of those officers until he had some evidence to connect them to the two murders he was investigating. And that realization did nothing to improve his temper. Added to which, there was little doubt in his mind that Hugo Lawton and possibly Max Vilsack would already have told everyone else at the Gosport airfield that police were taking an interest in their relationships with the late Isabel Plowman.

Hardcastle crossed the office to a cupboard and took out a black tie with which he replaced the one he was wearing.

'Another funeral, Marriott,' he said with a sigh. 'Which reminds me. How's Mrs Crispin faring?'

'As well as can be expected, sir,' said Marriott. 'But she's worried about getting pushed out of her quarters now that Bob's dead.'

'Bloody typical,' muttered Hardcastle. 'Well, I hope the Receiver's got some compassion, but I somehow doubt it.' The controller of the finances and buildings of the Metropolitan Police had a tendency to work strictly by the book.

By coincidence, Isabel Plowman was interred at the same church that had witnessed the burial of PC Crispin. But there was no pageantry accompanying this service.

Just a few members of the two families were there, notable among whom were Isabel's parents and her brother in the uniform of the Royal Marine Light Infantry. Seated alone at the very back of the church was Mary Hutchings, the Plowmans' maid. To Hardcastle's surprise, Major Edward Plowman was supported by no less a figure than Captain Hugo Lawton.

'Well, if that don't beat cockfighting, Marriott, I don't know what does,' muttered Hardcastle. 'Lawton freely admits having jig-jig with Mrs Plowman and then turns up at her funeral bold as brass.'

'D'you think Major Plowman knows, sir?'

Hardcastle scoffed. 'I doubt it. I reckon it'd be pistols at dawn if he ever found out that his wife's bed was being shared by that scallywag.' But even as he said it, the DDI wondered if Plowman did know of his wife's infidelity and did not care.

'That other fellow with Captain Lawton, sir,' said Marriott, 'looks very like him.'

'You're right,' said Hardcastle. 'Could be a brother. I seem to remember Major Plowman mentioning that Lawton had a brother. I wonder who the woman is with him. Looks a bit of a tart to me. Could be the wench that Vilsack mentioned. Where's Catto?'

'Across the street there, sir,' said Marriott, pointing at the lurking figure of the detective constable.

'Good. Get hold of him and tell him I want that fellow and his woman followed when they leave here. There'll probably be a wake somewhere, but he's to hang about and house 'em when they leave. And tell him not to get himself seen.'

'Right, sir,' said Marriott and crossed the street to pass on the DDI's directions.

It was several hours after Hardcastle and Marriott had returned to Cannon Row police station, via the Red Lion public house in Derby Gate, that Catto reappeared.

'Where have you been, Scotland?' demanded Hardcastle.

'No, sir, the Café Royal,' said Catto. 'It's in Regent Street.'

'I know it's in Regent Street. I used to be a sergeant at Vine Street, but what were you doing there?'

'Observing, sir.'

'God Almighty, boy, are you going to tell what you was up to, or do I have to drag it out of you?'

'No, sir. I followed the suspect as directed by Detective Sergeant Marriott, and him and the woman went to the Café Royal. The others from the funeral party went there an' all, sir. They had lunch in a private room where they seemed to be having a jolly time.'

Hardcastle raised his eyes to the ceiling. 'I don't give a damn if they was dancing the fandango, Catto. Anyway, how did you know they were having a jolly time, as you call it?'

'I had a word with the head waiter, sir, and he let me have a glim through a crack in the door from the servery.'

Although Hardcastle admired the young detective's initiative, he was not about to tell him. 'So who was the man and who was the woman with him?'

'They left the Café Royal at half past three, sir, and took the Underground train to Fulham Broadway. They walked from there to number twenty-seven Musgrave Crescent in Walham Green.'

'So who the hell are they?' demanded Hardcastle again, his exasperation now reaching a dangerous level.

'I made some enquiries locally, sir,' continued Catto hurriedly, 'and it seems the man's called Sebastian Lawton, and the woman is Vera Hammond. She's said to be a chorus girl, but isn't working at the moment.'

'At last,' exclaimed Hardcastle. 'And what does this Sebastian Lawton do, Catto? Did you find that out in the course of your local enquiries?'

'He's an artist, sir.'

'Is he really? And does he occupy the whole house?'

'No, sir, he's got rooms at the top. It was the woman who lives downstairs that I spoke to. Seems that Lawton's room's got skylights, sir, what's suitable for his painting.'

'Very resourceful of you, Catto. And he lives with this doxy, does he?' Hardcastle had no high opinion of artists and tended to regard them as immoral parasites.

'Yes, sir.'

'Right, get about your duties, lad.' The DDI paused. 'Well done.'

'Yes, sir, thank you, sir,' said Catto, his face breaking into a smile.

'And don't grin at me like a Cheshire cat, neither, Catto.'

'No, sir.'

'D'you think Lawton's brother's going to be able to tell us anything, sir?' asked Marriott once a relieved Catto had fled from the office.

'Don't know till we ask him,' said Hardcastle curtly, and paused in thought. 'You remember when we went to see that Charles Napier at Albert Hall Mansions, Marriott?'

'The antiquarian bookseller, you mean, sir?'

'That's the chap. Well, he had a painting of a mulatto girl in his sitting room.'

'Are you wondering whether Sebastian Lawton did that

70

painting, sir? This woman wasn't a mulatto. She wasn't even slightly dark-skinned.'

'In my experience, Marriott, artists usually have more than one model to pose for 'em, otherwise it gets a bit monotonous, having the same picture all the time. But I was thinking that if Sebastian Lawton knows Charles Napier, he might have given him that there picture.'

'But what would that prove, sir?' asked Marriott. 'We don't even know if Napier knows him.'

'Yes we do, Marriott,' said Hardcastle. 'Don't forget what Captain Vilsack said about the night he and Hugo Lawton went to the theatre in London. He said that Napier was there with Isabel, and so was Sebastian Lawton, along with that woman of his. I suppose it was the same woman that Catto followed to Walham Green,' he mused. 'It strikes me that they're all pals and the attraction was Isabel who, by all accounts, was very free with her favours.' The DDI glanced at his watch. 'Time we shook some of these people up a bit.'

The woman who answered the door of 27 Musgrave Crescent gazed searchingly at the two police officers. She wore a dirty floor-length apron over an equally grubby black bombazine dress.

'Yes?' The expression on her face was hostile, as was the tone of her voice.

'Mr Lawton, please,' said Hardcastle.

'I don't know if he's at home, I'm sure,' she said, hands on hips.

'Then perhaps you'd ask him,' said Hardcastle with a patience that surprised Marriott.

'Who shall I say it is?'

'Police.'

'Can't say as I'm surprised, living in sin with that flighty bit of fluff of his,' said the woman with a toss of her head. 'Calls herself an actress. Well, if she is, I'm the Queen of Sheba.' And obviously changing her mind about guarding Lawton's privacy, said, 'You'd better go on up, then. Top floor.'

'Bit of a harridan, sir,' whispered Marriott as he and Hardcastle mounted the uncarpeted staircase.

'I think she thought we were debt collectors,' said Hardcastle. 'She looked as though she might be expecting 'em.'

At the top of the second flight of stairs, Hardcastle banged on one of the two doors on the small landing. After a few minutes, the other door was opened, and the man they had seen at Isabel Plowman's funeral poked his head out.

'Yes?'

'Mr Lawton?' Hardcastle asked, well knowing the man to be Sebastian Lawton.

'Yes, what is it?'

'Police.'

'Oh! What d'you want?' asked Lawton, but made no attempt to admit the two detectives.

'I get the impression that the woman downstairs might be earwigging,' said Hardcastle, 'but if you're happy to have a discussion out here, that's all right by me.'

That was sufficient for Lawton. 'You'd better come in, I suppose,' he said, and with obvious reluctance opened the door. 'Too fond of minding other people's business, that one is.'

The room into which the policemen were admitted had been converted into a studio. Among other items, it contained a table bearing numerous pots of paint, a stone jar full of paint-brushes, a couple of paint-stained palettes, a couch, and next to it on a low platform, a chaise-longue, which presumably was where Lawton posed his models.

Several canvases were stacked against the walls and a painting stood on an easel in such a position that in daytime the skylight would illuminate it. There was no doubt about the identity of the woman who had posed for the artist. *It was a full-length depiction of a naked Isabel Plowman.*

'One of my better efforts,' said Lawton, nodding at the portrait. 'This way,' he added, and led the detectives across the bare floorboards to a door on the far side of the room. 'We're in a bit of a mess in here, I'm afraid, but we've been out most of the day.'

Lawton's comment proved to be an understatement: the room was chaotic. On a threadbare rug, a wooden table held the remains of a meal, and an unmade double bed was tucked in beneath the slant of the roof.

Reclining on the bed was the girl Hardcastle and Marriot had seen with Lawton at Isabel Plowman's funeral that morning. But now she was dressed in a silk robe that revealed most of her bare legs.

'This is my model, Vera Hammond,' said Lawton.

'Miss Hammond,' murmured Hardcastle, and faced Lawton. 'Mr Lawton, I'm Divisional Detective Inspector Hardcastle of the Whitehall Division, and I'm investigating the murder of Mrs Plowman.'

'I don't see how I can possibly help you.' Lawton gave the offhand impression that he was about to deny any knowledge of the woman. 'I don't think I know the name.'

Hardcastle sighed. 'Mr Lawton, there is a painting of the woman in the next room, and you were at her funeral this morning.' He glanced at Lawton's 'model'. 'As was Miss Hammond,' he added.

'Yes, of course. I'd forgotten her surname; I knew her only as Isabel at first, and she sat for me several times.'

'How did you meet her, Mr Lawton?'

'She was introduced to me by my brother Hugo. He said he'd met this girl who was willing to pose for me. She did so several times.'

'But you only produced the one portrait, the one next door.'

'No, two, actually.'

'What happened to the other one?'

'It was commissioned by her husband. Edward is a major in the Flying Corps. He was very pleased with it, so Isabel said.'

Hardcastle did not recall having seen a portrait of Mrs Plowman, clothed or unclothed, anywhere at Cowley Street, but let it pass. Maybe her husband had destroyed it – or she had – or, less likely, Edward Plowman had sold it.

'But your relationship went further than that of artist and model, didn't it, Mr Lawton?' said Marriott.

Surprised by the sergeant's intervention, Lawton stared at him and then sat down on the bed next to Vera Hammond. 'Yes,' he said quietly.

'That was before you met Miss Hammond, was it?' Hardcastle took up the questioning again.

'No,' said Vera Hammond suddenly, lowering a copy of

73

The Stage she had been reading. 'Seb screws most of his models. Artists do, you know.' It was the first time she had spoken, and Hardcastle noted what a coarse, cockney voice she had. He did not bother to ask whether she had taken exception to his sexual habits; it was fairly obvious that she did not care.

'You know that Isabel Plowman was murdered, of course,' the DDI continued, turning to Lawton again.

'Of course I did. I was at her funeral. A tragedy. I really can't understand why anyone should have wanted her dead,' said the artist. 'Was it a burglary?'

'I'm investigating that possibility,' Hardcastle countered, but by now he was convinced that a burglar was the least likely suspect for the woman's murder. 'Where were you on the night she was killed, Mr Lawton?'

'When did it happen?' Lawton asked innocently.

'Saturday the thirteenth of February.'

'I was here, with Vera. In fact, I was painting a portrait of her.'

'Did you do a painting of a mulatto girl at any time?' asked Hardcastle.

Lawton appeared to give the question some thought.

But before he could answer, Vera Hammond said, 'Yes, he did.' She turned to Lawton. 'Don't you remember her? She was called Maria something. You picked her up in Piccadilly.' Glancing at Hardcastle, she added, 'She was a prostitute.'

'And did you give that painting to Charles Napier, by any chance?'

'I may have done.' Lawton paused. 'Yes, of course. I did.'

'How did you come to know him?' persisted Hardcastle.

'I met him one night at the theatre. As a matter of fact, we got talking and I discovered that he had a very useful book on Cézanne that I'd been seeking for ages. I couldn't afford it, so we did a trade. I gave him the painting and he gave me the book.'

'Is there any reason why you're not in the army, Mr Lawton?'

'I've got asthma, Inspector,' said Lawton. 'Apart from which, I'm a devout coward.'

*   *   *

74

'What d'you think, sir?' asked Marriott as he and Hardcastle made their way to the Underground station.

'He's a born liar, Marriott, apart from when he claimed to be a coward,' said Hardcastle. 'He might have been at home with the Hammond girl, or he might not have been. But at least he admitted having shared Isabel's bed, and I'm beginning to wonder if there's anyone in the world who didn't.' He stopped, took his pipe from his pocket and tapped out the dottle on his heel. He hailed a cab. 'Bugger it, Marriott, we'll take a growler.' The taxi pulled into the kerb. 'Scotland Yard, cabbie,' he said, and turning to Marriott, added, 'Tell 'em Cannon Row and half the time you'll finish up at Cannon Street in the City.'

'Yes, I know, sir,' said Marriott wearily.

Eight

Hands in pockets, Hardcastle stared gloomily out of his office window at the snow falling lightly on to Westminster Underground station far below. It was now almost a fortnight since PC Crispin's murder, and eleven days since that of Isabel Plowman. And all he had learned was that Major Plowman's wife had been little more than a sophisticated amateur whore.

'Excuse me, sir.' Marriott tapped on the open office door.

Hardcastle turned from the window. 'What is it, Marriott?'

'Just had word from Mr Warrender at the War Office, sir. Captain Lawton was killed this morning at Gosport.'

Hardcastle sat down at his desk and took out his pipe. 'What happened? Get murdered by Major Plowman, did he?' he asked with a grim laugh. 'If he was, it'll be down to the local constabulary.' He opened his tobacco pouch and swore. 'Dammit, I'm out of tobacco. Get one of the lads to go down to that tobacconist in Bridge Street and get me an ounce of St Bruno.'

Marriott crossed to the detectives' office and sent a DC on Hardcastle's errand.

'Now then, what happened to Captain Lawton?' the DDI asked when his sergeant returned.

'Seems that his aeroplane crashed, sir.'

'How did that happen, then? Not shot down, surely? Not in Gosport, I wouldn't have thought.'

'Mr Warrender didn't know, sir. All he could tell me was that Lawton was dead.'

Hardcastle stood up and glanced at the clock: it was half past nine. 'We'll go down there, Marriott,' he said, making another of the instant decisions that so frequently nonplussed his staff. 'Kill two birds with one stone, so to speak. I'm interested in what happened to Lawton. Maybe someone tampered with that string and canvas contraption of his. I always knew them things were dangerous. T'ain't natural, going up in the air like that. I can just imagine what Mrs Hardcastle would say if I suggested it. She'd've said what she always says: if the good Lord had meant us to fly He'd've given us wings. Bloody madness if you ask me.' He stood up and put on his heavy chesterfield overcoat. 'Anyway, we'll go to Gosport and see what happened to Lawton, and while we're there we can have a word with them other officers whose names Sergeant-Major Warrender gave us.'

Marriott said nothing. There was little point in again correcting Hardcastle's inaccuracy over Warrender's rank, but what alarmed him was that the DDI seemed to think that Lawton might have been murdered. Although Marriott had to admit that Hardcastle was a skilled murder investigator, there were times when his course of action seemed to take on some bizarre flight of fancy.

The sergeant of the guard conducted the two detectives to the squadron commander's office. On the way they sighted the still smouldering wreckage of what they presumed was the end of Captain Hugo Lawton's last flight.

'Lost one of our pilots this morning, sir,' said the sergeant, pointing at the wrecked aeroplane. 'Captain Lawton. Very popular officer, he was.'

Particularly with Isabel Plowman, it would seem, Hardcastle thought, but he left those views unspoken.

'You've come on a bad day, Inspector,' said Perry Tyler as they were shown into his office. 'Captain Lawton was killed this morning.'

'So I understand, Major.'

Tyler glanced suspiciously at the detective. 'How did you know?' he asked.

'Your sergeant told me on the way over here,' said Hardcastle archly, choosing not to reveal where the information had originally come from. 'What happened?'

Tyler waved the two policemen to chairs and sat down behind his desk. 'He went up this morning, but while he was flying one hell of a fog came down. It's basic airmanship to avoid landing in the fog, but instead of finding somewhere else to land, the young fool tried to get in here. Came in too fast and found that the ground was higher than he'd thought. His undercarriage collapsed and the machine flipped over and caught fire. Killed instantly.'

'Sorry to hear that,' murmured Hardcastle. 'I suppose there was nothing wrong with his aircraft.'

'Good God, no! The fitters here are among the best in the RFC. What makes you ask a question like that, Inspector?'

'Call it a policeman's idle curiosity, Major,' said Hardcastle. But the DDI was really wondering whether, after his interview with Lawton, the young airman had actually committed suicide.

'We're losing enough pilots in France,' complained Tyler, 'without having them kill themselves here at home.' He shook his head wearily. 'Anyway, what brings you here?'

Hardcastle decided to show his hand, if only partially. 'From our conversation last time I was down here, Major, I think you realized that Lawton was having an affair with Isabel Plowman.'

'I rather gathered that,' said Tyler glumly, his face showing no sign that he too might have known Isabel more intimately than he should have known a brother officer's wife.

'And by all accounts, his brother Sebastian was dipping his wick with Isabel too.'

'I didn't know he had a brother, Inspector,' said Tyler, with a frown of distaste at Hardcastle's earthy description. 'Right now I'm busy trying to locate Hugo's parents. They'll have to be told, you see.'

'I thought the War Office did that sort of thing,' said Hardcastle.

'Yes, they do, but a chap's CO always has to write a letter. Brave young man, highly thought of by his comrades, died for his country, didn't suffer. All that sort of stuff, don't you know,' said Tyler, and lapsed into thought. He sounded cynical about the whole business, but Hardcastle surmised that he had written quite a few such letters since the start of the war. Emerging from his reverie, Tyler asked, 'Why exactly are you here, Inspector? It wasn't just to talk about Hugo Lawton, surely?'

'There are four of your officers I'd like to speak to,' said

Hardcastle. 'Have you got that list there?' he asked, turning to Marriott.

'Yes, sir. Lieutenants Baxter, Hartley, Morrison and Rowe-Smith.'

Tyler appeared puzzled by this request. 'Good God, you're not suggesting that they were all close friends of Isabel Plowman, surely?'

Hardcastle was secretly amused at Tyler's euphemism for Mrs Plowman's adultery. 'That's something I want to find out, Major. But they all served in France.'

'So did I,' said Tyler, 'but what has that to do with Isabel?'

'I'd rather not say at this stage,' said Hardcastle, 'but I can assure you it's relevant to my enquiry.'

Tyler looked as though he was about to refuse Hardcastle access to the officers, and probably, the DDI supposed, would cite some regulation about the secrecy surrounding RFC officers' duties in time of war. But if that had been in his mind, he relented. 'I'll get my clerk to find out where they are, Inspector,' he said, 'but I hope it won't take too long. We may not be operational, but we are fulfilling a vital training role and every minute is valuable.' He glanced at the clock. 'Perhaps you'd care for a drink while we're getting things organized.'

In the outer office – Tyler described it as the orderly room – they met Captain Vilsack.

'Ah, Skipper, I've just brought Hugo Lawton's kit over.' Vilsack waved a hand at a pile of clothing, equipment and other odds and ends that was spread out on a table. 'I suppose the personal stuff will have to be sent on to his folks.'

Hardcastle stepped across the room and examined a *pickelhaube*, the distinctive German spiked helmet, and a military belt, that were among the dead officer's possessions. This particular belt, however, was more ornate than the one the police had found at Cowley Street, and bore the motto of the Hohenzollern dynasty *Gott mit uns*: God with us. 'What on earth was Captain Lawton doing with these, Major?' he asked.

'He collected bits and pieces like that, Inspector,' volunteered Vilsack. 'We all did. What you might call trophies of war.'

'What about firearms?' asked Marriott.

'That was definitely frowned on, Sergeant,' said Tyler,

'although I don't doubt that one or two chaps managed to acquire them.'

'If you can't get what you want of this sort of stuff from the Hun, you can always do a swap with someone else, or even pinch it,' said Vilsack cheerfully. 'In fact, Hugo was only complaining a few weeks ago that someone had lifted some of his souvenirs.'

Hardcastle turned sharply. 'Did Captain Lawton say exactly what he'd had stolen, or who he suspected of having taken them?'

'Hell, no. It was no big deal,' said Vilsack. 'Anyway, you could always pinch some from someone else. Believe me, Inspector, there's plenty of it lying about in France.'

'And there'll be a lot more before we've finished,' said Tyler cynically.

Hardcastle, Marriott and Tyler spent a desultory half hour in the officers' mess, drinking beer and discussing the war, a subject not far from anyone's mind at the present time.

Tyler boasted about the two young pilots who had dropped bombs on German submarines at Zeebrugge last month. 'Aircraft are the coming thing, you know, Inspector,' he said. 'There'll soon be a day when nowhere is safe from the Royal Flying Corps.'

But impishly, Hardcastle pointed out that the RFC had not stopped the Zeppelin raids on Yarmouth and King's Lynn that had also taken place last month.

Eventually the mess corporal told Major Tyler that the orderly-room sergeant had sent a message to say that the officers he wanted to see had been assembled in the briefing room.

Hardcastle, Marriott and Tyler strolled across to yet another of the wooden huts that seemed to comprise the accommodation of the squadron. Inside were the four officers Hardcastle wished to interview. They stood up when their squadron commander entered the room, and glanced apprehensively at the two detectives. They had obviously heard that the police were interested in some of the squadron's officers' association with the dead woman.

'Well, I'll leave you to get on with whatever it is you want to talk to these chaps about,' said Tyler. 'Perhaps you'd pop in and say goodbye before you go. I'm not lecturing until half past one.' It sounded very much like a caution that the inspector should not tarry unduly.

'I won't keep you too long,' said Hardcastle to the four young lieutenants, once Tyler had departed. 'You probably know that I'm investigating the murder of Isabel Plowman, wife of Major Edward Plowman.'

There were mumbled assents, and one of the officers, Lieutenant Roderick Rowe-Smith, asked, 'What makes you think that any of us may be able to help, Inspector?'

'I've been told that you all served in France before you came here.'

'What of it?' asked Rowe-Smith.

'Did any of you collect any souvenirs while you were there?'

'Bloody hell, has the Hun complained about larceny?' asked another officer. 'Is that what you're investigating?' he added and laughed.

'And you are?' demanded Hardcastle.

'Richard Hartley,' said the officer.

'This is a serious matter, Mr Hartley,' said Hardcastle, not amused by the levity with which the flyers seemed to be treating his enquiry, 'and I'm not the slightest bit interested in how you laid hands on any of this stuff, but I particularly want to know if any of you brought home a pistol.'

'Christ no!' said Rowe-Smith. 'That's a court-martial offence. Not worth the risk, old boy. Anyway, we're all airmen. Not likely to pinch anything from a passing Hun flyer. Don't really get near enough.'

'But I believe that you were at Mons with the Royal Fusiliers, Mr Hartley, before you were attached to the Royal Flying Corps,' said Hardcastle, pointing his pipe at the lieutenant. 'Did you acquire any trophies?'

Hartley scoffed. 'I don't know how much you know about the retreat from Mons, Inspector, but we were too busy trying to save our own skins to worry about rooting for souvenirs on the battlefield. We certainly didn't have time to pick up anything to show an ungrateful public here at home, I can tell you that much. You can only do that when you overrun the enemy, not when they're overrunning you. But I daresay the Hun picked up a few souvenirs from us,' he commented sourly.

'I read the reports in the *Daily Mail*,' said Hardcastle, somewhat lamely. In common with the rest of the public at home, he was none too well informed about the débâcle of Mons.

'Yes, and if you believed that, you'll believe anything,' said Hartley. 'They made it sound like a victory, but we were marching all bloody day and half the night. In the wrong damned direction. Oh yes, the great British Army was brought to its knees at Mons. I finished up leading a motley bunch of soldiers from half a dozen different regiments: Seaforth Highlanders, Manchesters, Wiltshires, South Staffs. All lost they were, and just doing their desperate best to get out of the way of the Hun machine guns. It was a complete rout, a bloody shambles.' By now the young officer's face was etched with the horror of that awful defeat, and his voice reflected the bitterness that he and the other survivors of the retreat felt at having been let down by the high command's failure to reinforce them. It was a failure based upon the belief that the regular army's ability to fire fifteen rounds a minute would overcome anything that the Hun could throw at it.

'Were any of you aware that Captain Lawton had some trophies, and that some of them were stolen?' asked Hardcastle, regretting that he had questioned Lieutenant Hartley about Mons.

'Did hear something about it,' said Lieutenant Morrison, a languid, somewhat sarcastic youth, 'but I never paid too much attention. That sort of thing's always happening. It's definitely *infra dig* to pinch another chap's personal property, but souvenirs are fair game. Very much the public school ethos, don't you know.'

'Did any of you know Mrs Isabel Plowman?' Hardcastle had decided that his enquiries about souvenirs were getting nowhere, so he determined on a more direct approach.

'No, unfortunately,' said Rowe-Smith with a grin. 'Rumour had it that she was rather generous towards flyers.'

'Who did you hear that from?' asked Marriott, speaking for the first time.

'Hugo Lawton, as a matter of fact,' said Rowe-Smith. 'Not that he'll be visiting the fleshpots of London any more.'

It seemed that these pilots, young though they were, had already developed a cynicism about violent death that was far beyond their years.

'Well, that was a waste of time,' said Hardcastle, once he and Marriott were back at Cannon Row police station.

'I wonder if Lawton did possess the belt we found at Cowley Street, sir, and the pistol that Inspector Franklin said was used to kill Crispin and Mrs Plowman, and that it was those that were stolen from him.'

'Maybe,' said Hardcastle gruffly. 'On the other hand, he may have murdered them himself. Left the belt there to confuse us, and chucked the pistol in the river.'

Hardcastle's theorizing was, however, interrupted by the appearance of a constable in the doorway.

'There's a Major Plowman downstairs, sir. Asked he might have a word with you.'

'Send him up, lad,' said Hardcastle.

A few moments later, the immaculately uniformed figure of Edward Plowman strolled nonchalantly into the DDI's office. 'Good evening, Inspector,' he said, his face showing little sign of the grief he must be feeling.

'Evening, Major. What can I do for you?'

'I thought I'd let you know I'm returning to St Brouille first thing tomorrow,' said Plowman. 'I take it that there's nothing else I can assist you with.'

'Not that I can think of, Major, no,' said Hardcastle. 'As a matter of interest, what's going to happen to your house at Cowley Street now?'

'To be honest, I haven't given much thought to that. I've had other things on my mind, as I'm sure you'll understand. I think I shall keep it on in the hope that I may one day return once this damnable war is over. Though God knows when that'll be.'

'And the maid, Mary Hutchings?' queried Hardcastle.

'The maid? Why d'you want to know about her, Inspector?'

'She's a material witness, Major. I need to know where she is. She may, after all, be required to give evidence at the Old Bailey.'

Plowman raised his eyebrows in surprise. 'D'you mean

you've caught the fellow who was responsible for my wife's death?'

'And my policeman's,' Hardcastle reminded him.

'Ah, yes, of course.' Plowman gently stroked his moustache. 'And your policeman.'

'No, I haven't caught him yet. But rest assured, Major, I shall, and I'll delight in hearing he's taken the eight o'clock walk.'

'Quite so,' mumbled Plowman.

'The maid?' Hardcastle reminded him.

'Ah yes, the maid. I think it would be as well if I kept her on as a sort of caretaker for the time being. Don't like leaving the house empty.' He paused. 'I don't suppose you'll need me to give evidence, will you?'

'I think that's a touch unlikely, Major,' said Hardcastle. 'After all, you were in France when it happened.'

'Quite so,' said Plowman again. 'Well, in that case, I'll take my leave, Inspector.' He stood up and put on his cap. 'And perhaps you'd be so good as to keep me informed of the progress of your enquiries. The War House will always forward letters.' And with that he leaned across the desk and shook hands. 'Make sure you do get him, won't you?'

'I shall, Major, I shall.'

At the door, Plowman stopped and took out his wallet. He extracted a five-pound note and handed it to Hardcastle. 'Perhaps you'd put that in the fund for your policeman's family,' he said. 'I presume there is a fund.'

'Yes, there is. Most kind of you, Major Plowman. Most kind. I'll get an officer to make out a receipt for you.'

Plowman waved a dismissive hand. 'No need to bother with that, Inspector,' he said.

'I suppose you've heard that Captain Lawton was killed in an air crash this morning,' said Hardcastle.

Plowman nodded. 'Yes, I was talking to a fellow from Sutton's Farm field this morning. That sort of news gets round the circuit very quickly. A tragedy. Hugo Lawton was a good pilot. God knows how he made such a mistake. It's elementary airmanship not to try a landing in fog,' he said, echoing what Major Tyler had said only that morning. 'Should have made for the nearest field that was clear.'

'He doesn't seem too upset, sir,' said Marriott when the door had closed behind Major Plowman.

'Like he said, he's got other things on his mind, Marriott. I suppose that going back to fight the Hun means that he don't have much chance of lasting a lot longer than his missus did.'

'I suppose he could have known about Mrs Plowman's shenanigans, sir. He said that news of Lawton's crash got round the circuit, and by the same token I don't see any reason why he shouldn't have heard about his missus. And Sutton's Farm in Essex is a long way from Gosport in Hampshire.'

'They do have telephones and Morse code, Marriott,' said Hardcastle, 'but you're right. I doubt that his wife's carryings-on could have stayed a secret for too long.'

'True, sir,' said Marriott, 'but they do say that the husband's the last to know when his wife is playing fast and loose.'

'So I've heard,' muttered Hardcastle drily. 'This interminable war seems to be doing all sorts of odd things to people's behaviour.'

'Well, the Hun seems to think it'll last at least another year, sir. There was a bit in the paper this morning saying that they've cancelled next year's Berlin Olympics.'

'Don't affect me, Marriott,' said Hardcastle. 'I wasn't thinking of entering.'

Nine

Hardcastle glanced at the clock: it was a quarter to eight. He tapped out his pipe in the ashtray, stood up and made a decision. But just as he was donning his chesterfield, Detective Sergeant Marriott appeared in the doorway

'Ah, Marriott, I'm off home. Who's late duty in there tonight?'

'DC Catto, sir, but—'

'Good. I suppose the citizens of this division will be safe in his hands, although I have my doubts. You might as well push off yourself. I daresay Mrs Marriott will be pleased to see you home early on a Saturday night.'

'Yes, sir, thank you, sir, but what I was about to say is that Lieutenant Hartley is downstairs. He says he wants to talk to you about an important matter.'

Hardcastle sighed and took off his overcoat. 'Oh, well, there goes another early night. What does he want, Marriott, did he say?'

'No, sir, except that it was important. I tried to get him to tell me, but he said it was you he had to see.'

'Better fetch him up here then.'

Richard Hartley was wearing service dress and the collar badges of the Royal Fusiliers but, unlike Major Plowman, he wore slacks instead of breeches and field boots.

'And what can I do for you, Mr Hartley?' Resigned to a long interview, Hardcastle filled his pipe with his favourite St Bruno tobacco and sat back in his chair.

'It is rather confidential, Inspector.' Hartley darted an apprehensive glance at Marriott, who was standing behind him, leaning on the mantelshelf over the blazing fire.

'Detective Sergeant Marriott is my assistant in this enquiry, Mr Hartley, and he's always present at interviews. He takes notes, you see.'

86

Having received that oblique instruction, Marriott moved across to the only other vacant chair, sat down and took out his pocket book.

'I'm afraid I wasn't quite truthful with you when you came down to Gosport on Wednesday, Inspector,' Hartley began, nervously running his thumb up and down the inside of the cross-strap of his Sam Browne.

Hardcastle placed a half-crown coin over the bowl of his pipe and blew gently. 'Damn thing's not drawing properly,' he muttered, and put the pipe in the ashtray. 'I did rather think you were laying it on with a trowel when you were talking about Mons,' he commented, redirecting his gaze at Hartley.

'That's not what I was referring to, Inspector, although what I said about the retreat was absolute gospel. I meant when you were asking about whether any of us had collected any souvenirs.'

Hardcastle leaned forward, his interest aroused. 'Go on.'

Once again, Hartley glanced at Marriott, and was somewhat disturbed to see him making notes. 'It had got to the point where the Germans were actually chasing us down the streets of Mons itself. As I told you the other day, I was leading an assorted group of soldiers from all manner of regiments; I even had a dragoon with me at one time. Without his horse, naturally.' He gave an edgy sort of laugh. 'Anyway, at one stage I was in a doorway covering the lads of my platoon, when I saw this Hun officer. He was all by himself, so I took aim and shot him. As he fell, his pistol skidded across the road. I thought to myself, I'll have that, Hartley, just in case I run out of ammunition, so I picked up the pistol and stuck it in my pocket.' The young officer shrugged. 'When my secondment to the RFC came through I thought, what the hell, and brought it home with me.'

'D'you have this weapon now?' Hardcastle asked the question casually, as though it were of no great consequence.

'No, that's the odd thing. Someone stole the bloody thing.'

'Where from?'

'I'd left it with my kit in a cupboard in my room at Gosport, and forgot about it. It was in with all the other stuff I don't seem to have time for any more, things like a cricket bat, a tennis racquet and rugger boots. Anyhow, a week or two after

I arrived there, I persuaded the mess sergeant to allocate me a better room, one vacated by a chap who'd been posted to France. I gathered all my kit together and it was then I noticed that the pistol had gone.'

'So you don't know exactly when it disappeared,' said Hardcastle.

'No, I'm afraid not.'

'This first room you were in, Mr Hartley,' said Marriott, looking up from his pocket book. 'Did you share it with anyone?'

'Er, yes, as a matter of fact, it was with Roddy Rowe-Smith.'

'The officer who told me it was a court-martial offence to retain unauthorized weapons, if I remember correctly,' commented Hardcastle.

'Yes,' said Hartley.

'Did you ask him about the missing pistol?'

'Yes, of course. He said he knew nothing about it and that I was better off without it. He told me what he told you, that I could get court martialled if I was found to have it. That's why I didn't mention it the other day. Word soon gets round. I can tell you, Inspector, a Flying Corps airfield's like a leaky bucket when it comes to gossip of that sort, and I didn't want to get hauled up in front of the old man.'

'The old man?' queried Hardcastle.

'Yes, the CO, Major Tyler. Bit of a stickler for things like that.'

'When did you move into your new accommodation, Mr Hartley?' Marriott asked.

The young officer thought about that for a moment or two. 'Must have been about six weeks ago, I suppose,' he said eventually.

'And when did you last see this pistol?'

'At a guess, about two months ago, when I was posted to Gosport, Sergeant. But it's only a guess.'

'So it could have disappeared at any time after that,' said Hardcastle.

'I suppose so.'

'And what was the make of this pistol?'

'It was a Luger, point seven-six-three millimetres.'

'Did you by any chance lose a German Army belt at the same time you lost the pistol?' asked Hardcastle, concealing his elation that Hartley's description of the lost weapon matched Inspector Franklin's opinion of the pistol that had killed both PC Crispin and Mrs Plowman.

'A belt? No, Inspector, I didn't have a belt.' Hartley laughed. 'I was taking a risk grabbing the German officer's pistol, particularly as there were more Huns coming down the street. I certainly didn't have the time to take off his belt.'

'When I was at Gosport on Wednesday, I asked if any of you had known Mrs Plowman,' said Hardcastle. 'Mr Rowe-Smith answered for all of you, but you said nothing, neither did the other two. But I'll put the question to you again. Did you know Isabel Plowman?'

'You heard what I said about gossip at the airfield, Inspector,' said Hartley. 'Of course I said nothing.'

'Does that mean you did know her?'

Richard Hartley had the good grace to look shamefaced. 'Yes,' he said in a whisper, and reddened slightly.

'And you had a sexual relationship with her.' Hardcastle's statement was not so much a question, more a brutal accusation.

'Yes,' said Hartley again.

Hardcastle laughed, which did little to comfort the young flyer. 'I suppose you saw it as some romantic tryst, did you, Mr Hartley? Well, if you did, my lad, you was mistaken, because I'm beginning to wonder if there was anyone in the Royal Flying Corps who didn't share Mrs Plowman's bed at one time or another.'

'That's not fair,' protested Hartley. 'She was a charming girl.'

'It might not be fair,' said Hardcastle, 'but it's fact. If I was so inclined, I could name at least a dozen men who've admitted to bedding Mrs Plowman.' It was an exaggeration, but the DDI thought that it was not only near the truth, but more likely an underestimation. 'What are you doing in London this evening, Mr Hartley? You didn't come all the way up here just to speak to me, did you?'

'I'm going to the theatre with friends,' said Hartley.

'Who?' demanded Hardcastle.

Hartley bridled at the intrusive question, but eventually answered. 'Sebastian Lawton,' he said.

'Well, I won't keep you from your entertainment, Mr Hartley. What are you going see?'

'*Romance*, at the Duke of York's,' said Hartley, but failed to understand why Hardcastle laughed.

'When are you returning to Gosport?'

'Tomorrow morning, but not for long.'

'Oh?'

'No, I'm being posted to St Brouille on Tuesday. As a captain.'

'Congratulations, but if I was you, Mr Hartley, I shouldn't mention anything about your cosy nights with Mrs Plowman. Major Plowman's the squadron commander there.'

And with that word of caution from Hardcastle, a somewhat discomfited Lieutenant Hartley left for his meeting with the late Captain Lawton's brother.

'What d'you make of that, Marriott?' asked Hardcastle, once he had managed to get his pipe going again.

'Either he's telling the truth and someone did pinch this pistol, sir, which might or might not be the murder weapon, or he was the killer and got shot of it straight afterwards. But if that's the case, why bother to tell us at all?'

'Exactly my thoughts, Marriott,' said Hardcastle. 'And if it's true, it narrows the field a bit, don't it? It's beginning to look like someone on that station was the killer, but we haven't even thought about the rank and file.'

Marriott looked surprised. 'You surely don't think that one of the soldiers could've done it, do you, sir? Mrs Plowman might not have been too choosey who she went to bed with, but at least they all seem to have been officers.'

Hardcastle tapped the side of his nose with the stem of his pipe. 'You know me, Marriott. I never exclude anyone from the enquiry until I'm satisfied they ain't connected. And as Mrs Plowman was as free with her favours as we know she was, she might not have worried too much about rank. She might even have enjoyed a bit of rough, and no doubt our Mr Hartley had a batman who had free access to his quarters. On the other hand, the apparently innocent Mr Hartley might just have sold the weapon to some civilian. I know a lieutenant gets an extra eight bob a day for flying, but I expect he spends it. And why not? I reckon they deserve it. You'd never get me up in one of those things, and that's a fact.'

Marriott did not know how his DDI knew that a lieutenant received flying pay of eight shillings a day, but had to admit that Hardcastle's theorizing had, once again, opened up a case that to the sergeant had seemed as good as closed.

'What's next then, sir? D'you think it might be a good idea to have another go at these chaps down at Gosport?'

'What's next, Marriott, is that we knock Lieutenant Rowe-Smith off his perch. Bit too full of himself, is that young man. He knew what I was after when I was asking questions about trophies of war, but what did he do? I'll tell you, Marriott, he stayed silent.'

'Another trip to Gosport, then, sir,' said Marriott resignedly.

'No, I've seen enough of that windy airfield. I'll send for him. He can come up here for a change. Catch him off his own beat, so to speak.'

'But how are we going to manage that, sir?'

'Simple, Marriott, a word with the Provost Marshal. As you know, I'm not a man to be messed about.'

And with that statement, Marriott was forced to agree.

'There's an officer down at Gosport that I'm not too happy about, General,' said Hardcastle.

Brigadier-General Edward Fitzpatrick, Provost Marshal of the Army, sat back in his chair with an amused expression on his face. 'There are quite a few officers I'm not too happy about, Inspector,' he said, 'but we seem to be commissioning all manner of rag, tag and bobtail these days. Perhaps you'd care to tell me who he is and why you're not happy with him.'

'Lieutenant Roderick Rowe-Smith of the Royal Flying Corps, General.'

Fitzpatrick leaned forward and noted the name on a pad. 'And what's he been up to?'

Hardcastle summarized his investigation into the murders of PC Crispin and Isabel Plowman, and mentioned the mysterious question of the German pistol and army belt, and how the pistol had certainly been stolen from Lieutenant Hartley's room.

'It strikes me, General, that this particular officer hasn't been frank with me. Interviewing him at Gosport in the presence of other officers ain't very useful, if you take my point. Especially after young Hartley made a point of coming to see me while he was up in London.'

'This is a serious matter, Inspector,' said Fitzpatrick, leaning forward and linking his fingers on the desk. 'It's bad enough to learn of officers taking advantage of a serving officer's wife in the way you describe—'

'I don't think they was taking advantage so much as being encouraged, General,' commented Hardcastle.

'Yes, well be that as it may, the merest suspicion that one of these officers may have murdered your policeman and Major Plowman's wife is likely to cause a scandal.'

Hardcastle would not have described the murder of a police officer by an army officer as a scandal – in his book it was a bloody outrage – but he was pleased that the Provost Marshal had mentioned PC Crispin's death before that of Mrs Plowman. But then, Hardcastle thought, General Fitzpatrick was a policeman himself. Of sorts.

'So what d'you want me to do?' asked Fitzpatrick.

'I could arrest him and bring him to Scotland Yard,' Hardcastle began, naming the headquarters of the Metropolitan Police as being more impressive than his own police station, 'but that *would* cause a bit of a scandal. No, General, I'd like him to come to London voluntarily, in a manner of speaking. In other words, to be ordered to come here. Now, I can't do that without putting him on his guard, but you can. Provided you only tell him why he's been sent for *after* he gets here. Otherwise he'll have time to discuss it with his fellow officers, and perhaps make up some yarn.'

The whisper of a smile crossed the Provost Marshal's face. 'Yes, I most certainly can send for him, Inspector,' he said. 'Leave it to me. When would it be convenient for you to see him?'

'As soon as possible, General.'

'Good. Shall we say tomorrow afternoon at half past two, then?'

'That would be most suitable, General.'

*   *   *

Lieutenant Rowe-Smith's mood was one of uncontrolled incandescence. 'What the hell is all this about, Inspector?' he demanded, once he was shown into Hardcastle's office at precisely half past two.

'Why don't you sit down, Mr Rowe-Smith?' said Hardcastle mildly.

'I am a serving army officer engaged in matters vital to the war effort, but suddenly I'm summoned to the War Office by no less a person than the Provost Marshal himself and told to report to you here. What's the meaning of it, eh?'

Hardcastle stood up and walked to the door. 'Marriott,' he shouted, and waited until the sergeant had joined him. 'You know Detective Sergeant Marriott, of course,' he said to Rowe-Smith.

'You still haven't told me what this is all about,' said Rowe-Smith churlishly. His initial indignation now seemed to have been rather immature in the face of Hardcastle's bland reaction.

'It's about the murder of Isabel Plowman, Mr Rowe-Smith.'

'I've already told you, I know nothing about that.'

'So you said.' Hardcastle took out his pipe and searched his pockets for his tobacco pouch. Then he took a calculated gamble. 'But you wasn't telling the truth, because you were one of many what shared her bed an' all, weren't you?' He began to fill his pipe. 'And don't try denying it neither, because I've got proof.'

Rowe-Smith was unnerved by that statement and his face showed it, but he was slowly beginning to realize that this stolid policeman opposite him was not as dim as he had at first thought. It was one of the failings of people of Rowe-Smith's class and age that he assumed all policemen were mere Dogberrys.

'Well, yes,' said Rowe-Smith miserably. 'Isabel and I did—'

But Hardcastle was not interested in a description of Rowe-Smith's trysts with Isabel Plowman. At least not yet. 'And then there's the question of the pistol,' he continued relentlessly.

'Pistol? What pistol?' Rowe-Smith took out a silver cigarette case and appeared to give some consideration to the selection of a cigarette from it.

'The pistol that was used to murder my policeman and Mrs Plowman,' said Hardcastle, gazing calmly through his pipe smoke. There was no proof that Hartley's missing pistol was the murder weapon, but the DDI saw no reason to admit that.

'Well, I don't know anything about that, Inspector.' Rowe-Smith was beginning to wonder how much Hardcastle knew about this pistol. And for that matter, about his social life.

'Ah, but you do. You see, Mr Rowe-Smith, I have an informant who told me that Lieutenant Hartley had . . . er . . . shall we say, *captured* a pistol from a German officer during the retreat from Mons. And at some time in the past this pistol disappeared from the room he was sharing with you . . . Mr Rowe-Smith.'

'Yes, but I—'

But Hardcastle cut across what the lieutenant was about to say. 'Now I'd've thought you might have mentioned that when I came down to Gosport and was talking about trophies of war. But you never said a word. And that sort of withholding of information from the police makes me very suspicious, Mr Rowe-Smith. Very suspicious indeed.'

'Good God, man! I couldn't mention that down there. You heard what I said about it being a court-martial offence, and I didn't want to get Dick Hartley into trouble.'

'But you wouldn't have been the one being tried, would you? It would have been Mr Hartley.' Hardcastle paused. 'Unless it was you who stole the pistol, Mr Rowe-Smith, and murdered my policeman. Then, my friend, officer on vital duties or not, you'd be taking the eight o'clock walk, wouldn't you?' The DDI leaned back and gazed reflectively at the lieutenant through a haze of pipe smoke.

'Christ, I didn't have anything to do with that,' protested Rowe-Smith, his face showing the alarm that Hardcastle's statement had engendered. 'D'you think I'm bloody mad, or something?'

'As a matter of fact, I've thought for a long time that anyone what goes up in one of them flying machines must be queer in the attic.' Hardcastle stood up and walked to the window. For a moment or two he stared out at the unattractive view before turning once again. 'So what d'you know about this missing Luger pistol, eh, Mr Rowe-Smith?'

'Only what Dick Hartley told me. That the damned thing was missing when he went to shift his kit. I told him to keep quiet about it or he'd get into hot water.'

'Did you and Mr Hartley share a batman?'

'Yes, we did as a matter of fact. Why?'

'Could he have taken the pistol?'

'It's possible, I suppose, but Bates is a very reliable sort of chap. Frankly, I can't see him risking his cushy billet for the sake of a pistol, particularly when he would know the trouble he'd get into by just possessing the thing.'

'You served in France prior to going to Gosport, I believe.'

'Yes, but so did Baxter and Morrison. We were at Maubeurge airfield until the retreat. We were picked to come home and act as instructors. But I think we'll be off again soon. They're running out of experienced pilots in France, and they need chaps who can have a pop at German submarines in the Channel. They're creating havoc by torpedoing merchant ships.'

'And did *you* collect any souvenirs?' asked Hardcastle, dismissing Rowe-Smith's attempt to change the course of the conversation.

'Certainly not.' Rowe-Smith managed to sound offended by the suggestion.

'Where did Hugo Lawton get his *pickelhaube* helmet from?'

'I haven't the faintest idea. And you can't ask him now, can you?' Rowe-Smith fixed Hardcastle with a sarcastic sneer.

'Thank you, Mr Rowe-Smith, that will be all.'

'You mean that you've dragged me all the way up to London just for that?'

'Yes, and it may not be the last time I shall want to interview you neither,' said Hardcastle.

Ten

It was on a Monday morning that Hardcastle received the news that further complicated his enquiry.

A sergeant of the Military Foot Police appeared in the DDI's office. 'I've a message from the Provost Marshal, sir,' he said. 'He wishes you to know that Captain Richard Hartley was shot down last Friday, the fifth of March, at approximately eleven ack emma. General Fitzpatrick thought you ought to be told, sir, on account of Captain Hartley's name cropping up in this here murder you're investigating.'

'General Fitzpatrick got to hear of that quickly,' said Hardcastle, agreeably surprised that the army's senior policeman appeared to be monitoring the matter of the Crispin and Plowman murders insofar as it affected the military.

'He asked to be kept specially informed, sir,' said the MP sergeant.

'Is Captain Hartley dead?' asked Hardcastle.

'That's not been established, sir. By all accounts his squadron commander – that's Major Plowman, sir – reported that Captain Hartley went down somewhere behind enemy lines, but the officer who witnessed it never saw what happened after that.' The sergeant glanced down at the piece of paper in his hand. 'According to the report, that officer had a couple of Fokkers on his tail and pushed off back home a bit *jildi*. The general will let you know if he receives any further information, sir.'

Once the military policeman had left, Hardcastle crossed to the detectives' office. 'Marriott, a moment of your time,' he said.

'Yes, sir.'

'Hartley's been shot down in France,' said Hardcastle once Marriott had joined him. 'I've just had news from the Provost Marshal.'

96

'Was he killed, sir?' asked Marriott.

'They don't know,' said Hardcastle, 'but I wouldn't put money on his being alive, not coming down in one of them contraptions. Enough to kill anyone, I'd've thought. Apparently an unnamed officer was with him and witnessed it.'

'Was it on our side of the lines or the Hun's, sir? Do we know that?'

'Major Plowman reports that it was behind enemy lines.'

'D'you reckon the killings *were* down to Hartley, sir?'

'Right now your guess is as good as mine, but if he's dead we might never know,' said Hardcastle. 'Strikes me our suspects are going down like crossing-sweepers in a blizzard,' he added as an afterthought.

'So what do we do next, sir?' Marriott asked. 'If it's not too late.'

'I think we go back to Cowley Street and have a chat with young Mary,' said Hardcastle. 'Now that Major Plowman's out of the way, she might tell us a bit more than she's told us already. We've got to get to the bottom of this somehow. And before everybody who knew Mrs Plowman gets themselves killed.'

The Plowmans' house had an abandoned appearance, and at first Hardcastle thought that the major had changed his mind and sold it. Or perhaps locked it up for the duration of the war.

It was not until Marriott had knocked three or four times that the door was eventually opened a fraction, and the nervous face of Mary Hutchings appeared round the edge.

'Oh, it's you, sir,' she said as she recognized Hardcastle. 'I thought it might be the major come home on leave.'

'Yes, it's me, Mary. Can we come in?'

'Of course, sir. I've just made a pot of tea.'

The maid led the two detectives down to the basement kitchen and they were surprised to see a man seated at the table. He stood up as Hardcastle and Marriott entered.

'This is my father, sir.' Mary turned to him and said, 'These are the detectives I told you about, Pa.'

'Jesse Hutchings, sir.' The man spoke with a rich Dorset burr, and pushing out a callused hand, he grasped Hardcastle's in a firm grip. He was short, no more than five foot six inches in all probability, and had the strong shoulders that bore testimony to his trade of blacksmith. He was almost completely bald, a mere fringe running round the back of his head from ear to ear, and a bushy moustache. 'I'm staying here for the time being, sir, on account of young Mary not fancying being in the house on her own, not with them murders. One of them in the house an' all. That major what she works for shouldn't never have asked her to stay here on her own. But there you are, sir. I mean, work's not easy to come by these days. And as I bain't got much in the way of work myself now, what with the army having taken nearly all the horses in Clapgate village, to say nothing of Wimborne Minster, well, I thought I'd come up and keep her company.'

'My father's staying with me for the time being, sir,' said Mary, as she poured tea for the two policemen. 'To tell you the truth, I never wanted to stay on after the mistress was killed, but there's not many jobs where you can live in a nice house without having much to do and get paid for it.' She paused guiltily. 'If you happens to see the major, sir, I'd be obliged if you never mentioned to him that Pa's been here.'

'Your secret's safe with me, Mary,' said Hardcastle with a smile. He was inclined to share the fears of the girl and her father, given that the murderer of PC Crispin and Mrs Plowman was still at large.

'Is this your first visit to London, Mr Hutchings?' asked Marriott.

'No, sir, the first time was when I come up for the King's Coronation, back in nineteen-eleven. Stood for hours in The Mall we did, just to see Their Majesties go by.' Hutchings glanced at his daughter. 'Young Mary come up with me and the missus, too, but I don't s'pose you remember much about it, love,' he added, glancing at his daughter. 'You was only fourteen at the time.'

'I do so,' said Mary vehemently, a dreamy look in her eyes. 'I remembers it well. All them soldiers marching behind the King and Queen in their gold carriage. And the cavalry. There were even some Indians in their turbans an' all.'

'And you've not been to London since, Mr Hutchings?' queried Marriott.

'Bless you, no, sir,' said Hutchings. 'I'm a countryman, born and bred. Once was enough for me. I'm not one for the hustle and bustle of the big cities. A quiet pint in the local pub after a day's hard work is all I ask.'

'Sergeant Marriott and me have come here to talk to you about Mrs Plowman, Mary,' said Hardcastle, breaking into the Hutchings's reminiscences.

Sensing that Hardcastle wanted to discuss a matter that was likely to be confidential, Jesse Hutchings stood up. 'I'll just have a look round, Mary love, just to make sure everything's all right.' He glanced at the DDI. 'You can't trust the plumbing in some of these houses, you know, sir. Never know when they might spring a leak,' he said, and made his way upstairs.

'The men who used to call here to see Mrs Plowman, Mary,' Hardcastle began.

'I've told you all I know, sir,' said Mary.

'I'm not sure you have, lass. By the way, we've heard that one of them has been killed. Captain Lawton it was.'

'Glory be!' said Mary, her hand going to her mouth. 'Poor Captain Lawton. It's this terrible war, sir.'

'It wasn't really the war,' said Hardcastle. 'It was an accident, by all accounts. He crash-landed at Gosport in the fog and was killed outright.'

'Yes, but he wouldn't't've done if it hadn't been for the war, would he?' said Mary, with a philosophical insight that surprised even Hardcastle.

'No, perhaps not. Did you know of someone called Richard Hartley ever calling to see Mrs Plowman, Mary?'

But Mary did not answer. Instead she made an excuse. 'I don't think I ought to be talking about what the mistress did, not now she's dead, sir.'

'I can understand that, Mary,' said Hardcastle with a gentleness that he did not usually employ when questioning a witness, 'but this is important if I'm to find out who killed her. And between you, me and Sergeant Marriott here, I wouldn't be at all surprised if it wasn't one of them gentlemen who called here who was responsible.'

'Oh mercy! D'you think so, sir?' Mary was clearly shocked by this suggestion.

'So you've got to help me as much as you can, lass.'

Hardcastle continued to press the girl. 'The way I see it is that you owe it to your late mistress. And even the major.' He took out his pipe. 'Is it all right if I smoke in your kitchen, Mary?'

Mary smiled. 'Of course it is, sir. My pa always smokes his pipe down here.'

Hardcastle busied himself rubbing a flake of his tobacco in the palm of his hand, more to give Mary a chance to mull over what he had just said. 'Now then, you told me about Captain Lawton and Mr Napier and . . .' He paused, as if struggling to recall the third name, but in reality as an encouragement to Mary to open up.

'Mr Staples, sir,' volunteered Mary.

'That's him,' said Hardcastle. 'James Staples. Now were there any others?'

'Now you come to mention it, I did remember Mr Hartley. He was a nice young man. Always very polite to me whenever I opened the door to him. Not at all stuck up, that one.'

'I'm afraid he's missing in action, Mary. Somewhere in France.'

The maid shook her head. 'I don't know what's to become of us all,' she said, half to herself. 'I heard there's been raids by them Zeppelins up Norfolk way with people killed an' all. I don't know what'll happen if they ever come over London.'

'Did she have any other gentlemen callers?' asked Marriott, breaking into Mary's pessimistic view of the conflict.

'There was one I remember, sir. An American gentleman he was. Ever so nice. But he was in the Flying Corps.' The girl thought about that, and then said, 'Although he might've been a Canadian I s'pose, 'cos the Americans aren't in the war, are they?'

'D'you remember his name?' Hardcastle asked, even though he was certain that the maid was talking about Captain Max Vilsack.

'No, sir. I never heard what he was called, but he never seemed to mind I was the maid. Always teasing me, he was, whenever I let him in. Asked me if I ever went out dancing. He reckoned I'd be good at the cakewalk, whatever that is. I've never heard of it.'

'I'm sure you would,' said Hardcastle, who had not heard

of the dance either, 'but I want you to think about my next question very carefully, Mary, and don't forget what I said about helping me to find out who killed Mrs Plowman. Did any of these gentlemen stay the night?'

'Would you like another cup of tea, sir?' Mary stood up and turned to the range.

'Sit down, Mary.' Although Hardcastle spoke in kindly tones, it was obvious that he intended to brook no interruptions. 'The tea can wait. Now then, did any of them stay the night?'

The maid resumed her seat at the kitchen table. 'Yes, sir, quite a few,' she said, finally abandoning her reticence about her late mistress's social life.

'And did they share Mrs Plowman's bed?'

'Yes, sir,' said Mary quietly. 'I saw them when I took tea up in the mornings. But like I told you before, the mistress said she was only a young woman and what with the major being killed—' She gave a convulsive sob and dabbed at her eyes with a tea towel. ''Cept he weren't dead, were he?' she added. It was obvious that Isabel Plowman's lies about the major's death had upset the girl, to say nothing of her mistress's betrayal of her husband. 'And to think of that poor man being in all that danger in France. It's downright wicked, that's what it is.' She looked up with a defiant expression, the loyalty she had once felt for Isabel Plowman at last taking second place to the truth. 'It ain't Christian, sir.'

And Hardcastle, not much of a churchgoer himself, had to agree. 'How many of these men had keys to the house, Mary?'

'I don't rightly know, sir, but it was quite a few. I don't think the American gentleman had one because he always knocked. But there was another one I've just thought of, and he had a key. He was in the Flying Corps too.'

'Do you know his name?'

Mary furrowed her brow. 'Ah, I remember. That was Major Tyler, sir.'

'This list of Mrs Plowman's men friends gets longer and longer, Marriott,' said Hardcastle despairingly. 'A real ragtime girl she's turning out to be. And who'd've thought it, the first time we set eyes on her?'

'Bit of a turn-up, Major Tyler being one of her gentlemen friends too, isn't it, sir? Puts a whole different slant on it.'

'Don't come as no surprise to me, Marriott. Bit of a shifty cove in my book, that one. All high and mighty about officers having affairs with other officers' wives, and all the time he's at it himself.'

'Are you going to talk to him, sir?'

'Case of having to, Marriott. For a start, I want to know where he was the nights of the two murders.'

'Another trip to Gosport then, sir, I suppose.'

'You suppose right, Marriott,' said Hardcastle.

Major Perry Tyler was not at all pleased to see the return of the two detectives.

'Surely, Inspector, you've learned all you can down here?'

But Hardcastle was even less pleased to be at Gosport than Tyler was that they had returned for the third time. 'I don't like being messed about and I don't like wasting my time, Major,' he began.

Tyler blinked at Hardcastle's forthright attitude. 'I'm not sure I know what you mean,' he said, affronted that he should have been spoken to in such a manner.

'You were having an affair with Isabel Plowman, Major, but you didn't bother to mention that when I was down here last. Now why was that? Is it what we in the police call guilty knowledge?'

Tyler began to bluster immediately. 'I don't much care for that accusation, Inspector, nor for the tone in which you delivered it.'

'I don't suppose you do,' said Hardcastle. 'In my experience them as is caught out in a lie are never very happy. But I have proof that you called at the Plowmans' place in Cowley Street on several occasions. And you called there when Major Plowman was on active service in France and you was sitting here in your cushy billet in Gosport.'

'Now look here—'

'Major Tyler,' said Hardcastle patiently, 'I've been a police officer for twenty-four years, and a detective for twenty of them, so don't try selling me the pup. It won't wash. And I would remind you that I'm investigating the murders of a police officer and Mrs Plowman, and anyone obstructing me in the execution of that duty is likely to get himself arrested, army officer or not. Is that understood?'

Perry Tyler had never in his life been spoken to in such a blunt manner. He leaned back in his chair, a resigned expression on his face. 'What d'you want to know, Inspector?' he asked quietly.

'For a start, you can tell me where you were on the evenings of Thursday the eleventh of February and Saturday the thirteenth.'

Tyler leaned forward and thumbed through his desk diary. 'In London,' he said, having found the appropriate page. 'I was called to the War Office on Thursday morning and decided to stay in town until the following Monday.'

'And what was it you were called to the War Office for?'

'I'm afraid I can't divulge that, Inspector,' said Tyler, pleased that he was able to hide behind military secrecy, for no better reason than what he had just said was untrue.

'Never mind,' said Hardcastle. 'It's easily found out. If it's true. And where did you stay in London?'

'The In and Out,' said Tyler, worried about Hardcastle's apparently countless number of well-placed informants. 'It's in Piccadilly.'

'Yes, I know the Naval and Military,' said Hardcastle, affording the club its correct title. 'And I presume there is someone there who can vouch for you?'

'I've no doubt, Inspector, if you think that necessary. But I would remind you that the word of an officer and a gentleman is his bond.'

'Does the name Preston mean anything to you, Major?'

'No. Should it?'

'He was the last army officer to be hanged, but not the first by any means. Murdered his mistress in nineteen-twelve. And I'm thinking this case of mine is beginning to shape up the same way.'

'Really?' Tyler lifted his chin slightly.

'You say you were at the Naval and Military. Was that for the nights from Thursday to Sunday?'

'Exactly so.'

'But you likely went out in the evenings of Thursday and Saturday.'

103

'As a matter of fact, I did. I went to the theatre on both of those nights.'

'What did you see, Major?'

'I saw *The Ware Case* at Wyndham's on Thursday, and on Saturday I saw *The Angel in the House* at the Savoy.'

'I hope you've noted all this, Marriott,' said Hardcastle, and facing Tyler once again, asked, 'Did you go with anyone?'

'No,' said Tyler.

'Do you have the ticket stubs?'

'I don't keep such trifles,' said Tyler scathingly.

'Have you heard that Captain Hartley was shot down last Friday?' Hardcastle went on to a different tack.

'Of course, Inspector. The Royal Flying Corps is like a family. What happens to any one of us is of concern to all of us.'

'What do you know of the theft of a German pistol, a Luger, from Captain Hartley's room some time ago?'

'Nothing whatsoever. As I'm sure you're aware, the possession of illegal firearms is a very serious offence. If I had known that Captain Hartley possessed such a weapon, as you are suggesting he did, I would have dealt with him most severely. It would probably have meant a court martial.'

Hardcastle stood up. 'Well, thank you, Major. I may have to see you again, of course.' At the door, he paused. 'Do you have a key to Major Plowman's house in Cowley Street?'

'No,' said Tyler, 'I certainly do not.'

Hardcastle was never in a good mood when he returned from Gosport, but Marriott attributed it to the attitude of the military. On more than one occasion the DDI had confided to him that he found army officers to be a stuck-up bunch, tending always to look down their noses at mere policemen.

'Catto,' bellowed Hardcastle as he passed the open door to the detectives' office.

'Yes, sir.' Catto, shrugging on his jacket and attempting to button up his waistcoat at the same time, followed Hardcastle at a run.

'Get yourself up to the In and Out Club—'

'Where's that, sir?'

'If you shut up for a minute, I'm about to tell you, Catto.

It's the Naval and Military Club in Piccadilly, and it's called the In and Out because that's what it says on the gate pillars. So even you'd have a job missing it. Find out if Major Perry Tyler stayed there. Sergeant Marriott will give you the details.'

'Now, sir?' asked Catto, glancing at the clock on Hardcastle's office wall.

'No, next Christmas. Of course now. There are times, Catto, when I think the Metropolitan Police would be better served if you was walking the streets in a tall pointed hat.'

'Yes, sir, very good, sir.' And with that Catto fled in the direction of Piccadilly.

Eleven

'Well?' barked Hardcastle as Catto entered his office the following morning.

'I made enquiries at the Naval and Military Club, sir.'

'I should hope you did, Catto. That's what you were told to do. And?'

'There is a record of Major Tyler being a member there, sir.'

'I daresay there is,' said Hardcastle. 'And are you going to tell me when he stayed there, or do I have to drag it out of you?'

'No, sir.' Catto took out his pocket book, dropped it, picked it up, mumbled an apology and flicked through its pages.

'God Almighty, Catto, I haven't got all day.'

'No, sir.' Catto eventually found the page he was looking for, and continued. 'The major was there on the nights of the eleventh, twelfth, thirteenth and fourteenth of February, sir.'

'Go on.'

Catto looked perplexed. 'That's it, sir.'

'Did he go out at all during the time he was there?'

'They didn't know, sir. I spoke to the hall porter and he said that they don't keep a record of comings and goings.'

Hardcastle snorted. 'Slapdash, that's what it is. And what about the theatres? Did you check them?'

'No, sir. You never said nothing about theatres.'

Hardcastle let out a sigh of exasperation. But despite his usual bluster, he was a fair man, and he realized that he had not, indeed, mentioned theatres. 'Go and see Sergeant Marriott, lad. Major Tyler attended a theatre, so he claimed, on the night of Thursday the eleventh and again on Saturday the thirteenth.'

'The nights of the two murders, sir.'

'Ah, so you do pay attention, Catto. Exactly so. See if you

106

can find any evidence that Tyler did, in fact, go to the theatre on them nights. He might have paid by cheque, or they might've remembered him on account of his probably being in uniform. It's a long shot, because there's quite a few people wandering around London in uniform at the moment. And don't hang about. This enquiry's got whiskers on it already.'

'Yes, sir.'

'Well don't stand there, lad. Get going.'

'Yes, sir,' said the relieved Catto, and departed to do his DDI's bidding, almost colliding with Marriott in the doorway.

'What is it, Marriott?' asked Hardcastle as he lit his pipe.

'Message from Commissioner's Office, sir. You're to see Mr Wensley as soon as possible.'

'What the hell does he want?' muttered Hardcastle. 'I thought he was still down the East End.'

'Apparently he's acting head of Central Office, sir. Seems Mr Ward's been taken ill. But the messenger didn't say what he wanted.'

'No, I don't suppose he did.' Hardcastle put his pipe down in the ashtray and stood up. Donning his chesterfield and bowler hat, he seized his umbrella, even though Wensley's office was just across the courtyard from Cannon Row police station. In Hardcastle's view it always boded ill when the head of the Central Office sent for him.

A uniformed police constable pulled open the heavy door and saluted Hardcastle as he mounted the broad steps that led into that part of Scotland Yard occupied by its most senior officers.

Detective Chief Inspector Frederick Wensley occupied a large room overlooking the River Thames. He had a severe face, emphasized by a waxed moustache and a long nose, and his black hair was styled into a quiff. His well-tailored suit, old-fashioned stand-up collar, and black tie with a diamond tiepin completed the picture of the man feared by criminals the length and breadth of the Metropolitan Police District, if not beyond. His enquiry into the murder on Clapham Common of Leon Beron, a receiver of stolen goods, that resulted in the conviction of Steinie Morrison in 1911, was already a *cause célèbre* and a classic example of criminal investigation. There was, however, some suggestion that Morrison had merely pointed out Beron as the victim and that some other person had murdered him. This doubt had caused the then Home Secretary, Winston Churchill, to commute Morrison's death sentence to one of life imprisonment. But that decision had done nothing to tarnish Wensley's career.

'Going somewhere, Mr Hardcastle?' Wensley looked up with an amused expression on his face as the A Division DDI entered his office.

'No, sir.'

'I wondered why you were wearing an overcoat.' But Wensley knew that in the winter months, Hardcastle was rarely seen outside his office unless so attired, even for the short walk from his police station. 'Sit down and tell me how you're getting on with the murders of PC Crispin and Mrs Plowman.'

As succinctly as possible, Hardcastle outlined the progress of his enquiry so far.

'I take it you're of the opinion that the murder weapon was stolen from this Captain Hartley's room in the officers' mess at Gosport, and that the German belt was left there to lay a false trail.'

'Yes, sir, but enquiries are proving to be difficult because one of Mrs Plowman's lovers, a Captain Lawton, has been killed, and Captain Hartley has been posted as missing, if not dead as well.'

'Difficult,' said Wensley, crossing to a side table and pouring two glasses of sherry. It was well known in the Force that Wensley had been a teetotaller, but had discovered, early in his career, that informants did not trust a detective who would not drink with them. 'Do you need any assistance?' he asked, seating himself once again behind his desk.

'No, sir, thank you.' Hardcastle always regarded offers of help from the Central Office as implying that he was not up to the task. He took a sip of his sherry, a drink he did not like, but it was deemed impolitic not to accept a drink from Wensley. The DDI would have preferred a Scotch or, better still, a pint of best bitter.

'Mr Thomson was interested to know of your progress. He felt that the murder of a police officer was a matter that should take priority over anything else you may have on hand.'

Hardcastle was uncertain whether the Assistant Commissioner for Crime had expressed such a view. It was common knowledge that Basil Thomson's only interest at the present time was the activities of Special Branch, the duties of which had of late occupied him almost to the exclusion of everything else.

'I'm aware of that, sir,' said Hardcastle stiffly. 'All other enquiries on the division have been allocated to my deputy, Detective Inspector Rhodes, so that I can concentrate on Crispin's murder. And Mrs Plowman's, sir.'

'Yes, good, but we need to see a result quite soon.' Wensley withdrew a file from his in-tray, indicating that the interview was over.

Hardcastle was in a foul mood when he returned to Cannon Row. Wensley's veiled criticism of his conduct of the murder investigation did not please him.

He opened the door of the detectives' office. 'Marriott.'

'Yes, sir?' Marriott slipped on his jacket and joined Hardcastle.

'Come down to the Red Lion and buy me a pint. Get the taste of the chief inspector's sherry out of my mouth.'

'Is there a problem, sir?' asked Marriott hesitantly, once he and Hardcastle had pints of beer in front of them. He knew that the DDI would never criticize a senior officer to a subordinate, but he could see that the interview with Detective Chief Inspector Wensley had not gone well, and that it was not only the taste of Wensley's sherry that was upsetting him.

'The Assistant Commissioner's taking an interest in this wretched case of ours, Marriott. Seems to think we're not going fast enough.'

'It's a bit difficult, sir, what with our suspects getting bumped off.'

'And most of them'll likely be in France before you can say Jack the Ripper,' said Hardcastle gloomily.

'I don't see there's much else we can do that we haven't done already, sir,' said Marriott.

'No, you're right there, Marriott, and I'm not sure which way to turn next,' said Hardcastle in a rare admission of

uncertainty, 'but there's one thing you can put money on: I'll
see this murderer dancing on air if I have to stay on after I've
got my time in. People don't murder one of my policemen
and get away with it.'

With a sigh, Marriott ordered two more pints of bitter, having
given up all hope of Hardcastle ever buying a round.

Hardcastle was in no better humour after his liquid lunch, and
DC Catto's arrival with more negative information did nothing
to lift his sombre mood.

'I visited Wyndham's and the Savoy theatres, sir, and they
can't confirm whether Major Tyler was there or not on the
evenings of the murders. No one remembers him. They went
through their cheques and there wasn't one from him. Of
course, he could have paid cash. The manager at the Savoy
reckoned that most people do these days.'

'I thought that'd be the case, lad. On your way out, ask
Sergeant Marriott to come in.' Hardcastle waved a hand of
dismissal, took off his shoes and began to massage his feet.

'Yes, sir?'

'I've decided it's time to put a squib up the arse of some
of these snotty-nosed buggers who think they can run rings
round Ernie Hardcastle, Marriott. I might even arrest one or
two, just to see what happens. One of 'em will squeal when
I start talking about gripping the dock rail at the Bailey, you
mark my words.'

'Who are you going to start with, sir?'

Hardcastle thumbed through his daybook. 'James Staples,'
he said. 'We haven't seen him yet.'

'But we don't know where he lives, sir.'

'No, but Major Plowman said he was a friend of the Lawton
brothers, so we'll start with Sebastian Lawton down at Walham
Green.'

'I didn't expect to see you again, Inspector.' Sebastian Lawton,
wearing a paint-bespattered smock, was clearly discomfited
by the arrival of Hardcastle. 'I'm in the middle of painting a
nude of Vera, but you'd better come in,' he said, somewhat
grudgingly.

In the studio, a completely naked Vera Hammond was

reclining on a chaise-longue, but gave no sign that she was embarrassed by the arrival of Hardcastle and Marriott, and made no move to cover herself.

'I should take a break, darling,' said Lawton. 'The police want to ask me some more questions.'

'About time,' said Vera, 'it's bloody freezing in here.' She swung her legs off the couch, unhurriedly donned a worn peignoir and walked through to the other part of the studio-cum-flat.

Hardcastle and Marriott followed. The living area was still in the same state of disarray as it had been on the occasion of the detectives' last visit, and Hardcastle wondered what excuse Lawton would make this time. But he said nothing.

Vera walked across to where the artist had hung his jacket and took a packet of cigarettes from a pocket. Once sprawled on the bed, she lit her cigarette and regarded the three men with what could only be described as a wantonly sulky expression.

'I was sorry to hear about your brother,' Hardcastle said.

Lawton turned to face the DDI. 'I don't suppose you heard exactly what happened, did you, Inspector? All I got was a brief letter from some chap called Tyler. Apparently he was Hugo's commanding officer down at Gosport, but he didn't give anything away.'

Marriott answered the question. 'It was an accident, by all accounts, Mr Lawton,' he said. 'It seems that your brother tried to land in thick fog, misjudged his height and turned his aeroplane over.'

'Damned fool,' muttered Lawton, and walked across to a table. 'Fancy a drink?' he asked. 'I've only got Scotch.'

'No, thank you.' Hardcastle was surprised at Lawton's indifference to the death of his brother Hugo, and wondered whether some jealousy over either Vera Hammond or Isabel Plowman had been the cause of a rift between the two, if in fact there had been one. 'I'm told you know James Staples.'

Lawton took a sip of his whisky. 'Yes, I do. Hugo knew him too. And so did Vera. In fact, I think she and James had a bit of a grand passion going at one time.' He spoke as though the girl was not in the room.

'He means James was screwing me,' said Vera with cockney bluntness.

111

'In that case, you'll know where he lives,' said Hardcastle, ignoring the model's coarse interruption.

'Why d'you want to see him, Inspector?' asked Lawton.

'Because I intend to interview him.' Hardcastle thought that much was obvious.

'I see. D'you think he might have had something to do with this awful business? Isabel's murder, I mean.'

'I don't know,' said Hardcastle. 'That's why I have to see him.'

'I think he lives in Westminster somewhere.' Lawton turned to his model. 'You'll know where, won't you, sweetheart?' he asked, his endearment sounding vaguely sarcastic.

'No,' said Vera. 'But he's a journalist with the *Morning Post*.'

Hardcastle thought that the girl was being deliberately obstructive. If she and James Staples had enjoyed a sexual relationship, they must have gone somewhere to do it. But he let it pass.

'We'll beard him in his den, Marriott,' said Hardcastle as the pair emerged from the house where Lawton had his studio. He waved his umbrella at a passing cab. 'Know where the *Morning Post*'s offices are, cabbie?'

'Yes, guv.'

The cab set them down at the corner of Aldwych and the Strand, right outside a building that the architectural press had described as being of 'French classical' construction.

There was a small plaque on the desk of the doorkeeper that described him as the 'concierge'.

'I'm looking for James Staples,' said Hardcastle. 'I'm told he's a journalist here.'

'If it's a story you've got, I'd best put you in touch with the news desk,' said the concierge.

'I've got a story all right,' said Hardcastle, producing his warrant card, 'but it ain't for publication.'

'Ah!' The concierge brushed his moustache and thumbed through a book. 'He's on the first floor, sir,' he said, pointing at a broad staircase. 'Go on up. You'll find him in the reporters' room.'

At the top of the stairs, Hardcastle pushed open one of the

double doors and was confronted by six or seven journalists hammering away at typewriters. 'James Staples?' he demanded in a voice loud enough to be heard over the cacophony of typing reporters, ringing telephones and the hubbub of conversation.

'I'm Staples.' A young man, probably no more than twenty-two, rose from a desk at the far end of the room. In his single-breasted light grey lounge suit, striped shirt – an abomination in Hardcastle's view – and fancy watered-silk waistcoat, he looked every inch the dandy. 'Can I help you?' he asked, walking towards the two detectives.

'I'm Divisional Detective Inspector Hardcastle of the Whitehall Division,' said Hardcastle once Staples was near enough to obviate the need to shout. 'Is there somewhere a bit quieter we can go to talk?'

Staples led them into a small glass cubicle near the entrance to the large room and closed the door. 'Got something good for me, Inspector?' he asked, his journalistic eagerness coming to the fore.

'Depends what you have to say, Mr Staples,' said Hardcastle, relishing the thought that the young reporter imagined that he was on the brink of a scoop.

'Take a seat.' Staples waved at a couple of hard wheelback chairs before sitting down himself and lighting a cigarette. 'You were lucky to catch me,' he said. 'I'm off soon.'

'Off where?' asked Hardcastle.

'The Front. I've been assigned as a war correspondent. Winston Churchill was one, you know. In the Boer War.' The young man was bubbling over with enthusiasm about his new job.

'I've come to talk to you about Isabel Plowman, Mr Staples,' said Hardcastle, metaphorically bursting the young man's balloon.

'Oh!'

'You obviously know about her murder, and the murder of one of my policemen.'

'Yes, of course. We ran quite a few column inches on it. You must have seen it.'

'I take the *Daily Mail*,' said Hardcastle crushingly. 'How well did you know her, Mr Staples?'

113

'Know her?' Staples affected a mystified air of innocence.

'Mr Staples, let's not waste your time or mine. I spoke to Captain Hugo Lawton before his death, and I left his brother Sebastian not thirty minutes ago.' Hardcastle paused. 'And Miss Vera Hammond, who claims to know you rather well. All three of them told me that you knew Isabel Plowman. I also have another witness who told me that you were a frequent caller at Mrs Plowman's house in Cowley Street while her husband was away at the Front you're so looking forward to reporting on.'

'But he's dead. Her husband, I mean.'

'No he's not. I spoke to him last Wednesday, the day after his wife's funeral.'

'Oh my God!' The blood drained from Staples's face and he sat forward, bowing his head and clenching his hands between his knees.

'But I'm not really interested in your bedding her while her husband was away fighting for King and Country. I'm interested in who murdered her and one of my policemen.' Hardcastle took out his pipe and began filling it. 'I'll give you a word of warning though, young man. When you go off reporting on the war, I'd steer well clear of the Royal Flying Corps squadron at St Brouille. Major Plowman's the commanding officer there.'

'What can I say?' Staples looked up, an imploring look on his face. 'I had nothing to do with her death.'

'Didn't you?' Hardcastle stared at the pathetic young journalist.

'For God's sake, I'm not a murderer.'

'When were you last at Gosport?' asked Hardcastle suddenly. 'The First Reserve Squadron.'

Staples looked up in surprise. 'How did you know I'd been down there?' he blurted out.

'I didn't,' said Hardcastle, 'but I presume you've done *some* war reporting, otherwise they wouldn't be sending you off to Flanders, would they?'

'As a matter of fact, I went down there just before Christmas. Hugo Lawton put in a word with his boss, a chap called . . .' Staples furrowed his brow, trying to recall the name. 'Tyler. He was a major I think.'

'But why did you go down there, Mr Staples?' asked Hardcastle.

'Well, I, er . . . to get an insight into how our pilots were being trained. I even got taken up in one of their planes.'

'What did you hear about a missing pistol while you were there, Mr Staples?' Marriott decided to follow his chief's lead by asking an apparently irrelevant question.

'Nothing. Why?'

Marriott shrugged it off. 'Just another little enquiry we're working on,' he said. 'But I would advise you to be completely truthful with my inspector.'

'Right, let's get back to your relationship with Mrs Plowman,' said Hardcastle, tiring of the desultory conversation. 'How did you meet her and how often did you share her bed?'

Although Staples would have claimed that, as a reporter, he had grown accustomed to the sordidness of life, he was taken aback by Hardcastle's brash approach. 'I met her at a party.'

'And where was this party?'

'At Seb Lawton's place at Walham Green. Hugo was there and he'd brought Isabel with him.'

'Was this before or after you were having sexual intercourse with Vera Hammond?' Hardcastle had no intention of wasting any more time on this rather foppish young man who, he suspected, had probably obtained his present employment as a result of intervention by some influential relative. 'Or perhaps at the same time?'

'I'd been seeing Vera Hammond for about six or seven weeks then. It was before Christmas. About the time I went to Gosport, because it was at the party that Hugo said he'd speak to someone about getting me into the aerodrome.'

'But then you took a shine to Isabel. Is that it?'

'It was rather the other way round,' said Staples conceitedly. 'She let me know that she'd rather like to see me again. She gave me her address and told me to go round for supper on the Friday evening.'

'And what happened?' asked Hardcastle mischievously.

'She got supper for us. She actually told me she'd prepared it herself, because she had no staff.'

'And you finished up in bed with her, is that it?' Hardcastle was not surprised at Isabel Plowman's lie about her staff.

Staples blushed again. 'Yes,' he said in a whisper.

'And how many times did that happen?'

'About four, and then she told me she didn't want to see me again.'

Hardcastle laughed. 'Oh dear! So you'd been shoved to one side, had you? So I suppose you went back to Vera Hammond.'

'No,' said the crestfallen Staples. 'She said she didn't want to see me any more either.'

'Not having much luck with the fair sex, are you?' commented Hardcastle.

'Where were you on the nights of Thursday the eleventh of February and Saturday the thirteenth?' asked Marriott, looking up from his pocket book.

'Why? Is that when—?'

'Just answer the sergeant's question, Mr Staples,' cut in Hardcastle.

'I can't honestly remember,' said Staples. 'I'll need to look in my diary.' He left the office and crossed to his desk, returning minutes later clutching a small book. He sat down and skimmed through it. 'Thursday the eleventh, I was at home boning up on the war news in some back copies of the paper.'

'And the Saturday?'

'I went down to my local pub for a drink.'

'Who with?'

'Well, nobody. It was more for a walk than anything. I just stopped for one pint and then went home.'

'And where do you live, Mr Staples?'

'Queen Anne's Mansions in Broadway. I'm at number seven.'

'That must cost you a pretty penny, living there,' said Hardcastle. He knew the block of gaunt mansion flats; they were little more that half a mile from his police station and well within walking distance of Cowley Street.

Staples looked embarrassed. 'My father pays the rent,' he said.

'And did Mrs Plowman ever visit you there?' It had no bearing on her murder, but Hardcastle delighted in obtaining as many facts as he could.

'Only once.'

'And presumably she stayed the night.'

'No. She came in the afternoon, but left at about half past six.'

'And presumably you spent most of that afternoon in bed,' said Hardcastle.

'Yes.' Staples spoke softly, disconcerted that this policeman seemed to be destroying his confidence at every turn.

'You said you went to a public house on the Saturday,' said Marriott. 'Which one?'

'The Albert in Victoria Street.'

'Talk to anyone there?'

'No. I sat in the corner and had a pint. Then, as I said, I went home.'

'Go there often, do you?' Marriott enquired.

'Fairly often, yes.'

'And when are you going to France, Mr Staples?' Hardcastle was not much interested, other than to make sure that Staples did not escape from the jurisdiction too soon.

'Next week, if they can arrange passage for me in a troopship.'

The DDI stood up. 'A word of warning, Mr Staples,' he said. 'If any of this conversation appears in your newspaper, I shall come back here and personally wrap you in the Defence of the Realm Act before carting you off to my police station.' Hardcastle did not for one moment imagine that the Act would apply to a domestic murder case, but by the expression on Staples's face, it was obvious that he did not know that.

'Well, Marriott, what d'you think of that jumped-up little dandy?' asked Hardcastle once they were back at the police station.

'I think he's lying, sir.'

'So do I, Marriott. So do I. We'll make a few enquiries at the Albert, but to be honest I don't think he's got the guts to kill a fly, let alone his ex-lover and a policeman.'

Twelve

'Marriott, come into my office,' said Hardcastle. 'There might be a war on, but we've got to get on with these damned murders.'

However, Hardcastle was prevented from conducting yet another review of the evidence by the arrival of Staff Quartermaster Sergeant Warrender.

'Colonel Armstrong thought you'd wish to be informed of some news we received yesterday from the International Red Cross, sir,' said Warrender. 'It seems that Captain Hartley survived being shot down and was taken prisoner.'

'Good,' said Hardcastle. 'So where is he now?'

'Holland, sir.'

'What the devil's he doing in Holland?' asked Hardcastle. 'The Dutch are neutral, aren't they?'

'It's a bit complicated, sir,' said Warrender. 'Captain Hartley was apparently being taken to an *oflag* at Fallingbostel. That's in Germany.'

'What's an *oflag*, for God's sake?' demanded Hardcastle.

'An officers' prisoner-of-war camp, sir. But Fallingbostel is very close to the Dutch border, and Captain Hartley managed to escape from the lorry that was carrying him and made his way into Holland. But as you say, sir, Holland is neutral, and he was interned by the Dutch authorities. I daresay he'll be there until the end of the war.'

'Good God!' exclaimed Hardcastle. 'He could be there for years.'

'Quite possibly, sir,' said Warrender.

'Well, I don't know, Marriott,' said Hardcastle, once Warrender had departed. 'I'd rather like to have had another chat with Hartley, but I ain't going to Holland to do it.'

'No, sir, you'd probably get interned,' said Marriott, and received a black look from his DDI.

'I wonder if Hartley *did* get shot down,' mused Hardcastle.

'According to the Provost Marshal, sir, it was witnessed by another officer.'

'But how could that officer be sure?' continued Hardcastle. 'I don't know much about these things, but I should think that if he had a couple of Huns on his tail, which is what that provost sergeant said, he wouldn't've had much time for watching what was going on around him. Too busy trying to save his own skin, if he'd got any sense. You see, Marriott, we've been down to Gosport three times now, and that must've worried them a bit. Then Hartley comes up here to tell us this tale about picking up a Hun officer's pistol in Mons. But suppose our enquiries had rattled Hartley and he guessed we was on to him? So he deliberately crashes his aeroplane behind enemy lines, either trying to commit suicide, or hoping he'd be took prisoner, and that by the time the war was over we'd've forgotten all about him and Mrs Plowman. And now he's in Holland. For all we know, he might be intending to stop there. We can't apply for extradition because we haven't got enough evidence to persuade the Dutch.' He paused. 'For that matter we haven't got enough to convince a court over here. It's a bloody dog's breakfast, Marriott, that's what it is.'

Marriott wondered briefly how a dog's breakfast differed from a dog's dinner, Hardcastle's usual comment. 'But Hartley told us that someone had stolen the pistol from his belongings, sir.'

'That's what he *said*, Marriott, but no one else seemed to know anything about this supposed larceny of his, did they? Apart from Rowe-Smith, for what that's worth. Hartley could have done the killings and then pretended to have had his gun nicked, but actually chucked it in the river. Or even put it back where it came from.'

'Where it came from, sir? D'you mean Mons?' There were still times when Marriott, even though he had worked with Hardcastle for some time, was bemused by his comments and decisions.

'No, not Mons. But he could've chucked it out of his aeroplane, somewhere over enemy lines.' Hardcastle shook his head. 'It's all my eye and Betty Martin, if you ask me, Marriott.'

'But Rowe-Smith's not exactly off the hook, is he, sir?'

119

'No, he's not, Marriott, and I think we'll have another go at him when we've got a minute. But right now it's time we talked to Mr Cecil Yates again. He was a touch too high and mighty for my liking. Probably thinks he can run rings round a simple policeman like me.'

'But he said that he and Mrs Plowman had parted company before Christmas, sir,' said Marriott, secretly amused that Hardcastle should regard himself as 'a simple policeman'.

'I'd've thought by now, Marriott, that you'd worked out that quite a few people have been telling us lies. So we'll trot along to Eaton Place and see if we can find out the truth about him and Mrs P.'

'Is the master expecting you?' asked Yates's supercilious butler, looking down his nose at the two detectives.

'Never mind whether he's expecting us. Is he at home?'

'I shall enquire,' said the butler, leaving Hardcastle and Marriott on the doorstep.

But the DDI was having none of it. Stepping over the threshold into the entrance hall and slamming the front door behind him, he said, 'Well, don't be too long about it, cully. I haven't got all day.'

With a toss of his head, the butler disappeared into the drawing room to return moments later. 'If you'll come this way,' he said disdainfully, 'Mr Yates will see you now.'

'Inspector, what can I do for you?' It was almost as if Yates had not moved since the last time Hardcastle had seen him. Wearing the same plum-coloured smoking jacket, he was standing by the fireplace and there was a glass of whisky near at hand. 'Have you caught your murderer yet?'

'No, I haven't, and I'm not being helped by people who are constantly buggering me about,' said Hardcastle bluntly.

'I'm sure I've told you all I know about this awful business,' said Yates, taken aback by Hardcastle's forthrightness.

'Really? Well, for a start, I can tell you why Mrs Plowman had a reason for turning you down when you proposed marriage to her.'

Yates smiled condescendingly. 'I'm sure I'd be delighted to hear it, Inspector.'

'It was because she was already married . . . to Major Plowman.'

'But he's dead. I told you that the last time you were here.'

'What you said—' Hardcastle paused and motioned to Marriott to produce his pocket book. 'Yes,' he said, when he had found the place, 'you said she implied that her husband had died during the retreat from Mons, or words to that effect.'

'Quite right,' said Yates.

'Did she also tell you that he was a regular Royal Flying Corps officer?'

'Yes, I think she did mention something about that.'

'Then he was unlikely to have been involved in the retreat from Mons, was he?' Hardcastle returned Marriott's pocket book.

'Well, maybe she was confused. Women don't know an awful lot about the war, you know.'

'Oh she wasn't confused, Mr Yates. Mrs Plowman knew very well what she was doing. She was bedding any man who took her fancy, and she wasn't too discreet about it, neither.'

'That's preposterous.'

'And I spoke to her husband only a fortnight ago, Mr Yates. He's now back in France.'

Yates sat down, suddenly. He had clearly been shocked to hear that Edward Plowman was still alive. 'I'm afraid I knew nothing of this. Isabel told me she was a widow and I had no reason to disbelieve her. Alas, all too many women have been widowed since this terrible war began.'

Knowing what he now knew of Isabel Plowman, Hardcastle guessed that she had had little difficulty in persuading Yates that she was 'footloose and fancy free', as Mrs Hardcastle was fond of describing women of easy virtue. Neither did Hardcastle think that Yates would have needed much persuasion. Isabel Plowman had been an attractive woman, and a man some fifteen years her senior would undoubtedly have been flattered by her attentions.

'Where were you on the night of Saturday the thirteenth of February, Mr Yates?'

'I really don't recall, Inspector,' said Yates loftily.

'Then perhaps you'd look in that little diary of yours.'

121

Without a word, Yates crossed to the table upon which his newspapers and magazines were neatly regimented, and withdrew his diary from a drawer. He studied it for a few moments before returning it. 'I really can't say, Inspector. I don't have an entry for that date. I might have stayed in, or on the other hand, I might have gone to my club.'

'Which is?'

'I beg your pardon?'

'Which is your club?'

'Oh, I see. The Reform, actually. It's in—'

'I know where it is,' said Hardcastle. The club, which the Liberal Party regarded as its own, was in Pall Mall.

'As a matter of interest, why d'you want to know?'

'I shall see if their memory's any better than yours, Mr Yates. I shall ask them if you was there the night Mrs Plowman was murdered. If you wasn't, and, as you claim, you can't remember where you really was, we shall have to have a serious talk. Probably at my police station.'

'Now look here,' protested Yates indignantly, 'not only am I a respected member of the Reform, but I'm a person of some standing, and I—'

'So respected that you was screwing a married woman while her husband was at the Front,' said Hardcastle bluntly. 'And while we're on the subject, what do you for a living, Mr Yates?'

There was a long pause before Yates replied to the latest of Hardcastle's probing questions. 'I'm an architect. There'll be plenty of work once this war is over, now that half of France and Flanders is being laid waste.'

'Ah, I wondered why you wasn't in the army,' said Hardcastle sarcastically.

'There are other tasks of national importance, you know, Inspector,' said Yates defensively.

'I suppose so,' said Hardcastle, although he could not quite see how architecture contributed very much to the war effort. 'This man you saw with Mrs Plowman just before Christmas. It was at the Garrick Theatre, I seem to recall you mentioning.'

'What about him?'

'You said, last time we was here, that you didn't know him. Was that true?'

'Yes. I have no idea who he was, apart from the fact that he was in naval uniform. Oh, and he had a little device on his sleeve that looked like wings.'

'I don't know, Marriott,' said Hardcastle, settling behind his desk and searching his pockets for his tobacco pouch. 'Now we've got a sailor among Mrs Plowman's beaus.'

'But it seems he was a flyer too, sir,' said Marriott, 'if the wings on the man's sleeve that Yates was talking about is anything to go by.'

'Looks as though Isabel Plowman was free with her favours for airmen, don't it? Perhaps that was why Yates got thrown over by her, and, for that matter, Napier and Staples.'

'Maybe Mrs Plowman tried to persuade them to join the Flying Corps and they weren't having any, sir,' said Marriott with a laugh.

'Maybe,' said Hardcastle, 'but I think we'll have another word with Mary Hutchings. See if she can remember any sailors who came a-calling.'

'Yes, there was one gentleman in navy uniform, sir,' said Mary, once Hardcastle and Marriott were ensconced in the kitchen at Cowley Street. 'He come a couple of times just before Christmas. The last time was on Christmas Eve. Bit of a cheeky one, he was. When I let him in, he looked round and asked where the mistletoe was. Then he said it never mattered and give me a kiss on the cheek. Then he wished me a Merry Christmas. Fair made me blush, it did.'

'What was his name, Mary?'

The maid gave that some thought. 'Mr Mesley, sir, that was his name.'

'Now think carefully, Mary. Did he have a little badge on his sleeve that looked like a pair of wings, probably in gold?'

'Come to think of it, he did, sir.'

'And he had gold stripes on his sleeve as well, did he?'

'Yes, sir, two. But he never come again, not after Christmas. The mistress said something about him having gone to Dunkirk, wherever that is.'

'It's in France, Mary,' said Marriott.

'Oh, Glory be!' exclaimed Mary. 'I hope he's all right. Like I said, he was a cheeky one.'

'So now we've got the navy to worry about,' said Hardcastle. 'She certainly spread her wings, did Mrs Plowman,' he added, laughing at his own apposite little joke. 'I wonder she had any time to fit in her nursing.'

'If she did, sir,' observed Marriott.

Hardcastle looked keenly at his sergeant. 'Yes, Marriott, if she did. I think we'll make a few enquiries about that. Where was she supposed to be tending the wounded?'

'Charing Cross, sir.'

'We have a lot of these girls here, Inspector.' The matron at Charing Cross hospital pronounced the word 'gels'. 'VADs – Voluntary Aid Detachment – all come flocking along here wanting to do their bit for the war effort, but half of them can't stand the sight of blood. And there's plenty of it here, I can tell you.' She turned to a large register that was permanently open on her desk. 'What was her name?'

'Mrs Isabel Plowman,' said Hardcastle.

'Any idea when she supposed to be here?'

'As recently as Saturday the thirteenth of February, Matron, so I was told,' said Hardcastle.

The matron flicked through the pages of her book. 'Not here, she wasn't.' She looked up. 'Are you sure you've got the right hospital? There are a dozen others she could have been at. There's Number One General at Camberwell for example, and there's—'

'No, I'm certain it was this one.'

'Well, she wasn't here,' said the matron again. 'You could try the VAD headquarters. That's at Devonshire House in Piccadilly.'

But the two detectives had no better luck there. The formidable woman in charge assured them that her records were fully up to date and that the name of Isabel Plowman featured but once in them.

'She put her name down some time ago as being interested in nursing,' the woman said, 'but when we offered her a post, she said she'd taken up some other war work.' She slammed the book shut. 'Half the time they think it's the fashionable thing to do, you know, Inspector, but they're not really interested. Just flibbertigibbets, most of them.'

All week, Hardcastle had been reading the accounts in the *Daily Mail* of the desperate battle for Neuve Chapelle, a village some six miles southeast of the River Lys in France. The reports had described a small salient some two thousand yards wide and no more than twelve hundred yards deep that had finally been taken by British and Indian troops. But the cost had been high, leaving over eleven thousand Empire troops dead, wounded and missing.

On Friday morning, Hardcastle was the recipient of a distressing item of news that was one of the consequences of that battle. It seemed that these days there was no one that the war did not touch.

'There's a Mrs Kimber downstairs, sir,' said the station officer. 'She'd like a word with you if it's convenient.'

'Kimber, Kimber? Don't mean anything, Skipper. Did she say what it was about?'

'No, sir.'

'Better bring her up then.'

A minute or two later a woman in her forties was shown into Hardcastle's office. She was a tall, elegant woman, dressed all in black: a Raglan raincoat and a beret. In one hand she held a long umbrella, and in the other, a black leather handbag.

Hardcastle stood up. 'Mrs Kimber? Please take a seat and tell me what I can do for you.'

'It's about my son Edward,' Mrs Kimber began haltingly. 'He was one of your detectives.'

'Of course.' Somewhat belatedly, Hardcastle recalled the keen young CID officer who had been stationed at Cannon Row. At the outbreak of war, he had responded to Kitchener's 'pointing finger' appeal and had been commissioned into the Suffolk Regiment.

'I'm afraid he's been killed in action, Mr Hardcastle. I got the telegram from the War Office yesterday. I thought you would wish to know.' Mrs Kimber took a slip of paper from her handbag and handed it to Hardcastle.

It was a stark message: *REGRET TO INFORM YOU OF*

DEATH IN ACTION OF LIEUT EDWARD KIMBER 1ˢᵗ BATT SUFFOLK REGIMENT + FURTHER DETAILS TO FOLLOW + SECRETARY OF STATE FOR WAR + STOP

'Good grief!' Hardcastle was stunned by the news. Although of late mounting casualty lists had become commonplace, there was nevertheless a reluctance among the general public to accept that a war brought with it widespread death and injury. 'I can't tell you how sorry I am. Young Kimber was one of my best detectives.' The DDI was not exaggerating. Ted Kimber had shown remarkable promise, and Hardcastle was sure that he would have reached high rank in the Metropolitan Police had he lived to return to the Force. It was not a compliment that he bestowed lightly; neither was it in his character to have told Kimber that. But now he regretted not having done so.

'As you see from the telegram, Mr Hardcastle, the War Office didn't say how it happened, but I believe that he was at Neuve Chapelle. Before he went to France, we'd established a sort of code so that he could tell us where he was when he wrote home in a way that the censor wouldn't cut it out.' Mrs Kimber remained remarkably composed as she told the DDI of the death of her son, and he concluded that she was of a class for whom it was unseemly to display grief in public.

'If there is anything I can do, Mrs Kimber,' said Hardcastle, 'you have only to ask. Your son was one of us.'

'Thank you, Mr Hardcastle, but there is nothing.'

'Is your husband still alive?'

'Yes. He's serving in the Royal Navy with the North Sea fleet.' Mrs Kimber rose and held out a hand. 'Thank you for your concern,' she said. 'We shall feel Edward's loss grievously.' She paused at the door. 'He loved being a policeman, you know. It was his life's ambition. When he was a child, no more than ten, I suppose, he insisted on his father and I bringing him to London so that he could see Scotland Yard, and for ten minutes he stood just gazing at it.' She paused once more. 'He spoke very highly of you.'

Hardcastle escorted Mrs Kimber to the door of the police station and watched as her erect figure walked slowly out of Derby Gate and into Whitehall where one day would stand a simple Portland stone cenotaph as a memorial to the war dead, one of whom would be the former Detective Constable Edward Kimber.

Mounting the stairs, Hardcastle opened the door to the detectives' office. 'I've just had a visit from Mrs Kimber,' he said. 'She told me that Ted Kimber was killed in action a day or two ago. He was a lieutenant with the Suffolk Regiment.'

There were murmurs of condolence from the sergeants and constables who occupied the office, but Detective Sergeant Wood's voice could plainly be heard cursing 'this bloody war'.

Thirteen

The revelation that Isabel Plowman had not been a part-time nurse presented Hardcastle with another problem: where did she spend her days, and did she meet someone there, wherever it was, who may have had cause to murder her?

But first, there were two other outstanding enquiries to be tidied away.

'Nasty killing you've got on your hands, Mr Hardcastle.' The licensee of the Albert public house in Victoria Street pulled two pints of Young's best bitter and placed them on the bar. 'On the house,' he said. 'I knew Bob Crispin. Good copper, he was. Often popped in here for a wet. When he was off duty, like. Bloody shame, what with him having a young family an' all. We had a whip round in here, you know. Raised twenty quid.'

'That's very kind of you, Jim,' said Hardcastle, taking the head off his beer. 'D'you happen to know a youngster called Staples? James Staples. He's some sort of reporter on the *Morning Post*. Bit of a dandy.'

'Oh aye, I know him. Don't live far away. Round at Queen Anne's Mansions if memory serves me aright.'

'I know it's a bit much to ask, but d'you remember him being in here the night of Mrs Plowman's murder?'

Jim scratched his head. 'Blimey, that's nigh on four weeks ago. Much as I'd like to help, Mr Hardcastle, I couldn't put hand on heart and say as how he was in. I could ask my bar staff, but I doubt they'd say any different.'

'Fair enough,' said Hardcastle. 'He reckoned he was in here that evening, had one pint and sat in the corner.'

'Might well have been,' said Jim, clearly disappointed that he was unable to help the police.

'Never mind,' said Hardcastle. 'I've a suspicion he's a lying little toerag anyway.'

The two detectives fared no better at the Reform Club. The club's co-operative secretary summoned those members of his staff who might have been able to assist, but to no avail. They all knew Cecil Yates, but none of them was able to confirm that he had been in the club on the nights of the two murders. The secretary even went through the chits that members signed when they bought drinks, but none had been signed by Yates. 'It doesn't mean he wasn't here, though,' the secretary said and, echoing the words of the licensee of the Albert public house, added, 'He might have been here on those nights, Inspector. Then again, he might not.'

'To hell with it,' said an irate Hardcastle, once he and Marriott had returned to Cannon Row. 'It's Friday, and if the navy's anything like the army, they'll have gone home and won't be back till Monday. There's bugger all we can do till then. You wouldn't think there was a war on, would you?' he added, this time including the Admiralty in his usual complaint about the War Office.

'If this Lieutenant Mesley is in Dunkirk, sir, it's unlikely that we'll be able to get hold him anyway.'

'There's ways and means, Marriott,' said Hardcastle darkly. 'Ways and means.'

But for once Hardcastle did not have need to resort to what he flippantly referred to as 'The Ways and Means Act', a euphemism for circumnavigating difficulties. And occasionally sailing very close to breaching the law in the process.

He was tired of traipsing up and down Whitehall, and on Monday morning sent Marriott to the Admiralty.

'Lieutenant Mesley is at home convalescing, sir,' said a delighted Marriott when he returned. 'Apparently he got a bullet in the shoulder from a Hun machine gun while his squadron was attacking German submarines in the Channel.'

'And I suppose you're going to tell me that he lives in Manchester, Marriott, or somewhere equally far away?'

'No, sir, he lives in Brixton.' Marriott glanced at his pocket book. 'In Angell Town, to be precise.'

*   *   *

Lieutenant Vincent Mesley of the Royal Naval Air Service was a young man. Dressed now in an old jacket and grey flannel trousers, he appeared surprised at the arrival of the police.

'You'd better come in, gentlemen,' he said, and led the way into the parlour. 'I daresay my mother can conjure up some tea if you'd like some. Do sit down.'

'Thank you,' said Hardcastle.

Mesley left them for a few moments and when he returned, he said, 'Shouldn't be long.' He sat down opposite the detectives. 'Well, this is a mystery and no mistake. What on earth can the police want with me?'

'How's the shoulder?' asked Hardcastle. Mesley was showing no outward signs of injury.

'Good as new now. I'll be going back at the end of this week, but surely the police haven't come here just to enquire after my health? Or does the Admiralty think I'm a scrimshanker? If it did, it'd be the shore patrol they sent,' Mesley said with a laugh.

'I understand that you knew Mrs Isabel Plowman, Mr Mesley,' said Hardcastle, ignoring Mesley's attempt at jocularity.

'Yes, I did. What a terrible thing, her getting murdered.' Mesley leaned forward, an earnest expression on his face. 'D'you know who did it?'

'Not yet,' said Hardcastle, 'but we'll find him, don't fret about that. How did you know she's been murdered?'

'It was in the papers. Later on, I mean. The first reports spoke about two murders in Westminster, but a bit later they mentioned her by name.' Mesley seemed surprised that Hardcastle should have posed the question. 'Just because we're stationed in Dunkirk doesn't mean we're cut off from the outside world, you know. One of our chaps flies across every so often with the dailies and other goodies. Incidentally, did you see that the navy sank the German battleship *Dresden* in the Pacific yesterday?'

Hardcastle ignored Mesley's jubilation at his colleagues' success. 'How did you come to meet Mrs Plowman, Mr Mesley?' he asked.

But the answer to that question was delayed by the arrival of young Mesley's mother. A homely woman in a floral apron, she brought in a large tray on which were tea-things. 'I've put some biscuits on there as well,' she said. She smiled at the two police officers and turned to her son. 'I'll leave you to pour it out, Vincent, and don't splash the doily.'

Mesley busied himself pouring the tea and handing round the cups. Taking out a packet of cigarettes, he offered it to his guests.

'No thanks,' said Hardcastle, 'I'm a pipe man myself.'

'Do carry on,' said Mesley. 'Now then, about Mrs Plowman . . .' He paused to light his cigarette. 'I met her at a party.'

'Where was this?' asked Hardcastle.

'It was in Fulham. Musgrave Crescent.'

'At Sebastian Lawton's place.'

'Yes, but how did you know that?' Mesley raised his eyebrows in surprise. 'Actually it was Sebastian's brother Hugo I knew. I was stationed at Eastchurch on the Isle of Sheppey, but I was sent down to Gosport for a while. They wanted me to be an instructor, but I was only there for a week when the balloon went up and then I was off again. Anyway, Hugo invited me to this party at his brother's place. As a matter of fact, I went two or three times, and that's where I met Isabel.'

'And then you visited her at her place at Cowley Street.'

'I must say you've done some digging about me, Inspector, but why?'

'Because I'm trying to discover who murdered one of my policemen and then returned two days later to murder Mrs Plowman.'

'Good God, I didn't realize the two murders were connected. D'you mean the same man was responsible?'

'Almost certainly,' said Hardcastle.

'Yes, I did call at Cowley Street once or twice. Isabel was keen on the theatre and so am I. I took her out to supper and to see a show a few times.'

'And how many times did you stay the night at Cowley Street, Mr Mesley?'

'Never!' exclaimed Mesley, apparent shock at the suggestion etched clearly on his face. 'It was purely platonic. I was without a girlfriend, and Isabel had been widowed. It was an ideal arrangement as far as I was concerned, and I think it suited her too.'

Hardcastle did not for one moment believe that, but he let it pass; it was of no great moment. 'As a matter of interest,' he said, 'Mrs Plowman wasn't a widow. I met Major Plowman at her funeral, just over a fortnight ago.'

'Ye Gods!' Mesley leaned forward and ran his fingers through his thick shock of auburn hair. 'I'd no idea,' he said, looking up. 'Isabel told me that her husband had been shot down and killed over Amiens last September.'

It seemed to Hardcastle that there was no end to this woman's lying. She had told different people different stories about her husband's fictitious death: first it was Mons, then Lille and now Amiens. And in yet another lie, she had claimed to be a VAD nurse.

Hardcastle, who daily studied the war map with which the *Daily Mail* had provided its readers, and which was now on the kitchen wall at home in Kennington Road, looked askance at the young flyer. 'Didn't that strike you as odd, Mr Mesley? Amiens is well behind the front line. So who d'you think would've shot him down?'

'Blimey, I never thought of that.'

'Never thought of it, or too taken with this available young woman?'

Mesley had the good grace to appear embarrassed. 'Yes, I suppose so, but I never slept with her if that's what you're implying, Inspector.'

Mesley was at such pains to deny any impropriety that it merely served to harden Hardcastle's suspicion that the young naval officer *was* lying.

'You said just now that you went to these parties two or three times. How often?'

'Three times in about nine days, I suppose,' said Mesley without hesitation.

'Can you remember who else was there?'

'Well, Isabel obviously. In fact, she used to organize them, so Hugo Lawton told me. Hugo was there whenever he could make it, and a few of his chums from Gosport. I'd met most of them when I was down there. Among others there was Dick Hartley, Perry Tyler, some snooty beggar called Rowe-Smith and a Yank. Funny name, he had. Max something.'

'Vilsack?'

'Yes, Max Vilsack, that's the fellow. Life and soul of the party. He even tried to teach Isabel some American dance called the cakewalk. A real breath of fresh air, he was. You've got to admire a bloke like that. After all, it's not his war, but he paid his own fare to come over here, and got stuck in. I tell you, Inspector, we could do with a few more like him. Good chaps, the old Yanks.'

'D'you think that Isabel Plowman spent a lot of time at Sebastian Lawton's studio?'

'Oh, sure. In fact she posed for him a few times, so she said. But I'm not sure that Vera Hammond – that's Seb's girl-friend – liked her being there too much. There was a bit of friction between those two. Maybe it was because Isabel was refined, but Vera was a bit, well, common, I suppose you'd call it. Or maybe it was because Seb was obviously keen on Isabel.'

'Did Mrs Plowman ever mention anything about nursing?'

'Nursing? No. Was she a nurse, then?'

'So she claimed,' said Hardcastle.

'Shouldn't've thought she'd have had much time for nursing, not with the amount of time she spent at Seb's place.'

Marriott looked up from the notes he had been making, and asked, 'Where were you on the nights of the eleventh and thirteenth of February, Mr Mesley?'

The naval officer laughed. 'Not guilty, Sergeant,' he said. 'I was in Dunkirk looking for Hun submarines. Practically every day until I copped this' – he gestured briefly at his shoulder – 'on the sixteenth. They patched me up over there and then sent me home for a few days convalescence.'

'D'you think he was in Dunkirk when he said he was, sir?' asked Marriott as he and Hardcastle walked through to the Brixton Road in search of a cab.

'Be plain daft to tell us he was if he wasn't, Marriott,' said Hardcastle, waving his umbrella at a passing taxi. 'Easy enough to check with the Admiralty. If we can catch 'em on a day when they're open,' he added caustically. 'The only inter-esting thing to come out of our chat with young Mesley is that Isabel Plowman spent more time at Sebastian Lawton's place than he let on about. And that makes me suspicious. Very suspicious indeed. I think another chat with Sebastian's called for.'

'Where to, guv?' asked the cab driver.

'D'you know Musgrave Crescent in Walham Green?' asked Hardcastle.

'Course I do, guv,' said the cab driver in such a way as to imply that his professional expertise had been impugned.

'If it's the artist you want, you'd better go on up,' said the woman at 27 Musgrave Crescent, laying sarcastic emphasis on the word 'artist'.

'I want to have a chat with you first,' said Hardcastle.

'Oh you do, do you, and what might that be about?'

Hardcastle produced a portrait photograph of Isabel Plowman that he had seized from Cowley Street. 'Ever see this woman here before?'

'Seen her?' The landlady gave a derisive scoff and placed her hands on her hips. 'Practically lived here, did that one. A right little hussy if you ask me. Going up there and tearing all her clothes off before she was halfway through the door, I wouldn't wonder.'

'What makes you say that?'

'All them women what *Mister* Lawton had here was what he called his models. Well, I've got another word for it. Downright disgraceful, all them goings-on up there, I can tell you, Superintendent.'

'Inspector,' murmured Hardcastle, who was inured to such fruitless flattery. 'How often was this?'

'Almost every day, but then about a month ago she stopped coming.'

'That's probably because she was murdered,' said Hardcastle mildly.

But the revelation of Isabel Plowman's brutal end evinced no shocked reaction from the landlady. 'That comes as no surprise,' she said.

It was with a resigned gesture that Sebastian Lawton admitted the two detectives.

'I don't think you've been telling me the truth, Mr Lawton.' Hardcastle was pleased to see that Vera Hammond was not in the flat.

'I can assure you that—'

'When Sergeant Marriott and me I came here on—'
Hardcastle glanced at Marriott.

'The twenty-third of February, sir.'

'Yes, when Sergeant Marriott and me came here on the twenty-third of February, you first off denied knowing Isabel Plowman, despite having a nude painting of her on that there.' Hardcastle pointed at the easel upon which was now the canvas depicting a naked Vera Hammond, the painting that Lawton had been working on last time the DDI was there.

'But I told you at the time, Inspector, that I didn't remember her name was Plowman. She was just Isabel as far as I was concerned.'

'The other thing that you saw fit not to let on about was that she was frequently here, and organized parties to which all manner of rag, tag and bobtail was invited. Including Major Tyler, I've since learned.'

'They were mainly officers in the navy and the army,' said Lawton. 'Hardly rag, tag and bobtail as you call them,' he added, ignoring the fact that Hardcastle had caught him out over his lie about Perry Tyler.

'Don't stop them being of doubtful morals though, do it? By the way, where's your model?'

'Vera's gone for an audition.'

'Audition for what?'

'Some show in the West End.'

'So, these parties. What was the point of them, eh, Mr Lawton?'

'They were get-togethers for flyers. A bit of relaxation after the horrors of war.'

'With the possibility of a few loose women thrown in, is that it? You see, Mr Lawton, what you was doing comes precious close to running a brothel.'

'It wasn't like that, Inspector,' protested Lawton, unnerved that the DDI was now talking about the law. 'It was just a few drinks, some music and sometimes a bit of dancing. All quite innocent.'

'If it was all that innocent, why didn't you tell me about it the first time I was here, eh? Instead of which, me and my sergeant have had to traipse out here three times. And that makes me think that you've got something to hide.'

'I didn't think it was relevant, Inspector,' said Lawton lamely.

'Perhaps you'll let me be the judge of that,' said Hardcastle crossly. 'And now you can tell me what this disagreement was between your two models, namely Isabel Plowman and Vera Hammond. Over a man, was it?'

'Disagreement?' Lawton was foolish enough to smile.

'If you're going to bugger me about, Lawton,' said Hardcastle angrily, 'we can continue this conversation down at Walham Green nick, which ain't much of a stride from here, because I'm not wasting any more time jousting with some tuppenny-ha'penny artist who ought to be at the Front helping to defend this country against the bloody Germans.'

Lawton was shocked by Hardcastle's onslaught and actually took a pace back. 'They didn't get on, I must admit, Inspector, but I rather fancy it was because Isabel was a well-educated girl, and Vera was, well, I suppose—'

'A common tart,' said Hardcastle.

'That's a rather brutal way of putting it,' said Lawton, 'but I suppose it's a fair assessment.'

'So the up and down of it was that you invited these here flyers to your parties, organized by Isabel Plowman, and they had the pick of any of your models. How many of these models did you have here?'

'There were one or two, I suppose,' said Lawton.

'The sweepings of Piccadilly, no doubt,' surmised Hardcastle. 'And how much did these officers and gentlemen pay for the privilege of being introduced to your tarts?'

But Lawton was alive to the danger of admitting that he took money from his 'guests', and knew sufficient of the law to appreciate that such an admission would most certainly lay him open to prosecution. 'Nothing,' he replied. 'That would have been most improper.'

'Yes, it would,' agreed Hardcastle. 'How often did Isabel Plowman come here? And don't think of lying, because I'm just cross-checking, as you might say.'

'Almost every day, Inspector,' said Lawton softly.

'Yes.' Hardcastle drew out the word and nodded. 'And how often did you bed her?'

'A few times,' said Lawton, realizing that there was little the inspector did not know about his activities.

'Here or at Cowley Street?'

'Always here.'

'And that's what got up Miss Hammond's nose, was it?'

'So it appeared, but I don't really know why it should have done,' said Lawton. 'After all, she was not averse to entertaining some of our guests, *if you take my meaning*,' he added slyly.

'So Miss Hammond could have had good reason to murder Mrs Plowman,' mused Hardcastle, but did not really think that was the case. 'Or you would, I suppose.'

'Good God, Inspector, I wouldn't have harmed a hair of that girl's head.'

'Maybe,' said Hardcastle thoughtfully, 'but whoever murdered her and my policeman will be taking the eight o'clock walk down Pentonville.' He paused and turned to his sergeant. 'Or is it Wandsworth they top 'em now, Marriott?'

'I think it's Wormwood Scrubs, sir,' said Marriott, playing along with Hardcastle's game by naming another of London's prisons. None of which did anything to comfort the now distressed Sebastian Lawton.

But the two detectives got nearer the truth by a fortuitous meeting with Lawton's 'model' as they left the house.

Vera Hammond, who was wearing more clothes than Hardcastle and Marriott had ever seen her wearing before, recognized the detectives immediately, and tried to avoid them.

'Just you hold on, lass,' said Hardcastle. 'I want a word with you.'

'Oh, it's you,' said Vera, feigning surprise.

'Get the job, did you?'

'No, I never,' said Vera. 'All bloody stitched up afore I got there, weren't it?'

'In that case,' said Hardcastle, 'I reckon you could use a drink.'

Vera glanced suspiciously at the two policemen. She knew that the likes of Hardcastle did not buy drinks for the likes of her; it was more often the other way around. 'Yeah, s'pose so.'

'Good, we'll go to that pub round the corner in the King's Road.'

Fourteen

'What are you having?' asking Hardcastle.

'I'll take a sherry and lemonade off of you, ta,' said Vera.

'And I'll have a pint, Marriott,' said Hardcastle.

With an inaudible sigh, Marriott made his way to the bar while Hardcastle led Vera Hammond to a table in the corner of the saloon, away from the other drinkers.

'Well now, what was all this hoo-ha between you and Isabel Plowman, eh?' Hardcastle began, once Marriott had rejoined them with the drinks.

'I don't know what you mean, I'm sure,' said Vera, accepting one of Marriott's cigarettes without a word of thanks.

'I'm not stupid, girl,' said Hardcastle, lighting his pipe. 'I know you and her never got on, so what was it all about?'

Realizing that this abrasive inspector probably already knew something about her relationship with Isabel, and was unlikely to be satisfied with half-truths, Vera capitulated. 'It was Seb,' she said.

'What was?'

'It was him and that Plowman woman. Coming down here with all her airs and graces. That was bad enough, but it must have been about the third time she come down, I s'pose, that she waltzes in and takes all her duds off without a word, and then spreads herself on the couch. "Why don't you paint me, Seb darling?" she says, just like that, naked as the day she was born. I thought to meself, well, you get on with it then, you fancy tart. I get fed up with stripping off in that bloody cold place just so's Seb can do his daubing. I come round here to the jug-and-bottle to get some beer, and when I come back, more 'an likely a bit sooner than they expected, she hadn't only spread herself on the couch, she'd spread her legs

138

an' all, and Seb was on top of her, giving her what for. "Want me to paint the pair of you, then?" I says, all sarky like, and chucks his palette at him. Hit him on the arse, it did. Took him and her ages, and about a pint of turps, to get it all off.'

Hardcastle laughed. 'Oh dear,' he said.

'It ain't funny, mister,' said Vera, 'but she'd got money, see, and Seb ain't got two pennies to bless hisself with, and that's the gospel truth. He never makes nothing out of all that arty-crafty bollocks. But oh yes, up turns Lady Bountiful, sets her cap at Seb and throws money at him.'

'Why didn't you leave then?' Marriott asked.

Vera scoffed. 'Leave? And where d'you think I'd go, eh? Anyway, one day Seb says, "Why don't we have a party?" And quick as a bleedin' flash madam says, "Oh what a wonderful idea, Sebbie darling", and tells him she knows lots of flyers what'd love to come.'

'How many other women came to these parties?' asked Hardcastle.

Vera paused to finish her sherry and lemonade and looked hopefully at Marriott. Hardcastle nodded, and Marriott made his way to the bar again.

'Ta,' said Vera when Marriott had replenished her glass. 'There was about six altogether, I s'pose. Well, not together, I don't mean. Well, not always, but there was six different ones what come at different times.' She paused to consider her reply. 'Maybe there was more.'

'And where did they come from, these women?'

Vera shrugged. 'I don't know,' she said. 'Seb found 'em somewhere. Probably up the 'Dilly by the looks of some of 'em. They didn't need no prodding to get their clothes off, I can tell you that, mister.'

'Apart from Sebastian, was there any man in particular who took a shine to Mrs Plowman?'

''Ere, you ain't got another fag, have you?' Vera looked at Marriott, who reluctantly produced his packet of cigarettes again. 'Yeah, there was one,' she said, once her cigarette was alight. 'Some bloke called Perry something. He said he had the pick because he was a major and the others was only captains and lieutenants. He laughed when he said it, but you could see he meant it. Mind you, they all looked the same

139

with nothing on.' She blew a plume of smoke in the air. 'I wouldn't have minded having him get across me,' she added wistfully. 'He was well built, if you take my meaning. But it was only her ladyship what he was interested in.'

'Did Mrs Plowman ever stay the night at Musgrave Crescent, Vera?' Hardcastle asked.

'No, she never. Me and Seb shares the only bed, and she'd've had a fight on her hands if she'd tried putting me out. Anyhow, she said she had to get home or her maid would worry.' Vera scoffed. 'Maid! Well, believe that and you'll believe anything. Her *madam*, more like.'

'All we learned from Miss Hammond was that Sebastian Lawton was running an amateur knocking shop, Marriott. And we'd more or less worked that out from what Lieutenant Mesley told us.'

'But we're no nearer finding out which one of them topped her and PC Crispin, sir.'

'No, you're right there, Marriott, and that's a fact,' said Hardcastle gloomily.

'D'you think there'd be any profit in making enquiries round the Piccadilly area, sir?' Marriott asked.

'Take forever and a day,' said Hardcastle, 'and they wouldn't tell us anything we don't already know. If they told us anything.'

But, unbeknown to Divisional Detective Inspector Hardcastle, events were unfolding on the other side of the North Sea that would eventually solve his mystery for him.

Captain Richard Hartley had befriended a fellow flyer during his internment in the camp near Dordrecht, some forty-odd miles from the Netherlands capital at The Hague. *Ober-leutnant* Otto Vogel was a German pilot who had had the misfortune to fall victim to a failing engine while on a test flight, and had been obliged to make a forced landing in neutral Holland.

The camaraderie of flyers, however, prevented Hartley and Vogel from continuing the hostility of their respective nations, and the two became firm friends, playing chess most days, or walking around the perimeter of the camp, discussing anything but the war.

140

But Hartley's mind was dwelling on something else: escape. And ironically, and inadvertently, it was Vogel who was of some assistance in this venture. Both officers loved flying and were equally determined to get back in the air as soon as possible. For Vogel it was not so much of a problem; German-occupied Belgium was just across the border from Dordrecht, and all that he needed to do, once he had escaped from the none-too-strict confines of the internment camp, was to walk some fifty miles to the nearest German Army unit.

During the time that Hartley's friendship with Vogel matured, Vogel improved Hartley's smattering of German, and Hartley improved Vogel's English.

One evening, without a word to Vogel – there was, after all, a limit to friendship between enemies – Hartley simply crawled under the perimeter wire on the far side of the camp and disappeared into the Dutch countryside. Fortunately, he still had in his possession some English money; his German captors had dismissed it as useless and allowed him to keep it. 'When we conquer the great British Empire,' one of them had told him, 'you will be spending Reichsmarks.'

The next few weeks were ones of intense frustration for Hardcastle. During that time no further information came to light that would lead him to the killer of PC Crispin and Isabel Plowman. Even though he was convinced that he had already interviewed the murderer, he knew that he needed more to put before a jury than just a strong suspicion of guilt.

During that time, also, he learned that the Moulin Rouge in Paris had been destroyed by fire, amid dark hints that pro-German elements in the city had sabotaged it; a horse called Ally Sloper had won the Grand National, the last National to be held at Aintree until after the war; and the King had ordered that no alcohol was to be served in the Royal Household until the cessation of hostilities.

It was the last piece of news that caused Hardcastle some sadistic amusement. 'I'll bet that's taken the smile off the face of the King's protection officer,' he said. The DDI had always assumed that the inspector who guarded the King had an easy job.

* * *

141

The Dutch police were not really interested in escaping internees, and paid scant attention to descriptions that were, from time to time, circulated by the authorities.

Mainly because he was wearing British Army uniform, but also as practice for when he entered Belgium, Richard Hartley deemed it wise to move at night.

Skirting the southeast edges of both the *Oosterschelde* and the *Westerschelde*, he eventually found himself in the small town of Sluis. It should have had some significance for Hartley, for it was off the coast of Sluis that, over five hundred years previously, the British had destroyed the French fleet during the Hundred Years War. But Hartley, no student of history, was unaware of the battle.

It was on the outskirts of Sluis that Hartley took a chance. By now in desperate need of food, he entered a small shop and asked the owner if he would accept English money.

Fortunately the Dutchman was friendly towards the British and, in common with many of his fellow countrymen, feared that Holland's neutrality may not be respected by the Germans for much longer.

'After all, *mijnheer*,' said the shopkeeper, 'the Germans did not worry about Belgium's neutrality.'

Refusing to take Hartley's money, the Dutch couple gave him a good meal and a bed for the night.

The Dutchman also gave Hartley some old clothes, which he put on over his uniform, aware that once in German-occupied Belgium he could be shot as a spy if found in civilian clothing.

Even the Assistant Commissioner for Crime had to admit that there were occasions, despite the exertions of one of his best detectives, when a killer would not be caught. But it irked Hardcastle even more than it irritated Basil Thomson, and every so often the DDI would summon Marriott and insist that they go over, yet again, what they had discovered so far in their investigation into the murders of PC Crispin and Isabel Plowman.

'We must've missed something, Marriott,' said Hardcastle.

'I can't imagine what, sir. I've been through all the statements and the notes I made, and I can't see anything we've missed.'

'Well, we'd better try again,' Hardcastle said and lapsed into contemplative silence while he massaged his feet. 'By the way, what's the news on Crispin's family?'

'Mrs Crispin's been told she's got to quit her quarters by the end of this month, sir.'

'Bloody disgraceful,' protested Hardcastle. 'What do they think's going to happen to her, eh?'

'That's the police for you, sir,' said Marriott resignedly, 'but I understand the beat-duty men have been putting the arm on various people on the ground and they've come up with a place for her to live. I think she'll be all right.'

'Got no soul, the Metropolitan Police,' grumbled Hardcastle. 'If a man's chucked out because of illness or injury they mark him up in Police Orders as "discharged worn out". Did you know that, Marriott?'

'Yes, sir,' said Marriott, who was quite accustomed to being told things by his DDI that he already knew.

It was a tortuous and risky odyssey upon which Captain Richard Hartley had embarked.

Leaving the Dutch town of Sluis and continuing to travel at night, he opted to cross the border into Belgium just north of a tiny village called Schapenbrug. He knew from the sketchy lectures he had received in training that the very north of the war zone was only sparsely occupied, there being insufficient troops to realize the Kaiser's desire for the Germans 'to brush the coast with their sleeve'.

Over the next couple of weeks Hartley moved stealthily along the northern coast, but deemed it wise to skirt around the ports of Zeebrugge and Ostend.

But it was at Nieuwpoort late one night that Hartley came his closest yet to capture.

Taking a chance and walking along the main street, albeit in the shadows, he was confronted by a German soldier who appeared suddenly from a doorway.

'Where are you off to?' demanded the soldier in his native tongue. It was no casual enquiry, for Hartley found himself at the business end of a rifle to which was affixed a bayonet.

'I'm looking for another *estaminet*, comrade,' Hartley replied in German and staggered a little. He was careful to slur his words not only to give the impression that he was drunk, but also to disguise his English accent that he feared the soldier would recognize.

But the sentry merely laughed and lowered his rifle. 'Have one for me, friend,' he said, and paid no further attention to the escaping British officer.

It was, however, after Hartley had managed to cross the border into France, and out of German occupied territory, that he came very near to being shot out of hand.

Approaching the Royal Naval Air Service station at Dunkirk, he walked up to the main gate with confidence.

The sentry, a burly sailor, raised his rifle and shot the bolt. 'Stand bloody still, you,' he shouted in a strong Liverpool accent.

It was understandable. Although Hartley wore his uniform, dirty and torn though it was, it was still concealed by the civilian attire that the friendly shopkeeper in Sluis had given him, and those clothes were now so ragged that, coupled with the fact that he had not shaved for days, he looked like a tramp. But more dangerous still, he did not know that a number of similarly dressed German spies, all of whom spoke impeccable English, had recently been shot on sight.

'I'm a British officer,' Hartley shouted, raising his hands and walking slowly towards the aggressive sailor.

'Yeah, and Kaiser Bill's me uncle,' responded the rating. 'Keep yer 'ands where I can see 'em.' He then called loudly for someone he addressed as 'Chief'.

The chief petty officer who emerged from the guardroom, hand on holstered revolver, conferred briefly with the sentry and examined Hartley from a distance. 'And who are you?' he demanded.

'Captain Hartley of the Royal Flying Corps.'

'Is that a fact?' responded the CPO. 'So where's your bloody aeroplane?'

'Somewhere in Germany, Chief,' said Hartley.

Eventually the navy satisfied itself about Hartley's identity. He was taken to the officers' mess, which, perversely in his view, the navy insisted on referring to as the wardroom, offered a welcome bath and a change of clothes.

Twenty-four hours later, he was being flown back to the

United Kingdom, but despite the travails of the past weeks, he felt that it was an indignity to be conveyed there in a Royal Navy aircraft.

It was on Monday the twenty-sixth of April 1915 that the public learned that British, Australian and French forces had stormed ashore at Gallipoli, and there was renewed hope that the invasion would lead to a shortening of the war. But it was not to be; nine months later and at a cost of some two hundred and fifty thousand casualties, the peninsula was abandoned.

It was on that April day also that Hardcastle, with some degree of relief, left his house in Kennington Road to catch his tram to work. The weekend had followed the usual pattern, save for the fact that Mrs Hardcastle was still complaining bitterly that the price of a loaf had risen to eightpence-half-penny, and the Hardcastles' eldest daughter Kitty was still mourning the death from dysentery of Rupert Brooke, a war poet with whom she had imagined herself to be in love.

But it was Kitty who had been the cause of a minor upset in the Hardcastle household. Sticking gamely to her employment as a conductress with the London General Omnibus Company, a decision of which Hardcastle had disapproved vehemently, her shift pattern was such that she rarely saw her father.

On the Sunday, however, she arrived home in time for lunch dressed in her blue uniform: a cap similar to those worn by the troops, a smart tunic, skirt and knee-high boots. It was the skirt, coming to just below the knee, that caused the row.

'What in God's name do you think you look like, Kitty?' her father had fulminated. 'Just look at that skirt.'

'What's wrong with it, Pa?' Kitty pushed out one foot, placed her hands on her hips and smiled cheekily at her father.

'What's wrong with it? It's downright indecent, that's what's wrong with it, girl. What happens when you bend over? D'you want men staring at your legs?'

'I'm running up and down stairs on a bus all day collecting fares, Pa,' Kitty said patiently, at the same time thinking that the older generation would never understand precisely the problems faced by young women engaged in war work, 'and I couldn't do it in a skirt that was dragging on the ground.'

'Whatever will your mother say?' demanded Hardcastle.

145

'I'd say the girl's doing a valuable job, Ernest,' said Alice, emerging from the kitchen. She always addressed her husband by his full name when she lost patience with him. 'And she's quite right, she'd break her neck trying to run up and down stairs in a long skirt. Anyway the women ambulance drivers are wearing skirts that length. And another thing . . .' She mounted a hobbyhorse as a diversionary tactic. 'Have you seen these kids running about the streets in soldier and sailor uniforms? Five and elevenpence at Gamages, they are. You ought to be doing something about that, Ernest. It's not natural. Children should be allowed to be children.'

Alice Hardcastle winked at her daughter and carried on preparing the lunch.

'Pah!' snorted Hardcastle, realizing that he was both outnumbered and outgunned. Rattling his newspaper he continued to read it in irritated silence. He had once confided to a friend that he might be a divisional detective inspector at work, but that it counted for nothing at home.

Marriott entered the office as soon as Hardcastle had placed his hat and umbrella on the coat rack. The weather was such that he felt safe in abandoning his chesterfield overcoat, despite Mrs Hardcastle's admonition that one should 'Cast not a clout till May is out'.

'A message came in over the weekend, sir,' Marriott said. 'The Provost Marshal wishes to talk to you about Captain Hartley.'

'Did he say what it was, Marriott?' asked Hardcastle.

'No, sir, apart from saying that it might be of assistance in connection with the murder of Mrs Plowman.'

'Did he indeed?' Hardcastle took out his pipe and began to fill it with tobacco. 'These army policemen think they know it all, Marriott,' he said, 'but I'll wager they've never investigated a murder. Well, we'll give him till ten o'clock – I doubt he'll be in much before that – then we'll take a stroll down Whitehall and see what it's all about.'

'Ah, Inspector, come in, come in, and take a seat,' said Brigadier-General Edward Fitzpatrick.

'I understand that you have something to tell me about

Captain Hartley that may be of interest, General.' Hardcastle took out his pipe and held it up. 'D'you mind?'

'Not at all, Inspector, carry on.' Fitzpatrick took a file from one of the three trays on his desk and opened it. 'Captain Richard Hartley has managed to escape from the internment camp at Dordrecht in Holland,' he announced.

'Has he indeed?' said Hardcastle, rapidly revising his view that Hartley was a leading suspect for the murders and, in the DDI's view, likely to remain in the Netherlands for the foreseeable future.

'His escape was facilitated by his ability to speak German. Apparently he knew a little beforehand, and learned a great deal more of the language from a fellow internee while he was there.' Fitzpatrick looked up. 'He was a German.'

'Who'd've believed it?' said Hardcastle drily.

'However, he managed to work his way along the north Belgian coast and across into France, eventually fetching up at Dunkirk, where there's a Royal Naval Air Service station.'

'Interesting,' mused Hardcastle. 'That's where young Mesley is stationed.'

'Who's he?' asked the Provost Marshal, his eyes narrowing.

Hardcastle waved a hand of dismissal. 'Just one of many names that cropped up during my enquiries,' he said, unwilling to impart too much to the Provost Marshal, policeman or not.

'Captain Hartley sent me a message saying that he has something important to tell you, Inspector. He wouldn't tell me what it was, but he seems to think that it impinges on your enquiry into the death of Mrs Plowman.' It was evident from the tone of General Fitzpatrick's voice that he was somewhat put out that Hartley had declined to confide in him.

'Where is Hartley now, General?'

'He's staying at Regent's Park Barracks, but goes to Burlington House every day to be questioned about what he saw on his way home. Some officer in this new-fangled Intelligence Corps is dealing with him. A load of academics playing at soldiers, if you ask me.' Fitzpatrick had no high opinion of those who dabbled in military intelligence.

'When will I be able to see him?'

'This afternoon, I imagine. I'll tell them you're coming. When you get there, you'll be met by a man in the uniform of a Royal Academy attendant, but he's actually one of our chaps. Give him this pass' – Fitzpatrick scribbled his signature on an official form as he spoke – 'and he'll show you up. He's quite trustworthy.'

A comment that caused Hardcastle to grunt. He was becoming increasingly sceptical about the so-called trustworthiness of the military.

Fifteen

'All this cloak-and-dagger malarkey is a bit unnecessary if you ask me, Marriott,' muttered Hardcastle as the pair alighted from a taxi in Piccadilly.

As Fitzpatrick had forecast, a uniformed doorkeeper met them in the entrance hall. Without a word, Hardcastle thrust the pass into his hand.

'If you'll follow me, I'll show you up, sir,' said the attendant.

After the messenger had tapped deferentially on a heavy door and received a summons to enter, Hardcastle and Marriott were shown into a large room.

'Ah, Inspector, we meet again.'

'What on earth—?' Hardcastle was stunned to find that the speaker was none other than Sebastian Lawton, and he was dressed in army uniform with the badges of a captain in the Green Howards.

'It's the war, you know, Inspector,' said Lawton with a laugh. 'All sorts of people are doing all sorts of strange things these days.' He waved a hand at the other occupant of the room. 'You know Captain Hartley, of course.'

'What are you doing here, Mr, er, Captain Lawton?' asked Hardcastle, correcting the man's title as he recognized the rank badges on his cuffs.

'I'm with military intelligence, Inspector, and I'm having a chat to Richard about his swan around occupied Belgium and France. He has some intriguing stuff to tell. But I'd be obliged if you didn't mention to anyone what I get up to in my spare time,' said Lawton, laughing once more, 'particularly if you happen to run into Vera again and, more importantly, any of the officers from Gosport. However, General Fitzpatrick tells me that you wish to question Captain Hartley, so I'll leave you to get on with it.' Lawton stood up and made for

149

the door. 'I'll get one of my slaves to bring in some tea.'

'Did you know what Sebastian Lawton was doing, Captain Hartley?' asked Hardcastle, once he and Marriott were alone with the young Flying Corps officer.

'I had no idea, Inspector,' said Hartley. 'Just goes to show, doesn't it?'

'I understand that you have something you want to tell me,' said Hardcastle as he and Marriott settled themselves into the comfortable armchairs with which the office was furnished.

Even though there were only the three of them in the room, Hartley looked around furtively and then lowered his voice. 'It's about when I was shot down, Inspector,' he began, but was interrupted by a knock at the door. 'Damn!' he said.

A soldier carrying a large tray entered the room. 'The captain said you'd like a cup of tea, sir,' he said.

'Thanks. Just put it over there,' said Hartley. The soldier placed the tray on the desk recently vacated by Sebastian Lawton.

'You were about to tell me something about being shot down, Captain Hartley,' said Hardcastle, once the three of them were alone again.

Hartley leaned forward. 'I gather from what I've learned since I got back, that the official report said I'd been shot down over enemy lines, Inspector.'

'That's what I was told.'

'Well, that was true, but I'm pretty certain that it was one of our own chaps who shot me down. It was lucky shooting, for me anyway, because the rounds hit my engine and I was able to glide down. My undercarriage collapsed, but apart from that, there wasn't a great deal of damage done to the old crate. Mind you, I did get a rather nasty bang on the head that knocked me out for a few minutes.'

'Are you absolutely sure that it was a British aeroplane that shot you down?' Hardcastle asked, amazed at this latest turn of events.

'When something like that happens to you, you're under no illusion, Inspector,' said Hartley gravely.

'But according to the Provost Marshal, it was Major Plowman himself who reported you going down behind enemy lines.'

'Well, it would've been, Inspector,' said Hartley. 'As the

squadron commander it's Major Plowman's responsibility to report missing flyers to Wing HQ, but to the best of my recollection he wasn't in the air that morning. I suppose it was one of the chaps in my flight who saw what happened and reported it to him.'

'I see,' said Hardcastle. 'From his report, I assumed it was Major Plowman who'd witnessed it, although there was mention of an anonymous pilot who saw you go down. But the report also said that it was not seen exactly where you crashed because whoever made the report had a couple of Fokkers on his tail and was in a hurry to escape them.'

Hartley scoffed. 'I can tell you that there wasn't a Hun aeroplane in sight, Inspector. And what's more, the German Air Corps has hardly got off the ground yet. Literally. Otto Vogel told me that.'

'Who's Otto Vogel?' put in Hardcastle.

'A German officer who was interned with me in Holland,' said Hartley.

'The one who helped you improve your German, I believe.'

'How on earth did you know that?' Hartley raised his eyebrows in surprise.

'I'm a detective,' said Hardcastle archly. 'Have you informed the military authorities of your allegation?'

'Good God, no! That would mean a court of inquiry and probably result in whoever was responsible being court martialled. After all, I am in one piece. And what's more, as a result of improving my German and escaping through enemy occupied territory, I'm probably going to be transferred to military intelligence. All in all, whoever it was probably did me a good turn.'

'Whoever shot you down deserves to be court martialled, Captain Hartley, but as one used to weighing up the evidence, I have to ask what proof do you have? Were you able to recover any of the rounds from your aeroplane? British ammunition is different from German, isn't it?'

Hartley laughed derisively. 'Christ, Inspector, I was lucky to get out of the bloody aeroplane alive, and what was uppermost in my mind was to set fire to it. It's standard procedure.'

'So what you're saying is that there's no evidence other than your own belief.'

Hartley looked crestfallen. 'Yes, I suppose so.' He paused

to light a cigarette. 'But I'm absolutely bloody certain of it.'

'Could it have been an accident?' asked Hardcastle, intent on exploring all the possibilities.

'I very much doubt it. As I said, there were no enemy aircraft in the sky that morning, so the excuse that whoever shot at me missed a Hun doesn't hold water in my book.'

'Do you know who made the report of your crash?'

'No idea, I'm afraid, but it shouldn't be too difficult to find out.'

For some time, Hardcastle remained in silence pondering the quandary with which he had been faced. The dual revelation that Sebastian Lawton was engaged in military intelligence, and Hartley's allegation that a British flyer had tried to kill him, caused Hardcastle to think long and hard about what he should do next. As a police officer, he had had what appeared to be a case of attempted murder reported to him. But as it had taken place over or near enemy territory – if it had taken place at all – it was a matter for the military authorities. But he felt duty bound to advise the Provost Marshal, even though an investigation may well determine that it was an accident.

'And you've mentioned this to no one but me, and Sergeant Marriott here, of course?'

'No, no one.' Hartley looked straight at Hardcastle. 'And I hope you'll keep it to yourself, Inspector.'

Hardcastle laughed. 'Captain Hartley, I am a police officer. You have just made an allegation of attempted murder and that, if proved, is a felony under Section 15 of the Offences Against the Person Act of 1861. I am duty bound to investigate it. I can't forget about it, neither would I wish to do so.' But even as he said it, Hardcastle was fairly certain that his writ as a Metropolitan Police officer did not extend to the skies above war-torn France. And it was that doubt that made up his mind for him.

The following morning, Hardcastle and Marriott made their way, once again, to the office of the Provost Marshal.

'Did you learn anything from Captain Hartley that may assist your enquiries, Inspector?' asked General Fitzpatrick.

'Possibly,' Hardcastle said cautiously, 'but I also learned something else.'

'Oh?'

'Captain Hartley alleges that he was shot down by another British officer.'

'Good God Almighty!' Fitzpatrick was obviously shocked by Hardcastle's assertion. 'But surely—'

Hardcastle raised a staying hand. 'Before you suggest that it was an accident, General, I questioned Hartley as to that possibility, and he's certain that there were no enemy aeroplanes anywhere near his flight at the time.'

The Provost Marshal looked pensive. 'This is damned serious, Inspector,' he said eventually. 'Damned serious.' For a few moments he stared out of the window. 'It'll have to be investigated, of course.'

'I imagine so,' murmured Hardcastle, even though he was still convinced that such an enquiry would result in a cover-up. It would not do for such a matter to be made public during time of war.

'D'you think this has anything to do with the murders you're investigating?'

'I might be able to answer that if I knew who the other officers were, General.'

'That shouldn't be too difficult to find out,' said Fitzpatrick, at last faced with some positive task. 'I'll get one of my people on to it.' He paused again, his mind obviously in turmoil at the enormity of the allegation that Hardcastle had reported to him. 'It might be a good idea if I was to get one of your chaps to look into it.'

'One of *my* chaps?' Hardcastle did not much care for that suggestion; it might just finish up with him being sent to France if Fitzpatrick was able to persuade the Commissioner.

'Yes. There are ten of your fellows out there already, attached to the Intelligence Corps. Special Branch chaps, they are.'

'Really?' This was news to Hardcastle, but then he had often complained about the secrecy of the political branch of the Metropolitan Police, and was a little riled that this latest piece of arcane information should have come to him from the army's chief policeman, rather than from one of Hardcastle's own senior officers.

'They're attached to field intelligence, and it might look better if they were to poke around rather than the military police, if you take my meaning.' Fitzpatrick sounded enthusiastic as he warmed to the idea. 'And they're very discreet, your Special Branch chaps.'

'So I've heard,' muttered Hardcastle.

'In the meantime, as I said, I'll set the Provost Marshal of the British Expeditionary Force to finding out the names you wanted, Inspector.'

It was several days later that one of Brigadier-General Fitzpatrick's provost sergeants appeared in Hardcastle's office with a letter.

'The Provost Marshal's compliments, sir,' said the military police sergeant, 'and these are the names you wanted.'

'Thank you, Sergeant.' Hardcastle took the letter and, once the NCO had left, slit open the envelope. 'Well, I'll go to the foot of our stairs,' he exclaimed as he read through the list. Rising from his desk he crossed the corridor to the detectives' office. 'Marriott, come in here.'

'Yes, sir.'

'Have a seat, m'boy, and read that.'

Marriott skimmed through the list of names. 'How on earth did they get over there, sir?' he asked, looking up.

The list contained, among others, the names of Captain Vilsack and Lieutenants Rowe-Smith, Baxter and Morrison.

'If you read the rest of the letter, m'boy,' said Hardcastle, 'you'll see that they were posted over there in a bit of a hurry because they were running short of pilots. Looks as though they've practically cleared out Gosport.'

'I remember Major Tyler saying that it might happen, guv'nor,' said Marriott, matching Hardcastle's informality. 'So it could have been any one of these officers who took a pot-shot at Hartley.'

'If anyone *did* take a pot-shot at Hartley,' said Hardcastle. 'On the other hand, he might have made it all up.' He reached for his pipe. 'Look at it this way. Supposing Hartley thought the game was up and we were on to him. So he lands somewhere safe, like in Holland, not behind the enemy lines in France, and then escapes to tell us this tale. Don't forget that he said it was a lucky shot and he glided down. I don't know much about these aeroplanes, but it seems very lucky to me. What's more, he said he'd set fire to his aeroplane, so that bit of evidence has gone up in smoke, so to speak.'

'But if he's guilty why didn't he stay there, guv'nor, which is what you suggested in the first place?'

'Because that would have made it look as though he did do the murders,' said Hardcastle. 'But coming back and telling us this story about one of his own shooting him down makes him look innocent.'

'But didn't the Provost Marshal say that Hartley's capture had been reported to the International Red Cross by the Germans, guv'nor? He said it was the Germans who'd captured Hartley and that he'd escaped from the lorry taking him to a prisoner-of-war camp.'

'Trust you to bugger up my theory, Marriott,' muttered Hardcastle.

'D'you think it might be a good idea to have another talk with Sebastian Lawton, sir?' asked Marriott. 'Now that we know what he's up to, and he knows we know, he might be a bit more forthcoming about Isabel Plowman.'

Hardcastle looked doubtful. 'I think I'm likely to trust him less now that I know he's one them cloak-and-dagger lot than I did before, Marriott, but I suppose it won't do any harm.'

But before they were able to journey to Walham Green again, Hardcastle received a note from the Provost Marshal asking him to call at the War Office.

'An interesting development has occurred, Inspector.' Fitzpatrick reached across to a filing tray and selected a manila file, its papers secured with a treasury tag. 'The report of Hartley's crash was submitted by Lieutenant Roderick Rowe-Smith.'

'But does he suggest who might have shot down Captain Hartley, General?'

'No, but I understand from my sources' – the Provost Marshal looked up and smiled archly – 'that Hartley received his captaincy before Rowe-Smith, who was apparently senior to him, and Rowe-Smith was somewhat put out by it.' Fitzpatrick smiled. 'But then I suppose that sort of jealousy obtains in the Metropolitan Police, does it not, Inspector?'

'So I've heard, General,' said Hardcastle gruffly, 'not that it's ever affected me.'

'No, I imagine not,' said Fitzpatrick slowly, surveying the DDI with renewed interest. 'However, I mention it in case it provides an alternative motive if we subsequently discover that Rowe-Smith was the chap who pulled the trigger.'

'Have you by any chance found out who else was near Captain Hartley when he was shot down?'

'Yes. Baxter and Morrison. All three were members of the flight that Hartley commanded. And those two were at Gosport with Hartley and Rowe-Smith. But there's a problem insofar as our investigation is concerned. Rowe-Smith reported that there were other British aeroplanes in the vicinity when Hartley went down.'

'Where did they come from?' asked Hardcastle.

'We don't know. Certainly not from St Brouille, which is where the other four were based. I'm having enquiries made, but I'm told that when there are several squadrons in the sky, it's most unlikely that a particular note is made of who they are or where they came from. Our chaps are usually too busy to make a note of other squadron's markings. All they look for are the red, white and blue roundels. Apparently it's become much easier for them to identify their own people since roundels replaced the Union Jack, so these flying chaps tell me.'

All of which merely served to confuse matters in Hardcastle's view. 'So what happens next, General?' he asked.

'I'm having Rowe-Smith brought back to this country so that he may be questioned by a court of inquiry, Inspector. Perhaps you'd like to have a word with him at some convenient stage?'

'Thank you. That would be helpful.' But even as he said it, Hardcastle was unsure just how helpful such an interview may prove to be.

'I'll let you know when he gets back here, Inspector,' said Fitzpatrick.

That afternoon, Hardcastle and Marriott made their way to Walham Green and the studio-flat Sebastian Lawton shared with Vera Hammond.

'Ah, it's you, Inspector,' said Lawton with more warmth than he had displayed hitherto at Musgrave Crescent. 'You can speak freely,' he continued, as he led the two detectives into the living quarters of the flat. 'Vera's gone to another audition, but frankly I think she has delusions of grandeur if she thinks she'll land an acting part.'

'Why d'you let her continue to live here, Captain Lawton?'

'Er, I think *Mister* Lawton might be safer, don't you? Or Sebastian, if you prefer. But to answer your question, I allow her to stay here because she amuses me, she's a willing pillow-mate, and she poses for me whenever I want. Works out cheaper than hiring models.'

'Is this painting business a cover then?' Hardcastle still had a lot to learn about the arcane world of military intelligence.

'Good heavens no. Painting's my profession. The other hat I wear is merely a hostilities-only affair. I was approached by a chap I was up at Cambridge with and he said they were looking for fellows to get involved in the Intelligence business, so I put my name down.'

'Was there a purpose to these parties you held here, then? I mean something to do with your army job?'

For a moment it appeared that Lawton was not going to answer, but then he relented. 'On the understanding that this is strictly *entre nous*, Inspector, yes. The gorgeous Isabel was seeing quite a lot of Flying Corps chaps and it came to the notice of the powers-that-be, who wondered whether there was some ulterior motive, like the gathering of sensitive information. In short, that she might have been spying. Army chaps, flyers in particular, tend to be somewhat garrulous when they've had a few drinks. Add to that what they may say between the sheets and one has a dangerous cocktail. Fortunately my late brother Hugo knew Isabel, and we persuaded her to hold a few parties here. Keep it under one roof, you see. But as it turned out, she was just a good-time girl who was cheating on her husband.'

'Napier, the antiquarian bookseller,' said Hardcastle suddenly. 'Lives behind the Albert Hall.'

'What about him?' Lawton seemed surprised that Hardcastle had remembered the name.

'Was he one of your suspects?'

'No, he was the chap to whom I gave the painting of the mulatto girl in exchange for a book on Cézanne, but I told you that. I really was hard up then, but that was before I started drawing army pay.'

'Ah yes, the mulatto girl called Maria.'

Lawton smiled. 'You should be in my business, Inspector,' he said. 'You have a very good recall.'

'No I don't,' said Hardcastle sharply. 'I keep notes, or rather my sergeant here does. So where does this mulatto girl fit into all this cloak-and-dagger malarkey of yours?'

'Not at all. As Vera told you, the girl was a prostitute I picked up in Piccadilly. She was willing to pose for a few shillings and Napier obviously thought the painting was worth the Cézanne book I mentioned just now.'

Hardcastle lit his pipe and leaned back in one of Lawton's rather uncomfortable armchairs. 'I'm going to take you into my confidence now, Mr Lawton,' he said, 'and I hope you won't let on.'

'You can trust me, Inspector.'

Hardcastle had reservations about trusting Lawton, but continued anyway. 'Captain Hartley.'

'Ah yes. Dick Hartley's been very useful to us. Told us all sorts of interesting stuff about his journey through Belgium and France.'

'He also claimed that he was shot down by another British airman.'

Lawton let out a whistle. 'Did he, by Jove? He never mentioned a word of that to me.'

'He didn't tell anyone else at all, and I think he was hoping I'd sweep it under the carpet.'

'Then why didn't he keep it to himself?'

'Because he thought it might have something to do with Mrs Plowman's murder.'

'And d'you think it does?' Lawton was taking a keen interest in this piece of news.

'I don't know, but Hartley's crash, or at least his going down, was witnessed by Lieutenant Rowe-Smith.'

'The plot thickens,' said Lawton.

'However, I reported the matter to the Provost Marshal and he's making enquiries that may lead to a court martial. Rowe-Smith's been sent for and is coming back to this country shortly.'

Lawton laughed. 'That'll give the military police something to get their teeth into,' he said. 'Is there anything I can do to assist, Inspector?'

'Shouldn't think so,' said Hardcastle. 'I'll interview Rowe-Smith when the Provost Marshal gives me the nod, and I'll see what he's got to say.'

'Is there anything else you can tell us about Mrs Plowman, Mr Lawton?' asked Marriott. 'Now that we know what you were up to.'

Lawton pondered the question briefly. 'Don't think so,' he said. 'At least no more than I've told you already. The truth of the matter is that Isabel wasn't a spy, just a nymphomaniac. But I understand that you had a chat with Vera about her in the local pub some time ago.'

'Oh, you know about that.'

'Vera told me all about it, Sergeant Marriott. And what she told you about Isabel was quite true. About the second or third time she came here, she walked in and without a word stripped off all her clothes. Then she planted herself on the chaise-longue demanding that I paint her.'

'But it went a bit further than that, didn't it?' suggested Hardcastle, more out of devilment than a need to know.

Lawton laughed. 'Even captains in the Green Howards don't look a gift-horse in the mouth, Inspector. It was obvious what she really wanted and I was happy to oblige.' He laughed again. 'But I was off duty.'

'I understand that you used quite a lot of turpentine that day, too,' said Hardcastle mischievously.

'Oh, Vera told you about that too, did she?' But Lawton had the good grace to laugh.

'D'you still hold parties?' queried Hardcastle.

'No, not any more. There's no point. The target, as we say in the Intelligence world, is dead and buried, literally, and most of the gang of airmen that Isabel took a fancy to are over the other side of the plonk. And no doubt most of *them* will be dead before the year's out,' Lawton said mournfully. 'But if I should learn of anything that might be useful to you, I'll let you know. How can I reach you?'

Hardcastle had little hope that Sebastian Lawton would be able to contribute anything of value, but nonetheless gave him the address of his police station.

Sixteen

'Well, that was a waste of time,' complained Hardcastle, once he and Marriott were back at Cannon Row. 'All we really learned is that Sebastian Lawton was in the habit of picking up tarts in the 'Dilly and painting nude pictures of 'em. Seems a rum thing for an army officer in his position to do. I don't give a fig what the army thinks of him, but I wouldn't trust him as far as I could throw a grand piano. And to think he suggested I should be in *his* business, saucy bugger.'

'So what do we do now, sir?' asked Marriott, once Hardcastle had finished his castigation of the Walham Green artist.

'We wait until we have a chat with Rowe-Smith,' Hardcastle said. 'There's nothing else we can do in the meantime. Frankly, I don't see the pseudo Captain Sebastian Lawton coming up with anything useful,' he added, giving voice to his previous thoughts. 'Spends five minutes playing at detective and he thinks he knows it all.'

It was not until the following Monday that Hardcastle and Marriott were able to interview Lieutenant Rowe-Smith in a room at the War Office.

'The Provost Marshal has told me that I may speak freely to you, Inspector,' said Rowe-Smith, a supercilious sneer on his face, 'although I don't really see what I can tell you that will be of any value.'

'I'll be the judge of that,' said Hardcastle firmly. 'I'm a detective and you're not.' He was tired of the posturing of some of the army officers he had spoken to, and was in no mood to tolerate any obstruction from this particularly objectionable example. 'I'm told that you reported Captain Hartley going down on Friday the fifth of March at about eleven o'clock in the morning.'

160

Rowe-Smith looked a little surprised that Hardcastle was conversant with the details of Hartley's crash. 'That's correct. We were flying in formation and went over the enemy trenches to see if we could pick a fight with the Hun, but they wouldn't come out to play.'

'Tell me exactly what happened.' Hardcastle glanced at Marriott to satisfy himself that his sergeant was taking notes, but he need not have bothered; Marriott knew his job.

'Dick Hartley was flight commander and in the lead. The next thing I knew was that his engine was smoking like billy-oh and down he went somewhere behind the enemy lines.'

'Did anyone else see this happen?'

'I imagine so, but as I was Dick's deputy, I was the one who had to report it.'

'And what did Major Plowman say about it?'

'If I remember correctly, he took my report, read it and said something like "Rotten luck".'

'I've been told that there were some aeroplanes from another squadron somewhere near you. What d'you know about that?'

'Nothing. I didn't see any other aircraft, but I was a bit busy looking after my own tail.'

'That would be the Fokkers that were mentioned, I suppose,' said Hardcastle.

Rowe-Smith raised his eyebrows. 'I think you've been misinformed there, Inspector. As I said earlier, they declined to join in the fun. But that doesn't stop you keeping a sharp lookout. If you get slack, you're likely to be surprised by some damned Hun coming at you out of the sun.'

Hardcastle showed no interest that the enemy aircraft that Rowe-Smith originally reported now proved not to have been there at all. 'So what happened to Hartley, did you see that?'

'Beyond seeing that he was on the way down and didn't look as though he was going to come up again, no.'

'Did you think the crash was fatal?'

'Couldn't possibly tell, because I didn't see it,' said Rowe-Smith scathingly. 'But then the Hun Archies started up, so I signalled to the rest of the flight to break off and we returned to St Brouille. There was no point in staying any longer. Young Baxter's observer got a few photographs of the enemy trench system on that part of the front and we went home.'

'What are Archies?' asked Hardcastle, irritated at the slang used by soldiers in general.

'Anti-aircraft artillery,' said Rowe-Smith.

'You mentioned an observer just now. Did your observer see anything?'

'Not that he mentioned, no.'

'Have you been told why you were brought back to England to give evidence to a court of enquiry, Mr Rowe-Smith?'

'Not really. In fact, it's damned unusual for a court of inquiry to be held into a lost aeroplane. Happening all the time these days, and when we lose a chap, it's usually a toast in the mess to his immortal memory and then we get on with the war. But the colonel who's conducting this enquiry said something about Dick Hartley alleging that he was shot down rather than suffering engine failure.'

'And what do you think?' asked Hardcastle. 'Or could it have been one of these anti-aircraft guns you were talking about just now?'

'No. As I said, they didn't start up until after Dick started to go down,' said Rowe-Smith. 'In fact, they probably didn't realize he'd conked out and suspected he was going in for an attack. But quite frankly, I think Dick was imagining things. Engine failure is all too common I'm afraid, and I'm sure that was the problem.'

'I take it you don't think much of Captain Hartley.'

There was a long pause during which Rowe-Smith took a cigarette from his gunmetal case, and lit it. 'Since you ask,' he said eventually, 'I certainly don't think he had the experience to be promoted flight commander.'

'And that annoyed you?'

'Could always use the extra money,' Rowe-Smith said churlishly, but it was obvious that there was some underlying friction between him and Hartley that perhaps went deeper than missing out on promotion. And it might well have been something to do with Isabel Plowman.

'How many times did you go to one of Sebastian Lawton's parties, Mr Rowe-Smith?'

The sudden change in questioning seemed to disconcert the flyer, and he raised his eyebrows. 'I, er, well I suppose it must have been three or four times. How did you know?'

'I didn't,' said Hardcastle, 'but as half the Royal Flying Corps seems to have been there I assumed you had an' all. And that's where you took advantage of Mrs Plowman's generosity, was it?'

'Yes, if it's anything to do with you.'

'Oh, it is, my lad,' snapped Hardcastle. 'I shouldn't have thought you needed reminding that I'm investigating her murder. And the murder of one of my policemen. Who else was at these parties?'

'Perry Tyler, Dudley Morrison, Dougie Baxter, "Yank" Vilsack, oh, and Dick Hartley, of course.'

'Must have been a bit crowded,' observed Hardcastle drily. 'What did you do, draw lots and then disappear somewhere when your number came up for a bit of jig-jig with Mrs P?'

Rowe-Smith wrinkled his nose at Hardcastle's coarseness. 'As a matter of fact, the chaise-longue in Sebastian's studio came in quite useful,' he said, with an air of insufferable superiority that implied a mere policeman would not understand the finer things of life.

Hardcastle chuckled. 'Now you're at St Brouille, did Major Plowman ever mention these little sessions that his late wife indulged in? After all, he must've known about it, gossip in the RFC being what it is.'

'I shall not dignify that question with a reply, Inspector,' said Rowe-Smith loftily.

'No, I didn't think you would,' said Hardcastle, and laughed again.

But then Rowe-Smith relented, possibly because of the dislike he harboured for his squadron commander, rather than for a wish to assist Hardcastle. 'Plowman's wife was the one with the money, Inspector,' he said. 'Work it out for yourself.'

It was a week later that Hardcastle received a surprise visitor.

A constable appeared in the DDI's office doorway. 'There's a Sergeant Seamus Cassidy downstairs, sir, wanting to see you. He says he's a police officer, but he's wearing army uniform.'

'Is he a military policeman?' asked Hardcastle.

'Don't know, sir. He's not wearing any badges, apart from three stripes on his arm.'

'Better show him up then, lad.'

The man who entered Hardcastle's office was a tall burly character, and sported a walrus moustache. He wore khaki service dress but, as the constable had said, there were no collar badges on his uniform and no regimental badge on his cap.

'Mr Hardcastle, sir?'

'I'm told you're a policeman, Sergeant Cassidy.'

'Yes, sir. I'm a detective sergeant in Special Branch attached to the Intelligence Corps serving in France.'

'What on earth are you doing out there, Cassidy?' asked Hardcastle, although he recalled the Provost Marshal telling him that there were such police officers attached to the British Expeditionary Force.

'Field intelligence, sir. Home from home, really.'

'So, what can I do for you, Cassidy?'

'It's more a case of what I can do for you, sir.'

'Better sit yourself down.' Hardcastle walked to the door and shouted for Marriott. 'This here is DS Cassidy of Special Branch,' he said when Marriott had joined him. 'He's fooling about in France on some swan at the moment.'

Marriott acknowledged the SB sergeant with a brief nod of his head and accepted Hardcastle's offer to sit down.

'Now then, what is it that you think can help me with, Cassidy?' the DDI asked.

'Major Torrie sent for me, sir. He's head of Intelligence for the BEF.'

'What was that all about then?' Hardcastle knew what was coming, but was being his usual circumspect self.

'It's in connection with these murders you're investigating, sir. The major sent me to St Brouille to have a look round, ostensibly to check their security.'

'Ostensibly,' repeated Hardcastle with just the slightest hint of sarcasm. 'That's a nice word.' He had always thought that Special Branch officers had a good conceit of themselves and revelled in the secrecy they affected. 'So what did you learn, Cassidy?'

'Quite a lot, sir. I reported to Major Plowman, the squadron commander at St Brouille, and told him what I was there for.'

'Which was?'

Cassidy grinned. 'A standard security check, sir. So he put me in touch with the squadron sergeant-major, a chap called Martin. Ex-Grenadier Guards and a bit of a stickler for discipline. Well, of course I was fixed up in the sergeants' mess. Useful that, because I got to talk to the warrant officers and senior NCOs, and they're the ones who know what's going on.'

'Wish I'd been able to do that at Gosport,' muttered Hardcastle, 'but Major Tyler would hardly let me out of his sight.'

'That's the problem with your rank, sir,' said Cassidy. 'They're bound to treat you like an officer. But if you want the truth, the sergeants' mess is the place to find it. Anyhow, after beating about the bush, I got them to talk about this business of Captain Hartley's crash.'

'How did you know about that, Cassidy?' asked Hardcastle, surprised that the Special Branch man knew what to look for.

'I was briefed by Major Torrie, sir, who'd been briefed personally by the Provost Marshal.'

'Well, well,' said Hardcastle, surprised and pleased that General Fitzpatrick had taken so much trouble. But on reflection, he realized that the Provost Marshal needed to know as much about what went on at St Brouille as did Hardcastle. Although for a different reason.

'Anyway, it seems that Major Plowman is a bit of a maverick, although in the Flying Corps that seems to be the norm rather than the exception, if you take my meaning, sir.'

'I'd more or less come to that conclusion myself,' said Hardcastle. 'Funny lot, them flyers.'

'Anyway, they told me that Plowman was in the habit of taking off whenever he felt like it, and without telling anyone where he was going. But the mechanics could tell that on some occasions he'd been quite a long way.'

'How did they know that, Cassidy?'

'Fuel, sir. I got talking to the technical sergeant-major, a chap called Richards, and very helpful he was too, although he didn't realize it. But it seems there were two or three occasions when Plowman got back with almost empty fuel tanks. I played ignorant and asked what that proved. Well, Vic Richards – he's the sort of chief mechanic – told me that they were flying BE2c aeroplanes from St Brouille at the time, and that they carried enough fuel for three hours flying.'

'So how does that prove anything?' Hardcastle was becoming increasingly mystified by the technicalities that Cassidy was expounding.

'There were times when Plowman had been gone for considerably longer than three hours, sir, which means he must have landed somewhere else to refuel. And on those occasions, he didn't take an observer with him. In fact, they said he rarely took an observer with him. Now the chaps at St Brouille didn't know where he'd landed, and I wasn't in a position to ask on account of I wasn't supposed to be asking questions like that. But I got some dates out of Sergeant-Major Richards . . .' Cassidy paused to refer to his pocket book. 'Major Plowman was gone for lengthy periods on two or three occasions prior to the murders of PC Crispin and Mrs Plowman, but more significantly, he was on leave from Thursday the eleventh of February to Sunday the fourteenth. What's more, it's said that he took an aircraft with him.'

'And Crispin was murdered on that Thursday and Isabel Plowman on the Saturday.' Hardcastle picked up his half-smoked pipe and spent a second or two teasing the tobacco before lighting it. 'Any idea where he went, Cassidy?' he asked through a haze of smoke.

'The story was that he was going to Paris for a dirty weekend, sir, but there's no proof that he went there. Not that I could obtain anyway.'

'Is there an aerodrome near Paris, then?'

'I don't know, sir, but I should think it's likely. It wouldn't be too difficult to find out.'

'No, it won't.' Hardcastle turned to Marriott. 'Make a note to talk to the Provost Marshal about that. In fact, Marriott, in view of what Sergeant Cassidy has been telling us, there's quite a few things we need to talk to General Fitzpatrick about.'

'There was one other thing, sir,' Cassidy continued. 'I was told that on the day that Captain Hartley went down, Major Plowman took off immediately after Hartley and returned at about the same time as Lieutenant Rowe-Smith. But I got the impression there was a bit of doubt about that. There's so much coming and going that they tend to lose track.'

'Interesting,' said Hardcastle. 'Any indication where he'd been?'

'No, sir. It's not the sort of question the ground crew would ask.'

'What speed do these aeroplanes do, Cassidy?' asked Hardcastle, although he didn't know how that information would help him.

'Top speed is about seventy miles an hour, sir. Incidentally, as I said just now, Major Plowman is something of a maverick and has a reputation for being a bit of a reckless flyer. Takes chances in the air that the other pilots don't, and that's saying something for that lot. You certainly wouldn't get me up in the air in one of those things. Too bloody dangerous if you ask me.'

Hardcastle laughed. 'Me too, Cassidy,' he said.

At last Hardcastle had something to work on. That Plowman had been absent from the Royal Flying Corps base at St Brouille during the period when Crispin and Isabel Plowman had been murdered was of great interest. The detective in Hardcastle made him very sceptical about the story that Plowman had been to Paris for 'a dirty weekend'. Added to which, Rowe-Smith had mentioned that Isabel Plowman was the one with the money.

'I wonder if she left all her money to Plowman in her will, Marriott,' mused Hardcastle, but he did not expect his sergeant to know.

Following Sergeant Cassidy's visit, Hardcastle and Marriott made their way, once again, to the Provost Marshal's office.

'We'll be making a groove in the bloody footway if we go on at this rate,' complained Hardcastle.

'Have you heard about the *Lusitania*, Inspector?' asked Fitzpatrick the moment the two detectives arrived in his office.

'The *Lusitania*, General? What about it?' Beyond knowing that the vessel was a Cunard liner, Hardcastle had heard nothing that should interest him.

'Torpedoed by the Germans off the Old Head of Kinsale. Twelve hundred souls lost, so I hear, including Alfred Vanderbilt the yachtsman, and quite a few friends of President Wilson.'

'Sounds like the Germans want the Yanks to join in the war on our side, General,' said Hardcastle.

'That, Inspector, is a very profound comment. However, what can I do for you?'

Hardcastle spent ten minutes summarizing what Cassidy had told him, but it was the part about Plowman taking off immediately after Hartley and returning at the same time as Rowe-Smith that particularly interested General Fitzpatrick.

'So what's your next move, Inspector?' the Provost Marshal asked.

'I've been doing some working out, General,' said Hardcastle, producing a piece of paper from his pocket. 'These aeroplanes at St Brouille are called BE2c, whatever they are.'

'They're two-seater biplanes built at the Royal Aircraft Factory at Farnborough,' Fitzpatrick put in.

'Well, apparently they can fly at seventy miles an hour and carry enough fuel for three hours. According to my sums' – Hardcastle glanced down at his piece of paper – 'that means they can fly about two hundred miles maximum before needing to refuel.'

Fitzpatrick jotted down the figures on his blotter. 'Yes, I'd agree with that, Inspector, but what are you getting at?'

'It means that when Major Plowman said he was going to Paris for a few days, he could've flown from St Brouille to somewhere in this country. And those few days were when my policeman and Mrs Plowman were murdered.'

'Good God, Inspector, you're not suggesting that Plowman—' The Provost Marshal broke off as he grasped the enormity of Hardcastle's supposition.

'That's exactly what I am suggesting, General. But I'm going to need your help to prove it.'

'What d'you want?'

'I want to start at Gosport and be given permission to talk to the warrant officers and NCOs. When Marriott and me have been down there before, Major Tyler, the squadron commander, has always insisted that he answers our questions. Except when I talked to the five pilots who finished up at St Brouille. You see, General, I need to get Tyler off my back, otherwise I shan't get at the truth. And I think the ground staff might just have the answers I want. Apart from anything else, Tyler spent a few pleasant nights in Mrs Plowman's bed, so he ain't to be trusted.'

'Good God!' said Fitzpatrick again, and shook his head at this latest revelation. He stood up and crossed the room to a communicating door. 'Sergeant, get hold of Mr Macdonald for me, will you?'

'Yes, sir,' came the voice of the NCO in the neighbouring office.

A few moments later a young lieutenant entered the room. He was wearing the collar badges of the Royal Engineers and an MP brassard. 'You wanted me, sir?'

'This is Divisional Detective Inspector Hardcastle from Cannon Row police station, Macdonald. He's investigating the murders of Mrs Plowman and the PC who was killed a couple of days previously.'

'At Cowley Street, sir.' Macdonald was obviously conversant with the details of the slayings.

'I want you to accompany the inspector to Gosport. I shall speak to Major Tyler, the squadron commander down there, and tell him that you and Mr Hardcastle are making enquiries and need to speak to the other ranks on their own. And if you have any obstruction from him, call me immediately. That understood?'

'Yes, sir.' Macdonald turned to Hardcastle. 'When would you like to leave, sir?' he asked.

'Tomorrow morning would suit me, Mr Macdonald.'

'Tomorrow morning it is, sir. I'll call for you at Cannon Row at nine ack emma.'

'That's nine o'clock in English, Marriott,' said Hardcastle impishly, and grinned at Macdonald.

169

Seventeen

Major Perry Tyler had been disconcerted immeasurably to have received a telephone call from no less a person than the Provost Marshal, informing him that a military police investigating officer *and* the civil police were on their way to Gosport to carry out undisclosed enquiries.

As a result, a staff car with a corporal driver was waiting for the three policemen when they arrived at the ferry terminal in Gosport.

The corporal leaped from the driving seat and saluted as the trio approached him.

Hardcastle surveyed the smartly dressed soldier. 'He'd go down a treat at Peel House,' he said, naming the training establishment of the Metropolitan Police in Regency Street, Westminster.

'Not at the moment, he wouldn't, sir,' said Marriott.

'Oh?' Hardcastle stopped and faced his sergeant. 'And why not?'

'They've stopped training for the duration of the war, sir. It's been turned into a social club for Dominion troops.'

'How d'you know that, Marriott?'

'I live next door, sir,' said Marriott, risking a grin.

'You're a bloody know-all,' muttered Hardcastle as he clambered into the Vauxhall car.

The reception that Major Tyler accorded the military police officer and the two detectives was distinctly frosty.

'I understand from the Provost Marshal that you have more enquiries to make here, Inspector,' he said.

'That's correct, Major,' said Hardcastle, in no mood to joust with the squadron commander after yet another boring journey from London.

'Well I don't know what you hope to discover. I think you've been granted all the co-operation possible.'

'That might be your idea of co-operation, Major,' said Hardcastle bluntly, 'but it ain't mine. In fact it strikes me as being a touch nearer what we in the police call obstruction. And frankly, I'm not putting up with any more of it. Not from you nor anyone else neither. Now, if you don't mind, I want to speak to the—' He broke off and turned to the provost lieutenant, who was still recovering from the shock of hearing a major put in his place so sharply. Although as a military police officer, he had considerable powers even where a major was concerned, he secretly envied Hardcastle's ability to override army ranks. 'What's this fellow called that I have to see, Mr Macdonald?'

'The technical sergeant-major, sir,' said Macdonald.

'I don't know what he can possibly tell you that I can't,' said a petulant Tyler.

'I don't suppose you can, Major,' said Hardcastle, 'but then I'm a detective and you're not. And if you don't like it, you can take it up with General Fitzpatrick. But I will not have anyone, and that includes you, obstructing me in a murder enquiry. I hope that's clearly understood. Now, perhaps, you'll tell me where I can find this technical sergeant-major. What's his name, by the way?'

'Moore,' said Tyler tersely. 'I'll get my clerk to show you where you can find him.' The major shouted for the sergeant in the outer office, gave him instructions and then sat down at his desk intent on dealing with some paperwork. He made no secret of the annoyance he felt at Hardcastle's high-handed attitude, but even he realized that it would be dangerous to thwart the London detective, particularly now that the Provost Marshal was taking an interest in what went on at Gosport. Tyler's real concern was that he did not know precisely what Hardcastle was looking for.

The sergeant-clerk led the three policemen across the airfield. 'Mr Moore will likely be in the main hangar, sir,' he said.

'In the what?' demanded Hardcastle, unfamiliar with the term.

'It's that large building over there, sir,' said the sergeant. 'It's where they service the aircraft. The TSM's always knocking about there somewhere.'

171

And true enough the three policemen found the technical sergeant-major working on an engine that had been removed from a Maurice Farman Longhorn biplane.

'Excuse me, sir,' said the sergeant.

'What now?' demanded the TSM, his back still towards his visitors. 'Can't you see I'm busy?'

'There's an officer here to see you, sir.'

Sergeant-Major Moore stood up and turned, wiping his hands on a dirty rag as he did so. Sighting the provost lieutenant, he snapped to attention. 'Good morning, sir.'

'I'm Lieutenant Macdonald of the Military Foot Police, Sarn't-Major.'

'So I see, sir,' said Moore, glancing at Macdonald's brassard. 'How can I help you?' He did not seem nearly as disturbed by the arrival of the military police as his commanding officer had been. But then, Hardcastle surmised, he probably had nothing to hide.

'These gentlemen are civil police officers from London,' said Macdonald. 'They wish to ask you some questions.'

Moore glanced at the large clock over the entrance to the hangar, and then switched his gaze to Hardcastle. 'I daresay you could use a wet, sir, having just arrived from London like.'

'Indeed I could, Mr Moore,' Hardcastle agreed.

'Well, in that case, perhaps you'd accompany me to the sergeants' mess.' Moore glanced at Macdonald. 'It'd be a privilege if you was to join us, sir,' he said.

'Thank you, Sarn't-Major.' Macdonald looked at Hardcastle. 'If you'd prefer to talk to Mr Moore without my being there, sir, I'd quite understand.'

'I don't think the sergeant-major is likely to be worried by your presence, Mr Macdonald. Join us by all means.' Hardcastle doubted that Technical Sergeant-Major Moore would have been intimidated even if the Provost Marshal had been there in person.

Although the sergeants' mess was a wooden hut, the inside was better furnished than the officers' mess in which Hardcastle and Marriott had been entertained by Major Tyler on their previous visits. It was carpeted with a large rug, and possessed a piano and comfortable armchairs grouped around small tables. At one end was a bar. When Hardcastle commented on it, Sergeant-Major Moore pointed out that the regimental quartermaster-sergeant was a member of the sergeants' mess, not the officers' mess, and was responsible for all the furnishings on the aerodrome.

The only other occupant of the mess, a flight-sergeant with 'wings' insignia on his tunic, was reading a newspaper. He looked up and acknowledged Moore with a wave of his hand, but otherwise took no interest in the arrival of the three strangers, even though one of them was an officer.

'Four pints of your best, Charlie,' Moore shouted at the barman. 'And make sure it's not that watered-down piss you usually serve up.' And with that cautionary instruction, he led his three guests to a table near a window.

The barman quickly drew the beer and brought it to the table on a tin tray bearing an advertisement for Whitbread's beer.

'Well now, sir, what can I do for you?' asked Moore, having taken the head off his beer.

Hardcastle was a skilled interrogator and deployed those skills in much the same way when questioning a friendly witness as he would when dealing with a suspect. In other words, he posed his questions as though he already knew the answers. 'How often did Major Plowman land here from St Brouille, Mr Moore?' he asked confidently.

Moore took out his pipe and blew through it before filling it with tobacco. 'Major Plowman? Now let me see. Quite a few times, sir, but I'd have to check my records to give you exact dates.' He eventually got his pipe going and leaned back in his chair. 'Might I ask why you're interested in him, sir?'

'I'm investigating the murder of his wife,' said Hardcastle.

'Ah, I see. Yes, we heard about that. There's not much as happens in the Corps that the rest of us don't get to hear about.'

'I've discovered that already,' said Hardcastle drily. 'But the dates I'm particularly interested in are the period from Thursday the eleventh to Sunday the fourteenth of February this year.'

'Rings a bell, sir,' said Moore, 'but like I said, I'll have to look at my records to make sure.'

'And where are those records?'

'In my office in the main hangar, sir. The one we just left.'

'Perhaps we can have a look at them later on, but I gather that Major Plowman was quite a regular visitor.'

'Yes, sir, he was.'

'Did he ever say why he came here so often from St Brouille?'

'He did mention once that he had to report to the War Office from time to time.'

Hardcastle glanced at Lieutenant Macdonald and noted his frown. 'I wonder why he didn't land somewhere nearer London, then.'

'I don't think he wanted to risk running out of fuel, sir,' said Moore. 'He'd stop off here to fill up and then fly on, but I don't know where he went from here. Probably somewhere near London, as you say, sir.'

'And where would that be, d'you think?'

Moore gave that some thought. 'There's Hendon, or Brooklands at Weybridge. And there's Sutton's Farm at Hornchurch. But the nearest, I should think, would be Croydon. That was a civvy flying club, but the Corps has just taken it over.'

'Did he always land to refuel and then take off again?' asked Hardcastle.

'Yes, sir, apart from that three or four days you mentioned just now. I'm working from memory now, but I'm pretty sure he left the aircraft here then.'

The group finished their beer and returned to the hangar. On one wall was an office with windows on three sides, undoubtedly so that Sergeant-Major Moore could keep an eye on the activities of his mechanics.

'Come in, gentlemen,' said Moore, 'and I'll turn up my records.' He opened a large book and ran his finger down a page. 'Yes, here we are. Landed at ten-eleven ack emma Thursday the eleventh of February. Complained that engine was cutting out and requested thorough check. Examined engine and tested but could find no fault,' he continued, reading from his own notes in the book. 'Major Plowman returned to

Gosport at approximately one pip emma on Sunday the fourteenth of February and was airborne at quarter past two.'

'Well, Marriott, that rules out this bloody yarn that he'd gone to Paris for a dirty weekend,' said Hardcastle and turned back to the technical sergeant-major. 'But you said he landed here on other occasions, Mr Moore.'

'Yes, but just for refuelling. One moment, sir.' Moore walked to the door of his office. 'Corporal Granger, get me the fuel records will you, and a bit *jildi* an' all.'

When Moore's corporal returned with another large book, the TSM ran his finger down the entries. 'Major Plowman landed here to refuel three times between the tenth of December nineteen-fourteen and the eleventh of January this year, sir. Onward destination unknown.' He looked up. 'I seem to recall that the major said he didn't want his onward destination recorded because he was on secret business, sir.' But Moore's expression implied that did not believe what the major had said.

Having had Plowman's visits to the United Kingdom confirmed, Lieutenant Macdonald took the two detectives to lunch in the officers' mess.

'What d'you think about this story that Plowman was coming to England for a secret meeting at the War Office, Mr Macdonald?' asked Hardcastle, as he accepted a glass of port at the conclusion of their meal.

'Unlikely,' said Macdonald cautiously. 'The wing is commanded by a lieutenant-colonel, and the air brigade by Brigadier-General Henderson. He's the general officer commanding the RFC in the BEF. If anyone had to go the War House for a meeting, I think it would be Henderson.'

'So Plowman's story is all eyewash, you reckon,' said Hardcastle brutally. He had already received confirmation from General Fitzgerald that Major Tyler's earlier claim to have visited the War Office on official business was untrue.

Macdonald smiled. Since their first meeting he had warmed considerably to the abrasive DDI, and he liked the way he cut through military protocol. 'That about sums it up, sir, yes,' he said.

After lunch, Hardcastle decided that he wanted to interview Major Tyler again.

'Get what you came for, Inspector?' asked Tyler icily.

'Yes, at last, Major, and I could have been saved quite a lot of time if I'd heard about Major Plowman's frequent visits when I came down here first off.'

'I didn't think it was relevant,' said Tyler.

'Did Plowman ever stay here overnight?' asked Hardcastle.

'I believe so. Once in January, I think.'

'And that would have been in the mess, would it?'

'Of course. Why d'you want to know that?'

Hardcastle declined to answer Tyler's question, but effectively did so by his own. 'How near to the room that Hartley shared with Rowe-Smith was the room that Major Plowman had?'

'It would have been very close. All the officers' accommodation is in one hut. Why d'you ask?'

'I'm not prepared to say at the moment.' Hardcastle had not dismissed his suspicion that Major Perry Tyler himself might have been involved in the theft of Hartley's Luger pistol, or indeed, in the death of Isabel Plowman.

'Look here, Inspector,' began Tyler, with a show of irritation, 'I am the commanding officer here and I demand to know what it is you suspect my officers of having done. Or, for that matter, my friend Major Plowman.'

'Well, you'll just have to wait, won't you?' said Hardcastle mildly.

Tyler turned to Macdonald. 'Then you'll have to tell me,' he said.

'I'm sorry, sir, but I'm not at liberty to do so, and I would remind you that this is also a military police investigation as well as a civil one.'

Tyler thumped his desk with his fist. 'I do not need you to remind me of that, *Lieutenant*,' he said, laying emphasis on Macdonald's subordinate rank.

But some of Hardcastle's acerbity had obviously rubbed off on the young subaltern and he merely smiled.

'Major Plowman landed here on the eleventh of February, a Thursday, and did not return until the Sunday following,' continued Hardcastle. 'And he left his aeroplane here because he thought there was something wrong with the engine.'

'Happens quite often,' said Tyler dismissively.

'D'you know where he went? Or did he stay here again?'

'No, he did not stay here, and I've no idea where he went. In *my* service it is not the custom to question the movements of officers or what they do in their spare time.'

'Pity,' said Hardcastle mildly, dismissing the implied criticism. If any of his own officers were indulging in some activity of which he was suspicious, Hardcastle would very soon question them about it. And that even included Detective Inspector Rhodes, his deputy. 'He was telling your ground staff some cock-and-bull yarn about going to a secret meeting at the War Office.'

'Then perhaps he did.'

'Seems a bit strange,' said Hardcastle. 'He's only a major.' But before Tyler could respond to that slight to his rank, the DDI continued. 'Have you ever been called to a secret meeting at the War Office, Major?'

'No,' said Tyler tersely, clearly forgetting that previously he had claimed to have attended such a meeting.

'No, I didn't think so.'

'Have you learned anything useful, sir?' asked Lieutenant Macdonald during their train journey back to Waterloo.

'Only that Major Tyler is a pompous arse,' said Hardcastle.

Macdonald laughed. 'I don't somehow think you made a friend of him, sir.'

'I shan't be losing any sleep over that, Mr Macdonald, but anyone who treads on my toes in the course of a murder investigation is likely to get his collar felt, major or not,' said Hardcastle. 'However, I'm interested to know exactly where Plowman went during his four-day sojourn in this country. I don't believe this nonsense about secret meetings at the War Office, do you?' he asked, posing the question again.

'No, sir, I don't.'

'Think you can find out?'

'No, sir, but the Provost Marshal will.' Macdonald took out his cigarette case and offered it to Marriott before lighting a cigarette himself. 'D'you think Major Plowman killed his wife and the policeman, sir?' he asked.

'I don't know, Mr Macdonald. It's looking a bit too obvious. Either that or he's a bloody amateur and has made mistakes.

Still,' he continued, 'if you think about it, most murderers are amateurs. They usually only ever do it once, so they don't get much practice.'

Marriott, in the opposite corner of the carriage, smiled, but then he was accustomed to Hardcastle's dry sense of humour. Macdonald, however, lapsed into silence, and gave some serious consideration to what the DDI had just said.

'I shall certainly take steps to discover whether Major Plowman was called to a conference here at the War House, Inspector,' said the Provost Marshal, 'but I have to say that it sounds extremely unlikely. Officers of Plowman's rank, albeit he's a field officer, are rarely summoned here, particularly from active service, unless there is something of which only he would have knowledge. I know there's work being done at Martlesham Heath on parachutes for pilots and observers, but I wouldn't have thought that Plowman was any better qualified to discuss that question than a hundred other airmen. But leave it to me. I shall find out what he's been up to. In the meantime, is there anything else I can help you with?'

'No thank you, General,' said Hardcastle. 'Everything now rather hinges on what Plowman did while he was in this country. If he wasn't here on business, so to speak.' And after a pause, added, 'Or even if he was.'

Brigadier-General Fitzpatrick was as keen as Hardcastle to discover what Plowman had been doing on his frequent visits to Gosport and beyond. Within forty-eight hours, he had some of the answers and, by way of a change, it was he who called on Hardcastle at Cannon Row police station.

'I've had thorough enquiries made at the War Office, Inspector,' said the Provost Marshal, sitting down and lighting a cigarette, 'and there is no record of his ever having called there. I've also made enquiries of the outlying departments that, as a Royal Flying Corps officer, he may have reason to contact, and they know nothing of any secret meetings. In fact, as a result of my enquiries, those departments have taken an interest in his activities.'

'I hope they don't start trampling all over my investigation, General,' said Hardcastle.

The Provost Marshal smiled. 'Don't worry about that, Inspector, I've warned them off. I told them that if anything comes up they'll have to wait until you've finished, and then they can have any bits that are left over.' Fitzpatrick became serious. 'D'you really think that Plowman could have had anything to do with the death of his wife, Inspector?'

'I never count my chickens before they're hatched, General. But I'm not at all sure. If Plowman came over here with the intention of murdering his wife, he wasn't too clever about covering his tracks.'

'But why would he have wanted to kill her? That's the one thing that puzzles me.'

'That's easy to answer,' said Hardcastle. 'It seems that half the Royal Flying Corps was sleeping with her.'

'Oh dear! Well, it seems that what is sauce for the goose is sauce for the gander.'

'What d'you mean by that, General?'

'I have learned from Intelligence sources that Major Plowman has a fancy woman in London.'

Hardcastle was not surprised at that, but was surprised that he had not found out. 'Would that Intelligence source be a certain Captain Sebastian Lawton of the Green Howards?'

'How the hell did you know that, Inspector?' demanded Fitzpatrick, alarmed that Hardcastle had identified his source.

'You sent me to see him last month at Burlington House. He was interviewing Captain Hartley about his adventures in Belgium and France.'

'Ah, so I did,' said Fitzpatrick, somewhat relieved. 'Yes, as a matter of fact, it was Lawton.'

That did not please Hardcastle. 'I wonder why the bugger never mentioned it to me when I saw him?' he mused. 'And I've seen him at least three times.'

'You have?' The Provost Marshal affected surprise. 'How so?'

'In the course of my enquiries,' said Hardcastle mysteriously, determined not to reveal too much of his investigation. 'Did Sebastian Lawton by any chance mention who this filly was, General?'

'No, he didn't.'

'In that case I'll have to see him again and sweat it out of him,' exclaimed Hardcastle.

It was a comment that unnerved the Provost Marshal; he was accustomed to dealing with such matters in a much more gentlemanly way.

'D'you know what, Mr Lawton?'

Sebastian Lawton faced Hardcastle with a bemused smile on his face. 'I'm not really sure that I understand, Inspector.'

'I'm sick and tired of traipsing backwards and forwards to Walham Green, and I'm sick and tired of people who tell me lies or half-truths.'

'Go and get some clothes on, Vera, and close the bloody door,' snapped Lawton to his model.

Sulkily, Vera Hammond stood up and sashayed slowly into the sitting-room-cum-bedroom, giving Marriott one backward flirtatious glance before slamming the door.

'I don't know how the hell I'm supposed to get any work done with all these interruptions,' said Lawton angrily.

'Perhaps if you'd been straight with me in the first place, I wouldn't have to keep coming out here,' snapped Hardcastle, matching Lawton's anger with his own. 'But I can tell you this much: it's more of an inconvenience to me than it is to you.'

'I really don't know what you're talking about,' said Lawton.

'I'm talking about Major Edward Plowman, that's what. Why didn't you tell me he'd got a mistress?'

'Well, I er—'

'Because, I suppose, you'd been dipping your wick with her an' all, eh? Well, mister, I don't have the time to play silly buggers with the likes of you. You might think you're doing something important dabbling in your wartime hobby, but I'm investigating two murders, and I'm on the point of starting to lock up people what obstructs me. Got that?'

'Really, Inspector,' said the thoroughly shaken Lawton, 'I can assure you that I didn't set out to obstruct you. I really didn't think that what Ted Plowman did in his spare time had anything to do with the murder of his wife.'

'And the murder of my policeman,' Hardcastle reminded him.

'Well, yes, of course.'

'Right, so who is she and where can I find her?'

Lawton tore the corner off a sketchpad and scribbled on it. 'She's called Diana Douglas, Inspector. She's an actress and she lives at Prince of Wales Drive in Battersea. The details are on there,' he said, handing Hardcastle the slip of paper.

Hardcastle glanced briefly at Lawton's note. 'Does actress mean prostitute?' He had been told by Vera Hammond that Lawton was in the habit of picking up prostitutes to act as models for his painting.

'No, she most certainly is not,' said Lawton indignantly.

Eighteen

Marriott had suggested that it would be better to call on Diana Douglas during the morning, on the grounds that an actress was more likely to be at home then than in the evening.

'If she is an actress,' Hardcastle had somewhat cynically commented. 'Mind you, if she's on the game, she'll be out in the evenings anyway.'

The address that Sebastian Lawton had given Hardcastle was a block of mansion flats in Prince of Wales Drive, Battersea, less than a mile from the River Thames.

In her mid-twenties, the woman who answered the door was attired in a full-length oyster-white silk robe, her auburn hair loose to her shoulders. She put a hand to her throat and gazed at the two detectives with an enquiring expression.

'Miss Douglas?'

'Yes,' said the woman and smiled, her gaze lingering for longer on Marriott than on his chief.

'We're police officers, miss,' said Hardcastle.

'Good heavens! What on earth can you want with little me?' Diana Douglas affected an exaggerated expression of perplexity and looked away coyly, leaving little doubt in Hardcastle's mind that she was indeed an actress.

'We'd like to ask you a few questions about two murders we're investigating.'

'*Two murders?* Oh, my goodness! You'd better come in.'

The woman led the way into a richly-furnished living room in which were leather sofas, a riot of chintzes, a plethora of bric-à-brac – of the sort Mrs Hardcastle described as dust traps – and pictures galore, mainly of theatrical scenes.

Diana Douglas noticed Hardcastle looking at the pictures.

'They're not mine,' she said. 'I'm just living here while I'm in London. The flat belongs to an actor friend, but he's in Canada at the moment in some revue in Ontario. That one belongs to me though,' she added, and laughed infectiously as she drew attention, without any show of embarrassment, to a full-length painting of her unclothed self.

'I take it Sebastian Lawton painted that,' said Hardcastle.

Diana Douglas raised her eyebrows in surprise. 'How very clever of you, Inspector. It is "Inspector", isn't it?' But without waiting for confirmation, she prattled on breathlessly. 'He's very accomplished, don't you think?' She laughed girlishly and waved her hand at the sofas. 'Do please sit down, gentlemen. Would you like a cup of tea? I was about to have one myself.'

From the way that the actress was chattering on, Hardcastle concluded that the interview was likely to take some time, and that tea would not go amiss. 'Thank you, Miss Douglas, very kind,' he murmured.

'Do smoke if you wish,' said Diana, speaking over her shoulder as she left the room. 'I do.' She returned almost immediately. 'My maid will bring it in,' she said. Seating herself on one of the sofas so that she faced the two policemen, she smiled. 'So how can I help you?' she asked.

'Major Edward Plowman,' said Hardcastle.

'Oh, Teddy. Such a handsome man, and so brave.' Diana suddenly sat up in alarm. 'Oh my God, you don't mean that he's dead, do you?'

'No, Miss Douglas, but as I said just now, I'm investigating two cases of murder, one of which is Major Plowman's wife.'

If Plowman's marital status had come as a shock to Diana Douglas, she betrayed no sign of it. And neither did the untimely death of the major's wife appear to cause her any distress. In fact there was a flicker of an expression that could have been interpreted as one of relief. 'I didn't know about that,' she said calmly. 'When did that happen?'

'About the middle of February,' said Hardcastle, not wishing to be too precise.

'That was a long time ago. Was it in the newspapers?' she enquired, but then demonstrated that in her case it was a point-less question. 'Not that I read them, of course,' she added.

A young girl entered the room with a tea tray and placed it on a small table in front of her mistress.

'Thank you, Daisy. I'll pour it. Poor Daisy,' she said patronizingly when the girl was hardly out of earshot. 'She so wants to be on the stage, you know, but I'm afraid she'll never make it.'

'I take it you're in a play at the moment, Miss Douglas?' said Hardcastle.

'Yes. The *Belle of New York* at the Aldwych.' Diana handed the detectives their tea. 'I'm not sure how long it'll run though. The war makes everything so uncertain these days, don't you find?'

'I understand that you and Major Plowman had an affair,' said Hardcastle bluntly, deciding not to waste any more time on niceties. But if he had hoped for a spirited denial, he was disappointed.

'Not *had*, Inspector. *Are having*.' Diana beamed at the DDI.

'Did you know he was married, Miss Douglas?'

'Certainly I did.'

'Major Plowman's stationed in France, Miss Douglas, so how can you say that your affair is still continuing?' asked Marriott.

Diana afforded Marriott a mischievous smile. 'There are ways and means,' she said. 'You see Teddy is a pilot, and whenever he has a day or two off, he just flies over here.'

'And did he spend two or three days with you in February, by any chance?' asked Hardcastle, hoping that the girl would not connect those dates with the date of Isabel Plowman's murder.

'Yes, he did, as a matter of fact. Not that I saw much of him.'

'Why was that?' asked Hardcastle, playing the innocent.

'I'm in the theatre every night,' said Diana in a tone that suggested Hardcastle should have worked that out for himself.

'There wasn't much point in him coming, then.'

'There are always the mornings, Inspector,' said Diana with another of her coy smiles.

'So you saw him each morning.'

'Of course I did. He'd stayed the night.' Diana displayed no sign of shame or embarrassment at her admission, and took a sip of her tea, gazing with twinkling eyes at the detectives as she did so. 'Teddy would amuse himself in the evenings by going to his club or something of the sort, and then he'd either let himself in here or he'd meet me at the stage door and we'd have a late supper somewhere. He's very generous, is Teddy.' She fixed Hardcastle with a stare as if daring him to criticize her conduct. 'Oh, and there was one night when he actually came in to see the show.'

'Can you remember exactly when he was here for those few days?'

'Not precisely, but it was in February. He arrived on a Thursday morning and left again on the Sunday morning. He made some joke about them not being able to get on with the war until he got back.'

'And which of those nights did he come and see the show you were in?'

Diana looked pensively towards the ceiling. 'That would have been the Friday. We had a late supper at Rules that night. And we had supper after the show on Thursday and Saturday too. On Thursday it was Quaglinos and on Saturday he took me to Kettners.' Whatever else the actress may have been lacking, she was certainly familiar with the names of London's better restaurants.

'But he didn't see the show on those nights.'

'No. As I said, it was just the once.'

'And he left on Sunday morning, I think you said?' Not that Hardcastle had forgotten.

'Yes,' said Diana wistfully, but then she brightened. 'But then Sebastian took me out to dinner.'

'That would be the Sebastian Lawton who painted that, I assume?' Hardcastle nodded towards the Diana Douglas nude.

'Yes,' said the girl, gazing dreamily at the portrait. 'It's awfully good, isn't it?'

'Did Major Plowman ever mention his wife, Miss Douglas?'

'Not really, above telling me that he *was* married.'

'And it didn't concern you, having an affair with a married man?'

'Why should it?' said Diana. 'An awful lot of actresses do, you know. And if he felt like having a fling, who was little me to deny him a bit of fun? After all, he was risking his life every day in France. I thought of it as my contribution to the war effort.' And she giggled at what Hardcastle regarded as a thoroughly immoral comment.

'You mentioned just now that Major Plowman sometimes went to his club. D'you know which club?'

'I've no idea. They all sound such stuffy places that I don't know what you men see in them.'

'Nothing more than a wanton tart, Marriott,' muttered Hardcastle as they emerged into Prince of Wales Drive.

Marriott hailed a cab and the pair clambered in.

'Scotland Yard,' said Hardcastle, and turning to Marriott, said, 'Tell 'em Cannon Row and half the time you'll finish up at Cannon Street in the city.'

'Yes, sir, I know,' said Marriott with an ill-concealed sigh. 'What do we do now?'

By way of an answer, Hardcastle leaned forward and tapped on the glass screen with the crook of his umbrella. 'On second thoughts, make it the War Office, cabbie,' he said.

'I must say it's looking rather grave, Inspector,' said the Provost Marshal when he heard what Hardcastle had to say about Diana Douglas's affair with Edward Plowman. 'If I understand you aright, it's possible that Plowman committed these murders.'

'There's many a slip 'twixt cup and lip, General,' said Hardcastle cryptically, 'but I must admit that from what Miss Douglas said, the major was unaccounted for, so to speak, at the times when PC Crispin and Mrs Plowman were murdered.'

General Fitzpatrick leaned forward and toyed with a letter opener. 'We're in some difficulty here, Mr Hardcastle,' he said. 'If he told his commanding officer . . .' He paused. 'That'll be the lieutenant-colonel commanding his wing. If he told his colonel that he was going on leave to Paris, but went to London instead *and* took a military aircraft, he could be in serious trouble. From what Lieutenant Macdonald told me, the technical sergeant-major at Gosport found nothing wrong with the engine in Plowman's aeroplane, so I suppose it's possible that he was endeavouring to cover his tracks. Both in terms of your murders and the misuse of an aircraft.'

'What d'you propose doing about that, General?' Hardcastle was afraid that the inflexibility of the military machine, concerned as it was with comparative trivia, would inadvertently hamper his enquiry.

'That's entirely up to you, Inspector,' said Fitzpatrick with refreshing magnanimity. 'I don't want to obstruct your enquiries by anything that the army may do.'

'It would he handy if he could be questioned about his trip to London, General, but I'm not quite sure how you'd go about it.'

'You leave that to me, Inspector. Suffice it to say that I shall speak to the Provost Marshal of the BEF and tell him that anonymous information has come to light regarding this visit of Plowman's, and we'll see what he has to say about it. If it's unsatisfactory, I shall have him recalled to London. Then you'll be able to question him.' Fitzpatrick smiled. 'I don't suppose you'd want to pop over to St Brouille to talk to him, would you?'

'I wouldn't mind, General, but I suspect that Mrs Hardcastle would have a blue fit if I was to tell her where I was going.'

The Provost Marshal laughed. 'Your good lady sounds like a very shrewd woman, Inspector,' he said.

Brigadier-General Edward Fitzpatrick wasted no time in putting his proposal into effect, despite the war that was raging on the Western Front.

On the Thursday following Hardcastle's last interview with the Provost Marshal, Lieutenant Macdonald called on him to say that Major Edward Plowman was in open arrest at Wellington Barracks and would be available for interview. Macdonald emphasized, however, that the Provost Marshal had said it was imperative that he speak to Hardcastle first.

'I must say you got your skates on a bit *jildi*, General.' Hardcastle was surprised that the army had deemed it necessary to arrest Major Plowman.

The Provost Marshal smiled. Over the preceding months he had got to like this brusque detective, and enjoyed the way hc always got to the point, usually in language that dispensed with the normal refinements of genteel conversation. 'Cutting to the chase,' was the way Fitzpatrick described it.

'This is Colonel James Cunningham, Inspector.' The Provost Marshal indicated an officer reclining in one the armchairs. 'He's PM of the BEF, and he interrogated Plowman and then arrested him.'

'Colonel,' murmured Hardcastle and nodded in Cunningham's direction.

'I think it'd be better if you explained to the inspector exactly what you discovered, Jimmy,' said Fitzpatrick.

Cunningham, a man of about fifty, red-faced and moustached, leaned forward and linked his hands between his knees.

'The man's a scoundrel, Inspector,' he began. 'Danced all round the question till I got the truth out of the fellah. At first he denied ever coming here. When he asked his CO for furlough, he said he was going to Paris. Well, that's a bit bloody different from taking an operational aeroplane and flying the damned thing to England without so much as a by-your-leave. However, the upshot is that he eventually admitted taking a military aircraft for what would best be described as recreational purposes. So I've charged him with that and unauthorized absence and he'll stand a court martial. Unless you've got something up your sleeve that's more important, eh what?'

'Quite possibly, Colonel,' said Hardcastle. 'Did you ask him what he did with himself during the evenings of his visit to London?'

'He eventually admitted that he'd spent his time bedding some actress filly in Battersea, of all places. I don't know if that's an alibi that'll stand up, but that's your province, of course.'

'Did he tell you exactly where this actress lived, Colonel?'

'No. In fact he had the damned audacity to say that he didn't think it fair to compromise this tart, whoever she is. But it didn't seem relevant anyway. However' – Cunningham gave a triumphant grin – 'I searched his quarters and came up with this.' The colonel leaned down and picked up a briefcase. Opening it on his lap, he produced a pistol wrapped in oilskin and placed it on the Provost Marshal's desk. 'A Luger point seven-six-three.'

'Whereabouts in Major Plowman's quarters?'

'In his wardrobe, Inspector.'

'Did you find it yourself, Colonel?' Hardcastle asked, giving no indication of his excitement at such a discovery.

'Most certainly did, Inspector.'

'And has it been in anyone else's possession since then?'

'No. Why d'you ask?'

'It's a question of continuity of evidence.' Hardcastle sighed inwardly at having to remind a military policeman of the requisites of his trade.

'Ah, I see. Yes, good point.'

'It's not only a good point, it's bloody essential,' said Hardcastle, 'otherwise some clever Dick of a lawyer will say that it got muddled up between when you seized it and when we go to court. I wouldn't like to think you'd buggered it up.'

'Mmm, quite so.' Cunningham, a little taken aback by Hardcastle's gruff directness, tugged at his moustache. But Fitzpatrick smiled.

'How long can Plowman be kept in open arrest at Wellington Barracks, General?' asked Hardcastle, turning to Fitzpatrick.

'We won't be in a hurry to court martial the chap, Inspector. Apart from which, there'll be a summary of evidence to put together, and that'll take time, particularly as some of the witnesses are still in France.'

'Good. I've got to take that' – Hardcastle pointed at the Luger pistol – 'and give it to my ballistics inspector. With any luck, he'll be able to prove that it was the weapon that was used to kill my policeman.'

'And Mrs Plowman?'

'Yes, and Mrs Plowman,' said Hardcastle. 'I suppose you didn't find out which London club Plowman belonged to, did you, Colonel?' Hardcastle asked of Cunningham.

'No, I didn't,' said Cunningham. 'Just hope it's not mine. Why?'

'Miss Diana Douglas, the actress Plowman was having an affair with, reckons that he spent the evenings of Thursday and Saturday at his club, but she didn't know which club it was. But if he's got an alibi for those nights, it sort of rules him out of the toppings.'

'The toppings, Inspector?' Cunningham raised an eyebrow.

'It's what we in the trade call murder, Colonel.'

'Ah, I see,' said Cunningham, who was learning all manner of things the longer he talked to Hardcastle.

'Never mind. Once I start talking to Plowman in earnest, so to speak, he'll tell me everything I want to know, don't fret about that.' Hardcastle picked up the package containing the pistol and handed it to Marriott. 'Better give the colonel a receipt for that, Marriott, and get him to sign your pocket book an' all.' He faced Fitzpatrick. 'I'll let you know when I want to see Plowman, General. If he's up for the killings, I shall take him into custody.' And turning to Cunningham, he said, 'That'll sort of knock your court martial on the head, won't it, Colonel?'

'We can always deal with him when you've finished with him, Inspector,' said Cunningham.

Hardcastle let out a coarse laugh. 'If Plowman's as guilty as I think he is, Colonel, he'll be dangling from the end of a rope inside Pentonville prison when I've finished with him.'

'I'll wait to hear from you, then, Inspector,' said Fitzpatrick.

'Indeed you will, General,' said Hardcastle, 'and I'm obliged for your assistance in this matter. And yours an' all, Colonel. Come, Marriott.'

'Bit of a forthright fellah, ain't he, General?' said Cunningham when Hardcastle and Marriott had departed.

'Yes,' said Fitzpatrick mildly, 'but he has a way of getting things done. Could use a few like him in the Corps.'

Nineteen

It took Detective Inspector Franklin of the Ballistics Department less than an hour to confirm that the weapon seized by Colonel Cunningham was the pistol that had been used to kill PC Crispin and Isabel Plowman.

'Got the bastard,' exclaimed Hardcastle triumphantly.

But Marriott was a little more circumspect. 'The fact that he was in possession of the pistol doesn't necessarily mean that he pulled the trigger, sir,' he said cautiously.

Hardcastle laughed. 'By the time I've wrung him out to dry, Marriott, he'll be talking nineteen to the dozen, don't you worry about that.'

And of that, Marriott had little doubt, but whether Plowman would say what Hardcastle wanted to hear was another matter.

Hardcastle's jubilation was, however, short-lived, crushed by a visit from the Provost Marshal on the Tuesday following the Whit Monday.

'I'm afraid I've some bad news, Inspector,' said Fitzpatrick wearily. He sat down heavily in one of the DDI's chairs and lit a cigarette.

'Are you talking about the train crash?' asked Hardcastle. The day's newspapers had been full of the weekend tragedy at Gretna when three trains, one of them carrying two companies, the pipe band and the signallers of the Seventh Battalion of the Royal Scots, had collided in the early morning mist.

'I wasn't, no, although that's a terrible tragedy. Over two hundred of the soldiers were killed and an even greater number seriously wounded,' said Fitzpatrick, telling Hardcastle something that he had already read in the *Daily Mail*. 'On their way to reinforce Gallipoli.' He paused, staring for a moment out of the window before returning his gaze to Hardcastle. 'No, Inspector, it's about Major Plowman.'

'Don't tell me the bugger's snuffed it, General.'

'No, Inspector, he's escaped.'

'*Escaped?* How could he escape? Hadn't he been arrested? That's what Colonel Cunningham said.'

'He was in open arrest, Mr Hardcastle,' said Fitzpatrick. 'What that means in practical terms is that he was confined to his quarters, and another officer of equal rank was assigned as his escort. You see, Plowman was on his honour as an officer.'

Hardcastle scoffed at the thought that someone like Plowman, a man who had openly cheated on his wife and taken unofficial leave from a war zone, would have been put on his honour. 'So what happened, did he just walk out?'

'It happened yesterday. Being that it was Whit Monday, there weren't too many people on duty at Wellington Barracks and the consensus is that he probably did just walk out. There's not only the main gate, you see, where there's a sentry, but several other unguarded gates as well.'

'I know,' said Hardcastle sharply. 'Wellington Barracks is on my toby.' He was tempted to point out that there was a war on, but that it had somehow escaped the notice of the army's London District.

'Yes, of course.' The Provost Marshal was not happy at trying to defend the military, and his mood was not helped by Hardcastle's next utterance.

'If he'd been someone I'd arrested, he wouldn't've walked out, I can tell you that, General.'

'I imagine not,' said Fitzpatrick, 'but it's happened, I'm afraid. Plowman's escorting officer will doubtless be severely reprimanded for allowing it to happen.'

'Oh well, that's all right then,' commented Hardcastle sarcastically. 'So what happens now?'

'Military police patrols have been warned to keep a lookout for him and I sent Macdonald round to his house at Cowley Street, but the maid claimed that she hadn't seen him since he returned to France after his wife's funeral. If she is to be believed.'

'You can trust that girl, General,' said Hardcastle. 'She's

as straight as a die.' He lit his pipe and gave some thought to the problem the army had created for him through their inability to keep a murder suspect locked up. All because he was presumed to be an officer and a gentleman. 'If I remember aright, General,' he said thoughtfully, 'Major Plowman hadn't told your Colonel Cunningham where Diana Douglas lived, apart from saying it was in Battersea.'

'Diana Douglas?'

'She was the actress who Plowman was screwing.'

'Er, no, I don't think he did,' said Fitzpatrick, a little taken aback by Hardcastle's bawdy description of Plowman's dalliance with the showgirl.

'Good. I'll post an officer on her place, and for good measure I've a couple of other addresses where he might be hiding up. Somehow I doubt he'll go far from London.'

'What will you do if you find him, Inspector?'

Hardcastle's expression implied that the Provost Marshal had asked a fatuous question. 'I'll lock the bugger up in Cannon Row, General, as a deserter from military service in time of war. Then I'll have a chat with him about the murder of my policeman and Isabel Plowman.'

'I see. Perhaps, in that event, you'd advise me of his arrest, Inspector.'

'Certainly, General,' said Hardcastle. 'There is one other thing, however. I've interviewed Lieutenant Rowe-Smith about the time when Captain Hartley was shot down. However, Rowe-Smith struck me as being an unreliable, well-educated tosspot. But I'd like to have a word with the other two who were in the air that day: Morrison and Baxter.'

'I'll see what I can do, Inspector.'

'Marriott, get Catto and Wilmot in here. Bloody Plowman's escaped from Wellington Barracks. I don't know what those toy soldiers have been getting up to round there, but they managed to lose a prisoner.'

'Careless of them, sir,' said Marriott.

'Yes, it bloody well is. I can tell you this, Marriott, I've got reservations about them winning this war for us.'

The two detectives shuffled into the DDI's office and stood in a line in front of his desk.

'You both saw Major Plowman at his wife's funeral, so you'll remember what he looks like, won't you?'

Neither of the officers had the courage to deny Hardcastle's assertion, even though they doubted whether they would recognize Plowman if they saw him again.

'Right. Catto, you're to take up observation on this address.' Hardcastle pushed a slip of paper across his desk. 'That's where Diana Douglas lives, and the bold major's been shagging her on a regular basis. Since he's run from Wellington Barracks there's a good chance he'll be holed up there. If you see him, nick him. That understood?'

'Yes, sir,' said Catto, but not without some reservation.

'And you, Wilmot, will do the same outside Sebastian Lawton's place in Walham Green. I don't trust that bugger. Like as not he'll run one way and look another.'

The news about the two RFC officers that Hardcastle wished to interview was not good.

The same Military Foot Police sergeant who had called on Hardcastle previously brought a message from the Provost Marshal.

'General Fitzpatrick's compliments, sir,' said the sergeant, 'and I'm to tell you that Lieutenant Morrison was shot down and killed shortly after Captain Hartley was downed. And as for Lieutenant Baxter, he was shot down an' all, but he landed on our side. He was very badly wounded and he's convalescing at some place called Highclere Castle.'

'Where the devil's that?' demanded Hardcastle.

'I think it's somewhere in Hampshire, sir, but I don't know where exactly.'

Highclere Castle, ancestral seat of the Earls of Carnarvon, lay to the northwest of Basingstoke, and the two detectives eventually arrived there after a tediously long train journey and a seemingly interminable wait for a local taxi.

Hardcastle introduced himself and Marriott to the matron, a redoubtable Scotswoman.

The matron looked askance at the two detectives. 'Lieutenant Douglas Baxter, you say?' She turned to a ledger set on a lectern in the corner of her office. 'Yes, he's here.'

'I wonder if we might have a word with him,' ventured Hardcastle.

The matron pursed her lips. 'He's very ill, Inspector.'

'Yes, I understand he was badly injured.'

'Aye, he was. He's lost a leg, and we've fears for the other one. It's gangrenous, you see.'

'I'm sorry to hear that, but this is rather important. I'm investigating two murders and I think that Lieutenant Baxter may have vital information.'

'I'll speak to his doctor. If he says no, then the answer's no. I'll not keep you long,' she said, and swept from the room.

'I'd not like to argue with her,' muttered Hardcastle once the matron had left the office. 'She's enough to frighten the life out of anybody. I'll bet even generals are scared of her.'

The matron returned almost immediately. 'You can have five minutes with him,' she said, 'but you're not to tire him. Come with me.'

The matron led them into the Great Hall of the castle, a magnificent, high-ceilinged room, its walls adorned with paintings that included some of the present earl's ancestors and kinsmen. But now the room was lined with beds, a good half of which were occupied. Some of the fitter patients, however, were sitting at a table, playing chess or reading, while others were walking about or conversing with their less fortunate colleagues.

Lieutenant Baxter was lying flat in a bed at the far end, a large frame protecting his remaining leg, and the stump of the other, from the weight of the bedclothes. He looked pale and drawn, but managed to smile as the two detectives approached.

'What brings you here, Inspector?' he asked. 'Thought I'd seen the last of you when you came down to Gosport.'

'I'm sorry to hear about your injuries, Mr Baxter,' said Hardcastle.

'Put paid to playing cricket, I'm afraid,' said Baxter, forcing a smile. 'The best I can hope for is to become a champion at snakes-and-ladders.'

Hardcastle could not help but admire the young man's spirit, and looking around the ward at the other human detritus, wondered, yet again, what this awful war was all about and what it would have achieved once it was over.

'Major Plowman has been arrested.' Hardcastle decided that there was little point in prevaricating; in fact it may help the young wounded officer to be more frank about what Hardcastle hoped he had seen.

Baxter's eyes opened wide. 'Good grief!' he said. 'Whatever for?'

'Misuse of a military aircraft and absence without leave, so I understand from the Provost Marshal.' Hardcastle chose not to mention that he was also strongly suspected of murder, or that the military had allowed him to escape.

'Not surprised, really,' said Baxter. 'He was a bit of a show-off. I'm amazed he didn't kill himself the way he flew. He must have had a guardian angel somewhere up there.'

'D'you remember the day that Captain Hartley was shot down, Mr Baxter?'

'Yes.' Baxter's eyes narrowed. 'What about it? Dick Hartley was taken prisoner, so I understand.'

'Yes, he was, but he escaped from the lorry that the Germans were taking him to the prison camp in, and crossed into Holland. He was interned there, but escaped again and made his way to Dunkirk. He's back in this country now.'

'By Jove, good old Dick. I hope he gets a gong for that.'

'Captain Hartley claims he was shot down by another British aeroplane,' said Hardcastle slowly.

'He was,' said Baxter. 'It was Plowman.'

Hardcastle was astounded that confirmation of what he had suspected had come so easily. 'You're quite sure of that?'

'I'm in no doubt about it.'

'Why didn't you report it, Mr Baxter?'

Baxter laughed, and then grimaced at the pain it had caused him. 'Who to? Plowman was the squadron commander. I could hardly swan into his office and tell him I saw him shoot Dick down, could I?'

'Couldn't you have gone higher?'

'What, to the colonel? He'd've thrown me out of his office, Inspector. And I can tell you this: a subaltern who goes around making allegations like that is likely to find himself in very hot water.'

Hardcastle tried to liken it to a similar situation in the police, and was forced to agree with the young flyer.

'Would you be prepared to make a statement to that effect, Mr Baxter?'

Baxter smiled. 'I might as well. My days in the army are well and truly over. I've got nothing to lose . . . apart from my other leg,' he added with just a trace of bitterness. 'But I'm not up to writing much, Inspector.'

'My sergeant will take it down if you can manage to sign it.'

'Fire away,' said Baxter, and began to dictate.

'That's long enough, Inspector,' said the matron, appearing silently at Baxter's bedside.

'It's all right, Auntie,' said Baxter. 'Only a few more minutes.'

'I've told you before, Mr Baxter, that I do not approve of that sort of familiarity,' said the matron sternly.

Hardcastle suspected it was a pose, and that beneath that starched exterior there was a great deal of compassion for these crippled boys, most of whom were young enough to have been her sons.

'Very well, but don't tire yourself.' The matron looked at Hardcastle. 'I shall hold you personally responsible if he takes a change for the worse, Inspector,' she said, and turned on her heel.

'Is she like that all the time, Mr Baxter?' asked Hardcastle.

'Yes, but she's got a heart of gold ticking away underneath her corsets, Inspector.'

'Well, we don't want to get into trouble, Marriott,' said Hardcastle, 'so get writing.'

Ten minutes later, Baxter had finished his account and, with some difficulty, had managed to append his signature to it.

Hardcastle put a hand on Baxter's shoulder. 'I hope you get better soon, lad,' he said to the officer who was but a few years older than his own son Walter.

As they left the Great Hall, the matron was standing in the doorway to her office.

'Thank you, Matron, and goodbye.'

The matron merely nodded.

'Bloody war,' said Hardcastle as they reached the open air.

*　　*　　*

197

'Have you seen Major Plowman lately, Mr Lawton?' asked Hardcastle.

Sebastian Lawton looked suitably puzzled. 'No. He's in France, surely?'

'No he ain't. He was in so-called custody at Wellington Barracks, but he's run.'

'Well I'm damned. What was he doing there?'

'I'm surprised you didn't know, what with your connections,' said Hardcastle.

'Please, Inspector.' Lawton held a finger to his lips. 'Vera's in the next room.'

'If you do see him, let me know. I've got an officer posted outside, so if he does turn up he'll get his collar felt. And so will anyone harbouring him.'

'Wasn't much help, was it, sir?' said Marriott as he and Hardcastle left Lawton's flat.

'Matter of opinion, Marriott. I didn't expect to find Plowman there, but it fired a warning shot across Lawton's bows.'

But in fact, Hardcastle's journey to Walham Green proved to have been wasted.

Detective Constable Henry Catto did not like observation duty. Apart from the sheer boredom of such an assignment, he always had the guilty feeling that he was standing out like a sore thumb and that the subject of his surveillance would spot him in a trice.

Luck, however, was on Catto's side this particular morning. Within thirty minutes of taking up his post, an auburn-haired young woman emerged from the mansion flats in Prince of Wales Drive and looked around. But if it was a policeman she was looking for, she did not recognize the young detective in the curly-brimmed bowler hat, peering anxiously up and down the street as if searching for a cab.

Catto, who always had an eye for a pretty woman, spent a second or two admiring the girl's trim figure. Despite it being the end of May, she was dressed in a flared sealskin coat, and her ensemble was completed by a hat with a feather, a Dorothy bag suspended from her wrist and an *en-tout-cas* umbrella.

Apparently satisfied that it was safe, she beckoned to

someone inside the door to the flats and was joined by a man in the uniform of a major in the Royal Flying Corps.

Catto sped across the road. 'Major Plowman?'

The army officer turned. 'Yes?' he said, realizing too late that he had compromised himself.

'I am a police officer, Major Plowman, and I'm arresting you for being an absentee from military service.'

'What the hell are you talking about?' demanded Plowman, immediately going on the offensive. 'Who the devil are you, anyway?'

'Detective Constable Catto of the Metropolitan Police.'

'A *constable*!' Plowman sounded scandalized that so low-ranking an officer should be attempting to detain him.

'Don't make a fuss, sir,' cautioned Catto, 'or I shall be obliged to detain you forcibly.'

Plowman saw the sense of that at once. Apart from the fact that Catto was tall and well built, the sight of an army major in full uniform wrestling with a plain-clothes police officer in fashionable Battersea would do little for Plowman's standing. He turned to the woman. 'You'd better go back inside, Diana. I'll go with this constable and get this nonsense sorted out, and then I'll come back for you. There's obviously been some sort of misunderstanding.'

But Diana Douglas was not convinced. Without a word and with a scathing glance at her paramour, she hailed a cab and promptly got into it. Little did Plowman know it, but that would be the last occasion upon which he ever saw his actress lover.

'Where do you propose taking me?' Plowman asked, turning again to Catto.

'Cannon Row police station, sir,' said Catto.

'Well, I'm not bloody well going on a tram,' said Plowman. 'We'll take a taxi.'

'Only if you pay for it,' said Catto, mindful of what Hardcastle's reaction would be if presented with a bill for a cab from Battersea to Whitehall.

When Hardcastle returned to Cannon Row police station from Sebastian Lawton's place at Walham Green, a jubilant Henry Catto was awaiting him.

'You look like the cat what's got the cream, Catto,' said the DDI, 'and why ain't you still hanging about outside the fair Diana's place in Battersea?'

'Because I've got Major Plowman locked up downstairs, sir.'

'Have you, indeed? Well done, lad. Say anything, did he?'

Catto preened himself at receiving a rare word of praise from the DDI. 'He hooted and hollered a bit, sir. Was carrying on something cruel about being a major and didn't see why he had to be arrested by a mere constable. I think he thought the Commissioner himself should've knocked him off.'

Hardcastle laughed. 'That'll have brought him down to earth,' he said. 'Not that that'd be an unusual experience for him, being an airman,' he added, and laughed again at his little joke. 'Where did you find him?'

'Coming out of Miss Douglas's place, sir. She was with him an' all.'

'Was she now? Have anything to say, did she?'

'Not a dickie bird, sir. As a matter of fact, she looked daggers at the major. Sort of horrified, like that she'd been associating with a common criminal.'

'Where did she go?'

'Just hailed a growler and pushed off, sir.'

'That'll likely have put the kibosh on that love affair then,' said Hardcastle. 'Right, Marriott, time we had a word with our Major Plowman. Tell the station officer to get him up to the interview room.'

200

Twenty

To say that Major Edward Plowman was outraged would have been seriously to understate his frame of mind.

'I demand to know the meaning of this, Inspector,' he began angrily. 'One of your damned constables arrested me in the street, as though I were nothing more than a common criminal.'

'According to the officer who detained you, Major Plowman,' said Hardcastle mildly, 'he arrested you for being an absentee from military service.' He sat down opposite Plowman and placed a package on the table that separated them.

'Poppycock!' exclaimed Plowman. 'D'you seriously imagine that I would walk about the streets of London in full uniform if I'd deserted from the army? Apart from which, officers do not desert; they resign their commissions.'

'Not in wartime they don't,' said Hardcastle bluntly. 'You've met Detective Sergeant Marriott, of course,' he added, indicating his assistant with a wave of the hand.

But Plowman's anger continued unabated. 'Are you going to tell me what this is all about? I can assure you, Inspector, that I shall institute proceedings for wrongful arrest and false imprisonment. You might get away with browbeating common thieves, but I can assure you that in me you're dealing with a gentleman of substance.'

'The day before yesterday, Major Plowman, you escaped from military custody at Wellington Barracks. And that, in my book, makes you a deserter. As I said just now, that's what you was nicked for. However, Colonel Cunningham, who you probably know is the Provost Marshal of the British Expeditionary Force, carried out a search of your quarters at St Brouille and found this.' Hardcastle slowly undid the package to reveal a Luger pistol.

'I've never seen it before,' said Plowman predictably.

'What's it supposed to prove?'

'It was examined by a police ballistics expert who is prepared to testify that it was the weapon used to murder PC Crispin and your wife, Major.'

'Someone must have put it in my wardrobe.'

'Who said anything about a wardrobe?' But Hardcastle did not expect an answer. 'And the German Army belt? Where did that come from?'

'I've not the faintest idea what you're talking about,' said Plowman.

Hardcastle left the subject of the belt, even though he had told Plowman at their first meeting about finding it in the major's dining room at Cowley Street. But Plowman's blanket denial came as no surprise. 'I am told that you were absent from your unit in St Brouille from Thursday the eleventh of February until the Sunday following,' he continued, intent upon pushing Plowman into a corner, 'having told your commanding officer you was off for a jaunt in Gay Paree.'

'I don't know who told you that.'

'Miss Diana Douglas,' said Hardcastle.

Plowman emitted a derisive laugh. 'That woman is completely scatterbrained. You can't believe anything she tells you. She's probably mixing me up with that bounder Rowe-Smith.'

Hardcastle was careful to avoid showing surprise that Rowe-Smith also knew Diana Douglas. 'It's not a case of whether I believe her, Major. It's whether a jury at the Old Bailey will believe her.'

'What have Old Bailey juries to do with me?' Plowman raised his chin and fixed Hardcastle with a supercilious stare.

'D'you deny that you were in this country between those dates?'

'Most certainly, I do.'

'There is a technical sergeant-major at Gosport who will say that you landed there on the Thursday, complaining of engine trouble, and that you didn't return there until the Sunday. You then took off for St Brouille.'

'Do you really think that the word of a sergeant-major will be taken against that of a commissioned officer of field rank?' asked Plowman sarcastically.

'Yes, I do. What's more, he showed me the official records

of your arrival and departure. And what happened was that you spent a few nights in Miss Douglas's bed in Battersea before going back to France.'

Plowman decided to change his story. 'As a matter of fact, Inspector, and since you're forcing the issue, I was attending a secret meeting at the War Office, hence the deception. Not even my colonel knew about it.'

'So secret that even the War Office didn't know about this meeting,' said Hardcastle sarcastically. 'But I know you weren't there, because I checked.'

'You have been a busy little beaver, haven't you?' said Plowman, taking refuge in irony once more.

'On the Friday evening you went to see . . .' Hardcastle paused and turned to his sergeant. 'What was that show called, Marriott?' Even though he knew the answer, he was playing his usual role of being the dim-witted policeman.

'The *Belle of New York* at the Aldwych, sir.'

Hardcastle addressed himself to Plowman once again. 'And after that you took Miss Douglas to supper. On the evenings of Thursday and Saturday, Miss Douglas claims that you met her after her performance and took her to supper again.'

'And what's that supposed to prove?' Plowman was still attempting to maintain a haughty attitude, but it was obvious to Hardcastle, skilled interrogator that he was, that the major's confidence had begun to ebb. It might not have had anything to do with the murders, however; absence without leave while on active service was a serious enough charge to be laid against an officer.

'So where was you between kissing Miss Douglas goodbye when she went off to the theatre, and when you met her at the end of the show, eh?'

'If you care to give me a good reason for answering that question, Inspector, I shall attempt to do so.' Plowman was in the difficult position of not knowing whether Hardcastle was acting for the military in the question of his absence, or whether there were deeper questions to which he was seeking the answer.

'Easy,' said Hardcastle. 'If you can't come up with a satisfactory explanation, I shall charge you with the murders of PC Crispin and Isabel Plowman.'

A bleak smile crossed Plowman's face. 'I was at my club.'

'And what club's that?'

'The Rag,' said Plowman contemptuously, assuming that Hardcastle would not know which club he was talking about. 'But I doubt you know it by that name.'

'The Army and Navy,' said Hardcastle, who was not only familiar with all the gentlemen's clubs on his division, but also the informal names by which the members knew them. 'It was given that name by a certain Captain Billy Duff.'

'Oh, you do know it then.'

'Yes, and I also know that Duff later got six months in clink for assaulting a constable,' said Hardcastle with a certain grim satisfaction. 'Well, I shall have enquiries made there.'

'That's scandalous,' protested Plowman. 'If you can't accept the word of a gentleman, I can only conclude that you are not one yourself.'

'I'm not,' said Hardcastle flatly. 'I'm a common policeman investigating the senseless killing of one of my officers, and the brutal murder of your wife. And I'll tell you this much, Plowman' – the DDI deliberately omitted the major's rank – 'I doubt they'll want you through their precious portals once I've done with you.' He stood up. 'I'll give you the benefit of the doubt while I'm making those enquiries, but in the meantime, you'll be kept in custody here.'

'I'm on active service and you are preventing me from performing my duties,' said Plowman. 'I demand to speak to a senior army officer. He'll soon advise you that you can't go around arresting people like me.'

'Certainly,' said Hardcastle. 'I'll tell the Provost Marshal of your request, but after you walked out of open arrest at Wellington Barracks and dropped one of your fellow officers in the cart by doing so, I doubt he'll want to waste time on you.' He paused before changing the subject. 'As a matter of interest, Major Plowman, what happened to the nude painting of your wife that was done by Sebastian Lawton?'

'I know nothing of any such painting,' said Plowman, but it was clear that he was shocked that his wife should have posed naked for a portrait.

Hardcastle laughed. 'I thought you'd say that,' he said. 'Put him down, Marriott,' he added, turning to his sergeant.

*   *   *

The Army and Navy Club was in Pall Mall. Through its doors had walked some of the most famous admirals and generals in the nation's history, not least of whom was the Duke of Wellington.

Hardcastle and Marriott crossed the club's vast, echoing entrance hall to where the smartly-uniformed porter was on duty behind a counter. 'I'd like a word with the secretary,' said the DDI.

'Certainly, sir. Who shall I say it is?'

'Divisional Detective Inspector Hardcastle of the Whitehall Division.'

That the police had entered his illustrious club evinced no surprise from the head porter. 'If you care to wait one moment, sir, I shall enquire if he's available.' The porter raised the flap of his counter and crossed to a door in the far corner.

Two or three minutes later, the club's guardian returned. 'If you'll follow me, sir, I'll show you to the secretary's office.'

The secretary, a man of unmistakeable military bearing, was an affable fellow. He smiled and shook hands with Hardcastle, who introduced himself and Marriott.

'And what can I do for you, gentlemen?'

'A delicate matter, sir,' said Hardcastle, and went on to tell the secretary as much as he needed to know, which was little more than that Major Plowman was being investigated for unauthorized absence from the Western Front, from which he was also accused of taking a service aircraft without permission.

'Oh dear,' said the secretary, greatly understating the distaste he felt inwardly that one of the club's members should be suspected of such cavalier behaviour. 'I'm not sure that I'll be able to assist you, Inspector,' he continued. 'Members come and go as they please. They do not sign in, as it were, and it would only be possible to say whether Major Plowman was here or not if other members were able to recall having seen him.' For a moment or two, the secretary pondered the problem. 'I would be quite happy for you to speak to the head porter though. Simkins is a very reliable fellow. He was a sergeant-major in the Coldstream Guards and there's very little that misses him.'

The secretary conducted the two detectives back to the entrance hall and gave Simkins permission to answer any questions the police may ask. Shaking hands once again with

205

Hardcastle, he said, 'I do hope you're wrong about this Major Plowman, Inspector.' But even he realized that, with so senior a policeman investigating the matter, it was a pious hope.

'D'you know Major Edward Plowman, Mr Simkins?' Hardcastle asked, once the secretary had departed.

'Indeed I do, sir. A Royal Flying Corps gentleman.'

'I know it was a long time ago, but do you remember if he was in the club on the evenings of Thursday the eleventh of February and Saturday the thirteenth?'

Simkins took a dog-eared notebook from beneath his counter and thumbed through it. 'Yes, he was, sir,' he said without hesitation.

Hardcastle was surprised at the man's confidence. 'Are you sure?'

'Yes, sir, without a doubt. I daresay the secretary told you that members don't book in and out, but I keeps a private record. And I can tell you the major was in here from about seven o'clock each of them evenings and left again at about half past ten.'

'Is it possible that he could have left by a back door and returned the same way during the evenings on those dates, Mr Simkins? So's he wouldn't have been seen by you, so to speak?'

The head porter laughed. 'No, sir. I can tell you this without fear of contradiction, the major definitely ain't a back door sort of gent.'

'Well I suppose that puts the kibosh on that, sir,' said Marriott.

'Not in my book it don't, Marriott,' said Hardcastle. 'Just because Simkins says that Plowman ain't a "back door gent" don't mean that he couldn't have slid out and back again after doing the deed. See, Marriott, the problem with these here Coldstreamers is that they have an undying faith in their officers acting like gentlemen. Well, I've seen enough of Plowman to know that he ain't no gent. No, we'll just have to try a bit harder.' And with that sceptical assessment of the officer class, the DDI sat back in his chair, contentedly smoking his pipe, and wondering what to do next. But he did not ponder for long. 'We'll go and see Plowman's tarty actress again, Marriott.'

Diana Douglas was dressed much as she had been on the occasion of the detectives' last visit.

'What have you done with Teddy?' she demanded angrily. Somewhat reluctantly, she admitted them to her sitting room, but this time there was no offer of tea.

'Major Plowman's been arrested for being a deserter, Miss Douglas. What happens to him is a matter for the army.'

'I'm sure you haven't come all this way just to tell me that,' said Diana scathingly.

'Roderick Rowe-Smith was a friend of yours,' said Hardcastle, as usual making it sound like an accusation rather than a question.

'What of it?'

'And is he still?'

'No. When I met Teddy, he said I was to give him up. He said he wouldn't have me consorting with a junior officer.'

Hardcastle laughed. 'No, I suppose not,' he said, amused at Plowman's curiously paradoxical set of moral standards. 'So what happened? You just gave him the elbow, did you?'

'I told him I had no wish to see him again,' said Diana haughtily. 'In fact, he wasn't a very good lover.'

'When did you last see Rowe-Smith, Miss Douglas?' asked Marriott.

'Months ago, when he was still stationed at Gosport.' Diana cast a hostile glance in Marriott's direction as she replied.

'And you've not seen him since?'

'No, and I have no desire to see him again. He's a rather spoilt, immature young man. More of a boy, in fact.'

'Did he ever mention knowing Isabel Plowman, Major Plowman's wife?' asked Hardcastle.

'Yes, I think he did say something about her once.'

'And did Major Plowman ever say anything about his wife's behaviour?'

'What d'you mean by that?'

'Did he ever say that he was fed up with her associating with other men?'

Diana Douglas smiled at that. 'He said he didn't care, but then he was hardly in a position to complain, was he?' Then she paused before adding a final, cutting remark. 'Apart from which, he relied on her for his spending money.'

*　　*　　*

207

'I'm going to have another go at Captain Hartley,' said Hardcastle over a pie and a pint in the Red Lion in Derby Gate.

'What can you hope to learn from him, sir?' asked Marriott, mystified, yet again, at his chief's sudden decision. A decision that, like others he had made in the past, seemed almost irrational.

'Shan't know till I ask, Marriott,' said Hardcastle. 'When we get back to the office, find out where he is.'

Captain Richard Hartley was still living in the mess at Regent's Park Barracks, and Hardcastle sent a message asking him to call at the police station.

'I understand that you wish to see me, Inspector,' said Hartley when, at four o'clock that Friday afternoon, he was shown into Hardcastle's office.

'When you were shot down, Captain Hartley, back in March, you said that you thought it could have been another British aircraft that did for you.'

'Yes, I did, Inspector,' said Hartley cautiously. 'And I also said was that there were no Hun aircraft in the vicinity.'

'So you did,' said Hardcastle who recalled perfectly the conversation he had had with the young airman at Burlington House. 'I have since interviewed another pilot who was in your flight, and he told me that he was sure that it was Major Plowman who shot you down.'

Hartley's jaw dropped. 'God Almighty! Surely not.'

'Were there any other British aircraft in the sky that day? Aircraft that you didn't immediately recognize?' asked Hardcastle.

Appreciating just how serious the question was, Hartley gave it a deal of thought. 'D'you know, Inspector, it never occurred to me at the time, but I do remember now. Major Plowman's aircraft *was* up. It has red and white streamers on its struts to indicate that he's the squadron commander.'

'And was Major Plowman flying it?'

'Good God! No, he wasn't.' The young flyer's face paled as he realized the full implication of the question and his own reply. 'It was Roddy Rowe-Smith. It must have been that touch of concussion that I mentioned. I told you I was knocked out by a pretty severe crack on the head when I crashed. Come to think of it, the doctor told me it sometimes happens that you get a short-term partial memory loss. The business of Major Plowman's aircraft has only just come back to me. Roddy's aeroplane was unserviceable with some engine problem. The fitters only discovered it at the last minute, so he took the squadron commander's kite instead. The mechanics didn't bother to take off the streamers because they knew they'd have to put them back on again as soon as Roddy landed.'

'One more question, Captain Hartley. From what I've learned about these aeroplanes, the BE2c is a two-man aircraft.'

'That's correct. Pilot and observer.'

'So who is Major Plowman's regular observer?'

'He never took an observer with him, Inspector. And he'd had the Lewis gun mounting modified so that he could fire it from his cockpit. Ye Gods, it's all beginning to make sense.'

Which, more or less, is what Sergeant Cassidy had told Hardcastle about Plowman not bothering to take an observer with him. 'And what about Lieutenant Rowe-Smith?'

'I doubt he took an observer on the day he used the squadron commander's aircraft. Anyway, I think Major Plowman had had the seat removed from the observer's cockpit.'

Hardcastle nodded and stood up. 'Thank you, Captain Hartley,' he said. 'I don't think I need to keep you any longer.' It looked very much as though Plowman preferred to fly solo so that he could go where he liked, even to England, without anyone questioning what he was up to.

'I've come to the conclusion that Major Plowman is in the clear for the murders of my policeman and Isabel Plowman, General.'

'I'm pleased to hear that, Inspector,' said the Provost Marshal, 'but he's not out of the wood as far as his desertion in the face of the enemy and misuse of an aircraft are concerned.'

'No, but that's your business, General,' said Hardcastle, surprised that the charges against Plowman seemed to have been increased in severity. 'He's locked up in my police station at the moment, so any time you want him, you can come and collect him.'

'I'll arrange that immediately, Inspector. Sad business. Major Plowman is an experienced flyer and an officer with, hitherto, an impeccable record,' said Fitzpatrick. 'I really don't know what possessed him.'

'I think it was an actress called Diana Douglas who possessed him,' said Hardcastle drily, once again demonstrating that he had seen what most others had missed. 'There is something else though.'

'I rather thought there would be,' said the Provost Marshal with a sigh. 'What is it?'

'It's important that I interview Lieutenant Rowe-Smith as a matter of some urgency.'

'What in hell's *he* been up to?' Fitzpatrick was beginning to think that the Royal Flying Corps was creating more trouble for him than the rest of the army put together.

'For a start, I strongly suspect him of my murders, but I have witnesses who suggest that he was the one who shot down Captain Hartley. Now that's attempted murder, but as it happened over France, I reckon that's your problem rather than mine.'

'God, it never rains but it pours, Inspector.'

Hardcastle laughed. 'That's the policing business for you, General,' he said.

Fitzpatrick made a note on his pad. 'All right,' he said, 'I'll arrange it as soon as I can, but it may take a little while to get him back from France. I'll let you know when he's here.'

For yet another reason that eluded Marriott, Hardcastle decided to go from the War Office to Cowley Street.

'I'd like a very quick word with you, Mary,' said Hardcastle when the maid opened the door.

'Whatever is it, sir?'

'It's all right, lass, no need to look alarmed. Did a Lieutenant Rowe-Smith call here to see Mrs Plowman in early February? Tall chap with a lah-di-dah accent and a fair moustache.'

Mary had to think about the question for only a moment. 'Yes, he did, sir.'

Twenty-One

It was not until the last day of May, a day that had witnessed yet another Zeppelin bombing raid on London, that Hardcastle heard from the War Office that Lieutenant Roderick Rowe-Smith was back in the United Kingdom. To his astonishment, Hardcastle also learned from the Provost Marshal that Rowe-Smith had been on a fortnight's leave in the United Kingdom over the period of the two murders, but as he had told his squadron commander that he would be staying with his parents in Kingsbridge in Devon, over two hundred miles from Cowley Street, Fitzpatrick had not seen fit to mention it earlier.

'God Almighty preserve me from amateur detectives,' thundered Hardcastle. 'If only we'd known that, Marriott, we might have got to him sooner,' he complained. To the DDI's chagrin, the enquiry into the murders of PC Crispin and Isabel Plowman had, so far, taken nearly four months, but now, he hoped, a solution may be near at hand.

And so it was that on the first of June 1915 the languid Royal Flying Corps officer sauntered into Cannon Row police station and sneeringly told the station officer that he was supposed to be seeing 'some fellow called Hardcastle', as though he had not met the inspector before.

The Provost Marshal, at Hardcastle's request, had led Rowe-Smith to believe that the DDI wished to question him further about the incident that culminated in Captain Hartley being shot down and taken prisoner. But Rowe-Smith was about to receive a severe shock.

'Put him in the interview room, lad,' Hardcastle said to the constable who had brought the news that Rowe-Smith had arrived, 'and if he escapes I'll have your guts for garters.'

* * *

Roderick Rowe-Smith looked around the airless little room at the front of the police station and noted, with some misgiving, its high, barred windows.

'Why am I in here?' he demanded. 'I've come to see this Hardcastle man.'

The constable stood with his back to the door and said nothing. Rowe-Smith lit a cigarette. He did not much care for this turn of events.

A quarter of an hour later, Hardcastle, who had deliberately delayed the start of the interview, entered the room with Marriott.

'Now look here—' Rowe-Smith began.

'Sit down and shut up,' said Hardcastle, and took a seat opposite the officer.

'I am an officer in the—' Rowe-Smith tried again.

'I said be quiet.' Hardcastle made a pretence of going through the file he had brought with him. Not that there was any need; he had memorized all the facts. 'I have here statements from several witnesses, Mr Rowe-Smith,' he said eventually, looking up. 'First of all, you shot down Captain Hartley on Friday the fifth of March this year. That's attempted murder.'

'It was an accident,' Rowe-Smith blurted out.

'So you admit that you *did* shoot him down.' Hardcastle was delighted that that admission had come so readily.

'Yes, I had a Hun in my sights, but I didn't realize that Dick Hartley was on the other side of him. The Hun suddenly dived and I hit Dick by mistake.'

'Why did you not report that accident to your squadron commander?' But Hardcastle did not wait for an answer. 'I'll tell you why. Because there *was* no enemy aeroplane anywhere near you or Captain Hartley. And you said as much the last time I interviewed you.'

'I don't think I did,' interjected Rowe-Smith lamely, but he knew he was being caught out, step after step.

'The reason you shot him down,' Hardcastle continued, ignoring Rowe-Smith's interruption, 'was that you had, sometime previously, stolen a Luger pistol from his quarters at Gosport, and you were terrified that he knew you had and that he would tell the authorities.'

'That's absolute nonsense.'

'You also stole a German Army belt from among another officer's possessions and in an attempt to put me off the scent you left that at Cowley Street the night you murdered Isabel Plowman,' Hardcastle continued relentlessly. 'But you were also there two days previously. You were on the portico of the house next door, about to break in through an upstairs window of her house, when unfortunately you saw her leave.'

'This is all nonsense,' exclaimed Rowe-Smith, but his protestations lacked conviction.

'I wondered about that,' Hardcastle continued, as though the airman had not spoken. 'But eventually I decided that that could have been the only reason why you were on the portico. You knew the maid would be there and you didn't want to be seen. You were going to go in through that window, do the deed and then escape the same way. And even when you saw Mrs Plowman leaving, you thought you'd break in and lay in wait. But unfortunately for you, you *were* seen, Rowe-Smith, and Mrs Plowman returned with a policeman. And when that officer called on you to come down, you shot him in cold blood and made your escape. Well, my lad, you might be a dab hand at shooting down Germans, and even fellow officers, but you don't kill one of my policemen and get away with it.'

Rowe-Smith had firmly believed that what he saw as his own intellectual superiority would be more than a match for any difficult questions this apparently slow-witted detective might come up with, but he was being rapidly disabused.

'Diana Douglas told me that you were a lousy lover,' continued Hardcastle, 'and that she threw you out when Major Plowman told her to. Apparently he didn't like the idea of a subaltern screwing his mistress at the same time as he was screwing her, so to speak.'

'This is all a tissue of lies,' said Rowe-Smith, but his every answer sounded successively less convincing than his previous ones. 'Diana and I parted quite amicably.'

Hardcastle continued to ignore the flyer's pathetic interventions. 'But she wasn't the only one. You made frequent visits to Cowley Street, where you was having a fling with Isabel Plowman. But she threw you out an' all. Now why was that?'

'She was pregnant,' Rowe-Smith blurted out, but at once wished that he had kept silent.

'Ah, now we're getting to the nub of it, ain't we? So she threatened you, did she?'

'She wanted money. She asked for a hundred pounds in order that she could go to Sweden and arrange an abortion. But I hadn't got that sort of money. It was a crazy request, but she kept on at me.'

'And what else did she threaten you with, eh?'

Rowe-Smith stared down at the scarred table that separated him from Hardcastle, a miserable expression on his face. 'She said she'd tell her husband if I didn't pay up, and she'd also report me to the War Office, and that I'd be cashiered,' he said, almost mumbling the words.

Hardcastle's laughter at that statement did nothing to comfort Rowe-Smith. 'Well you've been had, my lad. The post-mortem didn't show any sign of a pregnancy or an abortion.'

'What?' Rowe-Smith looked up, white-faced with anguish at the deception Isabel Plowman had played on him. 'But she said that she'd seen a doctor and that he'd—'

'Doctor Bernard Spilsbury is one of the leading pathologists in the country, my lad, and he did the PM. If you want your counsel to have a go at him at the Old Bailey, you're more than welcome to let him try,' said Hardcastle, 'but I don't give much for his chances. I didn't know anything about this so-called pregnancy tale you're telling, of course, but now you've given us a motive it'll see you hanged.'

'It was an accident,' protested Rowe-Smith once again, and gripped the edges of the table in an attempt to stem the violent ague with which he had been seized at the prospect of going to the gallows.

'It wasn't no accident,' said the DDI bluntly. 'You might have been clever enough to take the cartridge case with you, but you left behind the cushion you placed over Mrs Plowman's face to deaden the sound of the shot.' He paused. 'Because you knew that the maid was in the house. So don't try telling me you put a cushion over Isabel Plowman's face and then accidentally shot her. Or was you trying to suffocate her instead?' he added sarcastically.

'You've got it all wrong. For God's sake, you don't understand what happened.'

'Let us now turn to the fingerprints found on the murder weapon, and on the cartridge cases left at the scene of PC Crispin's murder,' said Hardcastle. He opened his file to a blank sheet of paper that he was at pains to shield from Rowe-Smith. 'I have here a statement from the fingerprint expert at Scotland Yard who will testify that there were prints found on the gun seized from Major Plowman's locker in St Brouille. Which is where you put it.' He looked directly at the lieutenant. 'And when we take your fingerprints, we'll find they'll match, won't we?' He closed the file and placed it on the vacant chair beside him, thankful that Rowe-Smith knew nothing of the science of fingerprints. If he had, he would have known that the weapon had passed through so many hands since he had used it that it would have been impossible to identify any fingerprints.

'Yes,' said Rowe-Smith in a whisper.

'What did you say?' demanded Hardcastle.

'I said yes, damn you,' shouted Rowe-Smith.

Hardcastle stood up. For a moment or two he stared down at Rowe-Smith. 'You're nothing but a contemptible little nobody,' he said. 'A spoiled brat who's had everything in life and always got his own way, and who thought he'd join the army and cover himself in glory. And you murdered a policeman without any thought for him or his young family. And as if that wasn't enough, you returned two days later and killed a defenceless woman for no better reason than she'd spurned your advances. And you couldn't stomach that, could you? Because in your cosseted little life you always got what you wanted. But for a woman to more or less spit in your face like that was too much, wasn't it? I don't believe a word of your story about her being in the family way.' But that disbelief did not prevent him from later giving evidence of what Rowe-Smith had said.

Rowe-Smith said nothing. A pathetic figure, cigarette ash now marking the front of his tunic, he just stared at the table, tears welling up in his eyes.

'Marriott, take this officer and gentleman downstairs and charge him with the murders of PC Crispin and Isabel Plowman. Against the peace,' he added unnecessarily.

*　　*　　*

It was several months before Rowe-Smith appeared at the Central Criminal Court at Old Bailey. During that time, autumn had come, the trees had begun to shed their leaves, and yet more gallant soldiers were being cut down in the cloying mud of Flanders.

Little time was wasted on the renegade flyer. Despite his defence counsel's professional obligation to attempt to discredit the evidence, those attempts were to no avail.

Nor did Rowe-Smith's attitude help his case when, unwisely, his counsel put him in the witness box. His dissolute demeanour did little to endear him either to judge or jury.

Thirty minutes after being discharged to consider their verdict, the twelve men of the jury returned and pronounced Rowe-Smith guilty of both the murders.

The Court of Criminal Appeal dismissed Rowe-Smith's petition against verdict and sentence, and three weeks later he was hanged at Pentonville prison. But a few days before that, he had been cashiered from the army.

'It ties up the loose ends, Inspector,' the Provost Marshal had said, closing Rowe-Smith's file and tossing it into his outtray.

Ironically, on the day that Rowe-Smith was executed, Major Edward Plowman, MC, RFC, appeared before a general court martial held at Aldershot, and was reduced in rank to lieutenant for taking unauthorized leave, misusing a military aircraft and escaping from military custody at Wellington Barracks. The one mitigating factor that saved him from being shot was that his commanding officer had given him permission to take leave, but to go to Paris not to London.

It was also on that day that the newly-promoted Major Richard Hartley appeared at Buckingham Palace where the King invested him with the Military Cross in recognition of his daring escape from captivity. But it was a day saddened by the news that on that very morning, Hartley's chum, Lieutenant Douglas Baxter, had died of his wounds at Highclere Castle.